I0731854

SECRET SEEDS

A Gripping Psychological Tale

VINCENT DONOVAN

Black Rose Writing | Texas

©2025 by Vincent Donovan
All rights reserved. No part of this book may be reproduced, stored in a retrieval system or transmitted in any form or by any means without the prior written permission of the publishers, except by a reviewer who may quote brief passages in a review to be printed in a newspaper, magazine or journal.

The author grants the final approval for this literary material.

First printing

This is a work of fiction. Names, characters, businesses, places, events, and incidents are either the products of the author's imagination or used in a fictitious manner. Any resemblance to actual persons, living or dead, or actual events is purely coincidental.

ISBN: 978-1-68513-628-4
LIBRARY OF CONGRESS CONTROL NUMBER: 2025932562
PUBLISHED BY BLACK ROSE WRITING
www.blackrosewriting.com

Printed in the United States of America
Suggested Retail Price (SRP) $22.95

Secret Seeds is printed in Warnock Pro

*As a planet-friendly publisher, Black Rose Writing does its best to eliminate unnecessary waste to reduce paper usage and energy costs, while never compromising the reading experience. As a result, the final word count vs. page count may not meet common expectations.

PRAISE FOR
SECRET SEEDS

"Vincent Donovan writes a magnetically thrilling tale, a magnificent story not just about sacrifice but also growth…a definite attention grabber."
–Amy's Bookshelf Reviews

To Heather and Taylor with all my love.

SECRET SEEDS

Well, I'm going home
Back to the place where I belong
And where your love has always been enough for me
I'm not running from
No, I think you've got me all wrong
I don't regret this life I chose for me
But these places and these faces are getting old
So, I'm going home

–"Home" by Christopher Daughtry

CHAPTER ONE

Olivia stared at the turquoise 1965 Pontiac Catalina sparkling in the spring sun. She could never comprehend why Papa Dale was so captivated by a sixty-year-old steel horse.

Gazing upwards, a red-tail hawk circled overhead, appreciating the Catalina too, or maybe trying to decipher her thoughts.

"I would trade places with you in a heartbeat," she whispered as the bird floated in a blue sky no crayon could capture, "but I have bruised and broken wings."

The bird wanted no part of the sorry drama and headed toward the adjacent field in search of lunch. Running one hand through her blonde hair, she glanced at the car again, hating to see her favorite color on something that caused so much misery.

The sales guy at Pete's Roadside Extravaganza said turquoise radiated luck...peace... protection — three Wisemen that were strangers in their house. If her birthday was in December instead of February, she might persuade Mama to buy one of the chip turquoise necklaces. Before she came up with another angle, the twenty-year-old clerk, with long hair and painted nails, changed tactics and began describing how the Egyptians and Druids worshipped turquoise for its magical powers. Before he had the chance to open the display case and elaborate further, Mama took hold of her arm and proceeded towards the exit.

"Wait!" she pleaded when they got outside. "That guy is only jive-talking to impress us. I bet if we go back, he will offer to read our palms, hoping we buy something!" She looked at the stone dust driveway which led to the road and the long five-mile hike home and grabbed her mother's hand. "I'll do extra chores if you buy me one of the twenty-dollar turquoise necklaces. I will save it for special occasions and it would mean more than pearls!" The plea came out in one breath.

Her mother glanced at her and then back at the store, responding with a loud snort resembling a sick horse.

"Maybe next time, sweetheart. If we don't head home now, I'll never have time to cook the roast. And you know how Dale barges in like a starving bear."

Mama walked away, which meant the request was not up for further discussion. Olivia trailed behind as the heavy sensation in her chest resurfaced. Mama's sprint for home was a classic panic attack which popped up like thunderstorms in summer. But today, there was no build-up of heat to make clouds pop like corn over an open flame. They were enjoying a rare outing, so what triggered this anxiety? Mama could whip up dinner in fifteen minutes under pressure, resembling a short-order cook. Olivia glanced back at the store, thinking it might have been the display of second-hand jewelry that sparked a painful longing for Mexico. She fantasized grabbing her mother's purse and taking twenty dollars as partial payment for living in their hell house. But her hands remained frozen by her side. She might be sixteen but still young enough for Papa Dale's belt — or one very long timeout.

The flashback faded, and she noticed a shadow beside her on the uneven grass that would need a haircut soon. Identifying its owner did not require a detective. It was the woman who gave her life but seemed more focused on evading ICE and the menacing dragon they lived with, than anything else. It proved to be a steep price for room and board.

"If Dale gave me five cents out of every dollar he spends on Miss Pontiac, oh what a happy family we'd be," Mama said in a congested voice which masked some of the Spanish accent. She shuffled over to the front of the car and ran her middle finger along the edge of the front fender as if keying the car with foul contempt. "Wash and wax every Saturday, no matter the season," she continued in a matter-of-fact tone, as if reading the indictment for the hundredth time. "Which makes no sense because I've learned Maine only has two seasons: the fourth of July and winter and they're separated by mud, which paints everything turd brown." She glanced at her daughter. "Your father, God bless his soul, had a greater amount of common sense than anyone I know." She looked at the car again and slowly shook her head. "Back in Mexico, Luis never washed his truck because the rust and dried mud held it together."

Olivia wished Mama would talk more about her father, even if it caused all hell to break loose. She glanced at the car. Every Saturday morning, Papa Dale inspected the tips of her short nails before assigning her sponge duty.

"There's no rain in the forecast, so he will probably make me shampoo the rugs," she said wearily. The American flag air freshener dangling from the Catalina's rear-view mirror caught her eye, reminding her of how Papa Dale dressed up as Uncle Sam on the fourth of July. He said America was the home of the brave and free … except for Mama, because she snuck in.

Olivia threw the insult in the pit of her brain with the other snakes and gestured towards the spoiled set of wheels. "Papa says if any of the candidates want to become governor, they should arrive in style."

Her mother let out a short laugh. "Let's be real and translate what he really means. First, it can't be a woman and the guy could be the reincarnation of that FDR fellow he has framed down cellar, and Dale still wouldn't play chauffeur. He loathes Republicans and Democrats the same and allowing anyone to put extra miles on sweet Betsy is out of the question."

Olivia thought Mama's comments came with an extra dose of sarcasm this morning, though her shoulders drooped like they were carrying the weight of the world. The curated photos of Gabrielle Ruiz, from diapers to age eighteen, came to mind from the photo album hidden on the top shelf in the hall closet. Despite age, hairstyle or dress, each picture featured a radiant smile that had been absent since she moved to Maine. Mama's family were migrant farm workers and her father, after years of back-breaking work and thriftiness, proudly built a house in Mexico. While he had an H-2A temporary agricultural visa, the rest of the family worked in the fields undocumented. Mama said she was harvesting asparagus when she found out she was pregnant with her. Seeking a better life for their child, she and Luis took a bus to stay with Luis's cousin in Brooklyn. At the last moment, her brother Roberto discovered the secret plan and pleaded to join them. They no sooner reached New York when Luis and Roberto died in a carjacking, though she suspected there was a lot more to the story. Not surprisingly, there were no pictures of her father or uncle in the photo album because Papa Dale made it his mission to erase them. If looks could kill, she would be six feet under for even mentioning her father's name. She treasured one secret photo of her dad taken in Brooklyn. He was twenty-three and cut a tall figure in a dark suit which complimented the blonde hair she inherited. After years of studying his face, she believed his eyes and mouth exuded joy, hope, and life. To her, he was as rare as a lady slipper sporadically found in the woods behind the house. No matter how often she tried replicating the same look in the mirror, she lacked his spark. The reason was Papa Dale. He was a human wood chipper that shredded dreams and ambitions with delight.

"Maybe he could drive big wigs around town for a fee?" she asked, rejoining the conversation.

"Yeah, as long as it included a stop at his store to generate sales and please his distributors."

As her mother walked away from the steel mistress, Olivia let her eyes follow and complete a full body scan. Regardless of the day, the outfit never changed — an oversized gray sweatshirt, baggy blue jeans, slip-on no-name sneakers. She knew Papa Dale insisted on the drab clothes because he did not want any man ogling at the dark hair, ink well eyes and full lips even if their nearest neighbor lived a good half-mile away. Mama did not have a license and the nearest store a five-mile hike, and Amazon deliveries strictly forbidden. They were rats imprisoned on a ghost ship disguised as a white cape with black shutters. Papa Dale bragged the grays in life came here to die. It had been over a year since they even dressed up and attended church. Not that she liked the hard wooden pews at St. Thomas, but there were moments when she experienced a sense of being transported to another place. She struggled to name it, but after searching online at the school library, discovered the word *transcendental* described it best. But even when that sensation had its wings trimmed, she still found pleasure in many of the hymns that originated from the eighteenth century. The organ also provided perfect background music to study the smallest details of the congregation — the way Mary Jo Jenkins braided her hair differently each week, or how Mrs. Riley wore short skirts and drenched herself in perfume hoping a real man would overlook the three mouths she had to feed.

She held her gaze for too long, causing Mama to move further away. Even in church, few men could resist stealing glances at her. Mama appeared unaware, leaving Olivia pondering the experience of being admired. They were the same height and had similar features, but Mama had more depth and curves, like a sculptor poured his passion into replicating a woman he loved. When it came to framing her, the artist rushed the project, and it showed. Whenever she complained, Mama laughed and chalked it up to Luis being a rail with a flat butt. But there were few laughs since Mama cut her hair last month. The short-layered bob made her tired eyes sink in the slim face and called out bruises no coverup could hide. They should paint their house black and blue.

"Did you remember to pack your inhaler?" her mother asked, walking back.

Olivia replied with a single nod, following the same script they rehearsed for the past few weeks. The blue Samsonite stuffed with clothes, toiletries, and a few mementoes were collecting dust kitties under her bed. The small valet prioritized what mattered most.

Mama's eyes were black holes, never reflecting light. "Be sure and pack enough underwear," she added.

"Can we stop this? I can't take it anymore."

The words electrified Mama's index finger, which drilled the spring air between them. "Stop acting like a bratty two-year-old. This is serious. If you forget your meds, you can't call me!"

"What is essential is invisible to the eye," she recited from *The Little Prince.* She thought it funny that her mother read the book to her a dozen times but forgot the key lesson.

Mama waved at her. "Are you listening to me? You can't call."

"Yeah, because the king won't let me have a cell phone. The jerks at school put a Coke can up to their ears whenever they see me."

Mama cocked her head. "I don't get it."

She gave an exasperated look. "Because when they get bored making fun of my chipped front tooth, they say I use soup cans and string for a phone."

"Kids are cruel," she replied and rubbed the back of her neck. "You have a beautiful smile."

She pointed at the damaged incisor. "I used to... until Papa—"

"That was an accident! He thought you were paying attention when he threw that can of beans," Mama recited for the hundredth time this month.

"Saying it over and over doesn't make it true." She looked away. "Believe whatever. I don't want to make a fuss and end up in his prison again. But not having a phone is different. Aren't you tired of not having a say?"

"Why do you think I'm leaving him? As far as cell phones go, Dale can't understand why kids believe they're as crucial as air. He refuses to buy one for me too, which is no big deal. Who would I call anyway?

Your grandfather disowned me after Roberto died and prays Luis is rotting in hell."

But we're rotting here! Olivia thought.

Her mother leaned over and put her hands on her knees and took a couple of deep breaths. When she stood up, the stone mask was back in place, dominated by deep worry lines running like crooked trenches across her forehead. "I don't want to go through this again. I'm just saying triple check everything you packed because you'll be on your own for a couple of months. Once I have things settled, I will come and get you."

"By when? I want a date."

Mama bit her lip for a long moment. "Sometime in July. Meanwhile, you can have a fantastic getaway and miss the drama.

It was her turn to frown. "You keep checking the smallest details about my packing, but mighty vague about how you plan on pulling this off. Did you rob a bank?"

"Funny," she replied and pointed at the crater pocked driveway which meandered to the road a quarter mile away. "I know how to live on pennies. Remember, I started working on farms when I was fifteen. After your father died, I worked odd jobs until I met Dale." She took a quick look at the Catalina like it might be listening. "I have a bit saved up for a room somewhere, and will find a job."

"How do you plan on doing that without a social security number?"

"I borrowed one," she said, standing up tall, which looked forced. "Don't ask me the details. I'll work and save up for an apartment. We may need to sleep on air mattresses temporarily, but we'll manage."

"We'll manage." She longed to imprint that feeling on her heart and rely on it until they were together again. Words of hope were like a January thaw at the North Pole. It made her want to pump the air with her fist, but the purple bruise on her mother's face put it in perspective. "Bend, but don't break," Mama would whisper, while holding a frozen bag of peas on whatever body part he punched that day. But something besides her wrist broke last year, and the cast

mended the broken bone as well as her spirit. They began whispering in the dark about a future without Papa Dale. It was a mystery why it took so long.

Olivia backed away. "He won't let you leave." She never had faith in Santa, the tooth fairy or the Easter bunny and questioned movies with happy endings. The road ahead would be a minefield and it could get bloody.

"He can't make me stay," Mama countered.

She pointed at the rear of the Pontiac. "He will lock you in the trunk before you make it to the end of the driveway. I should stay here with you. At least it would be two on one."

"No way!" she replied, then walked away as if ending the conversation, but quickly turned back after a few steps. "I've considered the options, and I can't risk having you here. When he finds out I'm leaving, things will get ugly. If he gets abusive, I'll call 911. And if he contacts ICE, Dale can explain the last sixteen years, which included fathering a child with a deplorable criminal." Mama nodded fast, like she was trying to convince herself. "Whatever happens, I can't have you here complicating things, or having him use you to wear down my resistance. He plays the same game every time I threaten, thinking if he treats me like a human being for a while, I'll forgive and forget." She gestured towards her cheek. "I've learned the hard way that things never go quiet for long. Some of the worse scars are those you can't see."

Olivia sighed, knowing she would not win the argument. "Maybe he'll get so riled up with the idea that I disappeared, you can slip away through the back door."

"That's the plan — daze and confuse. Dale considers himself a tough guy, but I've withstood everything he has challenged me with," she said, followed by a congested laugh. "Who knows? There's a chance he will surprise me and say good riddance! Then he can book a drunken weekend in Atlantic City and find another desperate woman who will cook, clean, and…. satisfy his other needs."

Her mother's words were like lyrics to a song you play over and over as a balm for third-degree burns on your spirit. Over the past seven years, she discovered beauty by experiencing its shadow. She embraced sunlight because of the insufferable darkness inside the Pontiac's trunk. Papa Dale defined the rear of the vintage wheels as the ultimate timeout for children once they reached the age of reason. Lucky for her, he waited until she turned nine for the initiation ceremony, but her stepbrother had an introductory session at six when he stole a candy bar. Since then, his repeat visits were few. The first time she experienced the hole, it was only for twenty minutes, but she yelled so much; he tacked on another hour. When solitary confinement came again that summer, the air felt heavy and humid. Sweat pooled on her forehead and her legs stuck together. She fought the claustrophobia by closing her eyes and pretending to be in her bed. When the sentence repeated in winter after talking back at the dinner table, the temperature in the trunk made her teeth chatter and she curled into a fetal position and gathered her long hair around her face, hoping to stave off hypothermia. Over time, she found sleep to be the best antidote and cursed the car with its long hood but cramped rectangular trunk. Sometimes, her entire body would buzz as if electricity were coursing through it, which was strange. Each episode ended with Papa Dale raising the lid and asking if she repented. By then, she would have confessed to any sin, real or imagined, which made him smile with all his crooked yellow teeth. The ultimate insult was being warned that if she breathed a word about it to anyone, he would put her back in the trunk and throw away the key. But last month she feared being entombed for a different violation. After Papa Dale caught her kissing Ricky behind the bleachers at school, she cried in embarrassment, and when she got home, he banished her to the turquoise-colored coffin on wheels. The timing was unfortunate as she drank a Coke with Ricky. After three hours, she peed her pants. When freedom finally came, Papa Dale was furious and held the flashlight as she scrubbed the trunk.

Her mother glanced at her watch. "Go get ready," she announced. "You're leaving this afternoon."

She felt a light flutter across her chest and eyed a fist sized rock in the driveway and wanted to change places. "Today? It's Monday."

"Which is wonderful because on the second day, God created the sky and your future will be as wide."

"But what about school? I have stuff in my locker."

"I'll let your teachers know we had a family emergency. I'll tell them you have a tutor and won't fall behind."

She glanced at the back of the Pontiac and felt the moisture pool in her eyes.

Mama pulled her in, which felt timely as she had a sense she might implode. "What did you expect? That I'd send invitations for a bon voyage party for next Sunday afternoon?" She laughed at the idea. "Be real, honey. I didn't tell you last night so you could get a good night's sleep. Didn't you think it odd that I told you to take a day off from school to help me with some chores? Today is perfect. It's a beautiful spring day and Dale's locked in a hotel conference room for a sales meeting. This is the window of opportunity we've been waiting for!"

She pulled away and wiped her nose. "I can't wait to have him gone and never be called Sockeye again."

Mama nodded. "Apologies to all the beautiful salmon."

"I hate him saying I'll head south of the border soon and spawn." Olivia looked again at the Catalina glowing in the sun. Papa Dale's manager picked him up this morning in a new truck. "Do you know where he hides the keys?"

"What difference does that make? You know I don't have a license."

"Who's taking me to Sally's then?"

Her mother fished a crumpled pack of smokes out of her pocket and lit one up.

Olivia knew she limited cigarettes for stressful moments, but hated the smell. "Tell me how I'm getting to Sally's!" she said and stomped her foot for emphasis.

Mama took a deep drag and began coughing like she might need to borrow her inhaler. "That was never an option. Dale would rocket over there first. Sally is a good woman, but she would cave in five minutes."

"So, where am I going?"

She blew smoke out her nose and it hung around and caressed the bruise. "A couple months ago, I hitchhiked downtown to a small watering hole when Dale was away on his ice fishing trip and you were at school. I stopped at a bar and met a woman named Rezi. Strange name, isn't it? We had a few drinks and nachos." She smiled, leaving Olivia unsure if she was remembering the meeting or practicing the sales pitch. "Rezi helped me come up with a plan and, yes, got me documents so I can work. She told me about a new settlement."

"Settlement? You mean like back in the pioneer days?"

"No, a place of light and love—"

"And don't tell me! Sex, drugs and rock and roll!" she said, interrupting. "You're sending me to a commune?" Her skin started tingling.

"No, more like a piece of heaven on earth called New Roswell."

"Are you kidding me? Isn't that related to Area 51 and aliens?"

Mama shrugged. "Let's get this straight. I'm the only alien you will ever see. Rezi says it's a new community that welcomes those in need. You're going there and once things get settled, I'll come for you."

"Why not leave with me and we can both hide there?"

"I wish it were that simple, but I can't run. I have to consider your brother and make peace with him here. But if it's as special as Rezi claims, maybe we can make it our future home."

"So, you're taking advice from the stranger you got drunk with? Sounds like you're trading one nightmare for another."

She took a long drag of the cigarette, then tossed the rest and stomped on it with her sneaker. "I won't have you talking to me like that. Look at what I'm doing for us!" She gave her a once over, before locking onto her eyes. "You don't know what I'm saving you from! Lately, after Dale's had a few too many, he says you're growing up fast and could be a hottie like I was fifteen years ago. He says your eyes remind him of Hershey Kisses! If he tries anything, I'll kill him. But what if I'm too late?"

"It's bad enough when he throws me in the trunk." She shook her head. "My friends thought I was a dud last year when I didn't freak out about the total eclipse and seeing day turn into night. I couldn't tell them it happens all the time at our house. Trust me, if he ever comes into my room and tries anything …I'll use the rusty ax in the shed."

Mama's eyes filled, and she looked away.

She heard enough. "Can I say goodbye to Sonny?"

"Sometimes, I wonder if your brother believes Dale carried him in his belly for nine months instead of me. Bad enough he's named after his father. We called him Sonny to reduce the confusion in the house, but I didn't expect the name to become permanent. He adores his father. Say a word and the whole plan falls apart like the house of cards it is. No, everyone must believe you ran away."

"So, I'm leaving this afternoon?"

Mama nodded.

Olivia exhaled, like she had been holding her breath for as long as she could remember. "Well, since I can't kiss Papa Dale goodbye, I'll leave him a note." She picked up the hand size rock and ran over to the Pontiac. Before Mama could pull her away, she put a good-sized dent in the trunk around the lock and erased a section of the turquoise paint. *Let him try to buff that out!*

With any luck, Papa Dale would have a hell of a time locking anyone in it.

CHAPTER TWO

Thin fingered clouds caressed the sky as Olivia spotted a black sedan slowly crawling up the driveway, as if questioning why anyone would leave 107 Pleasant Street. Try as she might, she could not catch a clear glimpse of who was behind the wheel as the car bounced through one muddy crater after another. When it finally rolled to a stop, she noticed the car not only lacked a suspension system, but hubcaps, too.

The moment her eyes met the driver, a woman with weird white hair, Mama hurriedly rushed forward and opened the car door. Unexpectedly, a strong desire arose to find refuge in the Catalina's trunk. Better the devil you know than the one you don't.

Paralyzed, she watched her mother embrace the woman and then lead her over. Typically, she would subtly assess the stranger, but time was scarce. Instead, she swiftly scanned the woman from head to toe. She estimated her height to be around five feet, excluding the electrifying, coiffed white hair that defied gravity. Her skin was porcelain and contrasted with black marble eyes that were close together and in constant motion. The combination called her age into question. There were few lines on the forehead and less around her mouth, showing she kept her emotions in check and did not gift the world with many smiles. *Was she sixty or a dozen years younger?* Her clothing raised more questions — black jacket, jeans and boots.

Under different circumstances, Papa Dale would think her a kindred spirit and split a six-pack.

"Olivia, this is Rezi," her mother gushed, blind to the weird-looking human she entrusted to keep her daughter safe.

Normally, she would smile, but mirrored the stranger's blank expression.

Their awkward silence highlighted a blue jay squawking nearby, followed by a thin smile on Rezi's face that looked as shaky as the undercarriage of the car. "Nice meeting you," she said, extending a liver-spotted claw.

The hand would dangle until Halloween, if not for the glare on Mama's face. Taking it, she felt smooth, cold skin, eerily reminiscent of Papa Dale's father before they sealed the casket.

"Your mother has told me so much about you. I feel like I know you to some degree. Given what you've endured, I'm thrilled about escorting you to a better life," lady weirdo cooed in a tone above a whisper. "Do you prefer I call you Olivia or just Liv?"

It was a simple question, but difficult to answer. While she reserved the nickname for family and close friends, she did not know if Rezi was an angel of delivery or destruction.

The woman worked the springs on her lips to widen the smile and revealed a bottom tooth doing its best to hide behind the others. "Tell you what. I'll use your birth name until we become more familiar with each other. Okay?"

She nodded at the shy tooth and hoped the stay would not be that long. Breathing in, she glanced down at her sneakers. The cool girls at school wore crocs, UGGS and Nike. While her friends said nothing, others made fun of her red, white, and blue canvas sneakers. Papa Dale yearned to squeeze his size twelve dogs into a pair, too. She pondered the idea of baptizing them in mud, but knew Papa Dale would view it as ungrateful and deserving of another timeout. Instead, she said they were not good for gym and he barked, "those colors will make you fly like an eagle!" The only option left was to bleach them in the sun, which in Maine took a dozen years.

"Well, I suppose…" Mama said, causing her to raise her gaze and find her mother stroking the visitor's arm. "Under any other circumstance, I'd invite you in for something to eat after your long drive, but…" she hesitated and glanced toward the road, "it's just like Dale to fake the stomach flu so he can escape a conference room with no windows."

Olivia looked toward the woods. The Maine Turnpike was only a few miles away and she could hitchhike. If she wore her hair up and put on makeup, she could pass for eighteen and the shelter would not report her.

She pointed at the Catalina, its oblong eyes taking in this rendezvous and telling her to stall. "But Papa Dale can't come home. He didn't drive."

Mama let out a small chuckle, her signature shorthand that broadcast she was young and stupid. "You should know better than anyone how slippery Dale can be," she added. "He will call one of his buddies to pick him up. I don't want to think what he would say if he caught us standing here."

Rezi looked toward the road, and her eyes narrowed. "Yes, that would be most unfortunate," she added, sensing the danger. "I have trouble driving in the dark, so we should get going, anyway." She smiled at her mother. "When you come for your daughter, Gabrielle, we can have a meal of celebration."

Olivia watched them embrace and then turn like twins toward her. A stomach cramp made her consider running to the bathroom.

Rezi gathered her smile and lifted the suitcase, which looked so small after the long hibernation under the bed. "I'll let you say your goodbyes."

Mama stroked the arm of her hoodie. "I was hoping you left this behind so I could hang it in my closet and feel close to you."

Olivia sometimes wondered what else was in the cigarettes she smoked. This was her only spring coat.

"I know this is hard," her mother continued, "but staying here would make things impossible." She took a gold stud out of her right ear and handed it to her. "Let's both wear one until we're together again."

The gold earring blurred with her tears. Mama wore the earrings every day, the last present she received from her mother.

Mama pointed at the Catalina. "I should have been stronger when Dale began locking you and Sonny up. Called 911 and taken the beating when the police left." She wrapped her arms around her. "I'm sorry for not standing up for you...for us."

She could not control the tears. "Please don't send me away with that woman! Hide me around here with someone we know."

Mama did not answer, and they rocked back and forth. The smell of Herbal Essences shampoo combined with cigarette smoke brought back memories of her mother braiding her hair.

"Why can't we just leave together?" she asked, hoping for a Plan B.

"Because if he comes after me, I don't want him taking it out on you." Mama backed away and wiped her face on the sleeve of her sweatshirt. When their eyes met again, her face was New Hampshire granite.

"How can you trust that woman?" she asked, trying one last time. A sudden breeze punctuated the question and made her shiver.

"I suggest you treat her a lot better than you just did. She is putting herself in danger doing this for us."

"Right! And why is she? Did you think this through?"

Invisible magnets pulled Mama's hands to her hips. "You sound just like Dale, always doubting me. If you love me, trust me and get in the car."

At that moment, she wanted nothing more than a giant etch-a-sketch of her life so she could shake it good and hard until everything disappeared. But her mother's method was using an eraser to get rid of the black ink that outlined their lives. And if you rub too hard, all you get is a giant hole.

Her feet were cement stones, and Mama began pulling her toward the car. As they inched forward, Olivia took in the yard she grew up in... the lilac bush that would sweeten the air soon...the tire swing patiently waiting for another spin... the sandbox Papa Dale fashioned out of two by fours when his better angels made a brief appearance and where she corralled plastic dinosaurs that ripped each other and relied on her to bandage the wounds... and a little further back in the yard under the shade of a white birch, Squeaky the twenty-pound tabby passed last fall. More than once she heard the cat sitting on the trunk, waiting for her release.

In an instant, she was in the car with Mama closing the door. The leather seats felt cold through her jeans.

Before she could mouth goodbye, the car rolled forward and hit a crater and began rocking up and down.

"Better buckle yourself in," Rezi warned. "It's going to be a bumpy ride."

CHAPTER THREE

Rezi leaned forward in her seat, clutching the steering wheel, while her eyes darted back and forth along the edges of the road.

"What's the matter? Are you expecting someone will ambush us?" she asked, trying to ignore the musty smell in the car.

The question remained without a response. Olivia looked away, seeking solace in the passing landscape. The pines maintained their eternal green, and the maple and birch trees were fully clothed. She wondered if she would return in time to see the leaves changing colors.

The country road led to the town depot and a long row of abandoned buildings. Papa Dale said bricks may be stronger than hay, but the wolf still blew the paper mills overseas. Time held hands with nature and seasons of freeze and thaw, rain, and wind, led to rotted windows, cracked mortar, caved in roofs. Those that survived the first culling became havens for addicts, the homeless, and a rash of fires. In recent years, a renaissance revitalized the remaining relics, transforming them into trendy offices for lawyers, realtors, and a handful of high-end restaurants. Plans were being developed to convert some into condominiums for the one-percenters that wanted New England quaintness in their portfolios.

The road meandered this way and that, as if designed by a drunken mill worker trying to walk it off before arriving home. All the traffic lights were green, making her think the town's infrastructure somehow colluded with the strange lady. The quick exodus produced internal alarm bells. She needed time to think things through while still within known territory. Martha's barn came to mind as a possible hideout. They had been good friends since first grade, and Martha listened to the little she shared without judging. *Maybe Martha would know how to locate the underground railroad for abused children? Anything is better than hitching a ride with this anxious weirdo!*

Olivia inhaled deeply and reached for the door handle while focusing on a patch of grass to the right of the approaching intersection. The landing spot looked ideal — no bushes or trees. Try this on the highway and she would become road kill.

"When you jump, make sure you keep your head up as you roll, because you wouldn't want to spoil such a pretty face," Rezi said, and then let out a small chuckle. "But if you're unlucky, you can hide the scars behind your long hair…unless the DPW used rocky fill instead of sand. If that's the case, you might lose a piece of your scalp too. Whatever happens, I'll pull over and put what's left of you in the backseat and continue on. I made a promise to your mother … and to Seth."

She's just trying to scare you! the voice in her head screamed as her mind flashed her senior year picture with half her face missing. Sadly, the gross mug still highlighted her chipped front tooth. Rezi did not speed up, which made her wonder if this really was a stupid move.

The planned launch site came and passed.

"I'm glad you reconsidered," the driver continued in the same flat voice. "Keep listening and I will share with you everything I've learned. It will be the education of a lifetime."

Time for a new plan. "I need to use the bathroom," she whispered.

The driver's eyes continued scanning the road. "This is the best you can come up with? I'm disappointed. Your mother said you were creative."

It might be the plan of a seven-year-old, but she had nothing else to work with. Leaning forward in the seat, she let the seatbelt press into her stomach. "No, I'm not kidding! I have to go bad. My stomach is killing me."

For the first time, Rezi glanced at her. "There's an empty water bottle on the floor in the back. You can use that."

"Gross! But it's not my bladder!" She undid the seatbelt and unzipped her jeans. "If my mother told you so much about me, you'd know I have a sensitive stomach. If you don't stop, I'll go right here on the seat! I'm not kidding."

The car sped up. Seconds later, they pulled into a combo gas station and convenience store, and Rezi pulled up to the front door.

"You have five minutes." She pointed under the seat and then made a gun with her index finger and thumb. "Don't be stupid and try anything!"

She opened the car door and darted into the store. The place looked empty, except for a teenage girl standing behind the register, her head bent over a cell phone. The profile of slicked back black hair and red lipstick were familiar from school. *What's her name? ... Linda? ... Lisa? ... Lori?* Her thoughts felt stuck, and her heart raced so fast she was panting.

She hurried over to the counter. "Where's the bathroom?" she asked.

The cashier looked up and pointed toward the back of the store. "But it's for customers."

Her eyes scanned the counter, and she grabbed a pack of peppermint gum and threw it on the counter, along with a dollar bill.

The girl rolled her eyes and rang up the sale. Afterwards, she reached under the counter and handed her a wooden spoon with a key attached.

Olivia grabbed the crazy combo. "Is there another way out of here?"

The cashier looked confused and gestured towards the front door. "No. People go out the same way they came in."

"Don't be a smart ass. I don't have time!"

Linda, Lisa, or Lori pointed at the pack of gum. "Guess that's all a buck will buy in customer service these days."

The tattooed wings of the Harley-Davison insignia on the girl's forearm gave her hope. "Do you know Sonny Pearce?"

It was like the key found the lock and the cashier suddenly looked interested. "Yeah, he hangs out with my brother. So what?"

The face clicked. It was Lori. "I'm his sister."

The cashier nodded. "I know."

"Then what's with the attitude?" She glanced at the door. "Listen to me. When I leave, take the plate down and give it to Sonny."

The cashier looked confused. "Why?"

The door opened, and the bell chimed.

"Pretend you don't know me," she whispered to the cashier. Turning around, she watched the kidnapper approach with one hand behind her back.

Olivia held up the gum and the wooden spoon. "You don't have to check up on me, Rezi! I had to buy something to use the bathroom."

Rezi eyed the cashier.

"I told you I don't make the rules," Lori said, playing along.

"We're running late, so let's go!" Rezi barked, while giving the cashier a once over.

Olivia winked at Lori and handed her the bathroom key before following the kidnapper outside. Before she could run, Rezi pressed something against her side and pushed her into the car. They took off so fast, Olivia thought any cruiser on patrol would pull them over. As the car sped up onto the highway, she studied the driver's thin hands and painted black fingernails.

"Is Rezi your real name?" she asked.

"I expected a few days to pass before you got the nerve up to ask. I see your mother brought you up to be direct," she replied.

"More like Papa Dale. He doesn't like to waste time with unnecessary conversation." She frowned, hating to think she picked up any of his habits.

"From what I understand, he reserves his fists for Mama and the trunk for you and Sonny. Leaving might feel like a shock, but if I were in your shoes, I'd be thrilled to escape 107 Pleasant Street."

Olivia looked away as her fingers played with the door handle again. The sun was lower in the sky, camouflaging any rocks in the grass. It would hurt to jump, and there would be blood.

Rezi snapped her fingers, which startled her.

"Pay attention to what I'm about to say and write it on your heart," she said, enunciating each word. "Seth teaches you can remake yourself into more than the sum of your parts."

"Sounds like one of those word problems I suck at. If a train leaves Boston at nine o'clock....." she stopped and moaned.

Rezi ignored the brushoff. "Math has nothing to do with it. I'm talking about changing your approach. Your senses and experiences make you think perception is reality. Set them aside and open yourself up to the entire picture and gain perspective. If you're able to do that, you can't unsee what has been hiding in plain sight."

"That's a pretzel salad of words. Who is this Seth guy you keep mentioning?"

"You'll meet him soon enough and can judge for yourself." She nodded a few times, like she was having an internal conversation. "Seth gave me the name Rezi. Perhaps not as popular as Olivia, but I think its meaning fits my calling."

"Which is?" she asked.

"In Greek, it means the gatherer... and so I am."

The way the driver curled her tongue around the words gave her a chill. "Gatherer of what?"

"Troubled souls, but in reality, those that have been touched and will play a central role in our mission." She shot her a quick glance. "That includes you."

"Gatherer has a mysterious ring to it, but I prefer calling you a kidnapper. I also think it's weird how you and Seth don't have last names."

"I see you have the same spunk as your mother!" Rezi said with a smile. "Last names are so yesterday because they tie us to the past. And how can you call this a kidnapping when I had your mom's permission?"

"Because my mother only told me about you this morning and when I had second thoughts, you threatened me with a gun." She looked at the driver for a response, but the air remained dead. "She was pretty vague where you're taking me, though it sounded like a commune."

Rezi checked the rear-view mirror and sped up to pass a pickup truck. "Look at me. Do I resemble a heathen addicted to the world?" She pointed at the silent radio. "Put some tunes on if it will make you feel better."

She crossed her arms and waited.

Rezi noticed. "Okay, I give. We're heading south for a couple hours to—"

"Portsmouth?" she asked, interrupting.

"Close, and still in the Live or Die State. We're going to Salem."

She heard her friends talk about the town because of Canobie Lake Amusement Park and the crazy rides. "Do you live there?"

"I live wherever I am. Salem is where Seth broke ground for New Roswell."

"Let me guess, everyone is family and Seth has twelve wives?"

Rezi sighed. "I see your mom never explained the golden rule to you."

"That's not true. I treat others like I want to be treated," she replied. *Not that anyone else does, especially Papa Dale or the jerks at school. They play by different rules...more like King of the Hill where anything goes to get ahead.*

"Then you will love it in Salem, because it means peace," Rezi added.

"How did that work out in Salem, Massachusetts? I think history would disagree with you."

"Different town, state, and time."

Olivia frowned and looked at Rezi. Maybe she kept the broomstick in the trunk.

CHAPTER FOUR

Gabrielle waited until the angry water spilled over the side of the pan before turning the heat down on the potatoes.

"Peel, boil, smash, and whip with butter and milk so it can sit pretty on a plate," she mumbled to the drowning vegetable. Dale hated himself for being attracted to her olive skin and tried peeling it off with cutting words or a fist. Afterwards, he would try to make up by asking her to put on something pretty which was code for the coming attractions. If Roberto were alive, Dale would be several feet below the carrot roots by now. It was too painful dwelling on what Luis would think of the deal she made with the devil. Their love had no limits, and they risked everything to give their baby a better life. After he died, the only goal was survival. The encounter with Dale in Atlantic City transformed everything. When you're drowning, you do not ask for the resume of the lifeguard. Dale came across as a cocky man bordering on obnoxious, but she detected a soft center. She told herself if that hardened, she would leave. Wrong on both counts. The world became small and cold in Maine, and Olivia and Sonny kept her sane. She loved them more than life itself and could not understand her father's rejection. If her mother were still alive, it never would have come to this.

The front door groaned, as it did whenever King Dale entered. The worn wood could not comprehend why he did not use the back door, like the rest of the family. She checked the knot on her apron and glanced out the kitchen window over the sink. The spring sun was low in the sky, unveiling that special interlude when the day embraces the coming night and their kiss makes the sky glow orange. She embraced this in-between moment, licking the wounds from another day in the gulag and holding on to the promise of escape.

A throaty grunt echoed, and she turned around. Of all the beautiful ways to say hello or good evening in every language, the vulgarity of his greeting made her ears hurt.

"I didn't hear you come in," she said, swallowing the indictment.

Dale gave her a gaze that attempted to penetrate every nook and cranny of her brain. "Then you better have your hearing checked. The front door swelled last summer like always. Usually, a few days of January temps takes care of it, but maybe there's something to all the climate change nonsense after all. Whatever the reason, I don't have time to fix it." He opened the fridge, took out a longneck bottle of beer and guzzled half before closing the door. He looked at the stove and then at her.

She flashed him the Play-Doh expression of submission sculpted years ago and reached in her apron for another antacid, which she devoured by the gross. The trim six-foot, forty-year-old, that could pass for thirty if not for thinning gray hair, looked like a rabid coyote watching her every move. If she made the mistake of locking eyes, a sudden attack might begin and no one would come to her rescue. After all, Dale Pearce was an upstanding member of the community and managed the only auto parts store within fifty miles. The Chamber of Commerce regularly recognized him for his business acumen. Last month, the Herald ran a feature about how the civic citizen helped a struggling family with a set of all-weather tires. Dale said it saved him thousands in advertising.

"What's for dinner?" he growled.

Say something quick or he will suspect. "I thought they might serve you a nice lunch at the meeting, but made dinner anyway."

"Served me lunch?" he laughed. "Why, the cheap bastards ordered a few sandwiches and cut them in half, so you looked like a pig if you took two pieces." He took another swig of the beer. "Lucky for me, I was in front of the line and took three and knocked two into the trash. Then I sat down and almost peed my pants, watching the big shots at the end of the line. You know that stupid saying that leaders eat last? Well, today they had to pool their change and buy a couple packages of peanut butter crackers from the vending machine… You still haven't told me what's for dinner?"

Dale got upset when she did not applaud his antics, but took her chances. "Well, I made enough so you can bring it for lunch tomorrow." She pointed at the stove. "It's the last of the venison," … *and also of me,* she wanted to add.

Dale replied by draining the rest of the beer and letting out a loud belch. He placed the empty on the worn laminate counter and retrieved another bottle from the fridge.

"Where are the two pains in my ass?" he asked, making his way to a kitchen chair.

Hopefully, the oldest is in New Hampshire, she wanted to say, but found a sliver of an antacid stuck on a back molar and sucked on it instead. She turned up the burner, looking absorbed in cooking. "Sonny should be home any minute. He's helping Billy tune up his truck."

"Once he gets his license next year, we will have to send a posse to bring him home. What about Sockeye?"

She preferred when he called her the mouthy bastard instead. She and Luis planned to get married and Olivia was the antonym for illegitimate. Funny, he never put Sonny in that category when she got pregnant a year after they were together. He thought it beyond generous to name his son Dale junior, but had no intention of sharing his last name with his mother. Theirs was a contract of convenience — she cooked and cleaned and expected to service his other needs in the wee hours. In return, she got a home for her and Olivia. Even before Sonny was born, she realized it was a bum deal.

Gabrielle opened the worn pine cabinet and took out four plates and when she turned around, found him squinting at her. She thought of the meeting with Rezi and how they meticulously planned out every detail except this one. *How am I supposed to act so, he does not suspect something?* The element of surprise was crucial, not only for Olivia's safety but also for her own escape. One wrong word and he would hit her until she came clean.

"Earth to Gabrielle," Dale said, snapping his fingers. "Where is your clone?"

"Uh…. Olivia stopped at the library to do research for a term paper," she said matter of fact.

"Talk about gullible! It's a wonder you didn't get shot with your two amigos."

"You know they were much more than friends, Dale," she replied in a steady tone. "Roberto was my baby brother and Luis was going to marry me! May God grant them eternal rest!"

"I understand grieving for your brother… but the other one? Unless you pawned it at Taco Bell, I don't remember seeing any ring on your finger when we met."

She held her breath and felt the force-field around her heart weaken. Luis used to stroke her ring finger and promise to save up for a gold band. She did not care about a physical symbol because they had a golden love no element could replicate.

Dale laughed at her silence. "Gotcha!" His face darkened. "I bet Sockeye is making out right now with that hoodlum. If I find out she lied about the library, she will spend the night with the crickets, if she can hear them in the trunk." He glanced toward the window. "If I make a bonus this year, I plan on building a garage for my beauty."

She nodded, anticipating his explosive reaction to the dent in the trunk. It would take all of her reserves to feign ignorance and later, when Olivia did not come home, he would figure it out. But if he tried to take it out on her, she would run.

Her peripheral vision noticed Dale's right leg tapping the floor. He looked like a jealous boyfriend and catapulted to his feet. "I have a good mind to drive over there right now and check."

"Don't be ridiculous," she replied, knowing Rezi needed a bit more time for safe measure. If she blew it now, he would call his police buddy. They could radio an APB faster than she could make toast. "You must be exhausted," she added, knowing Dale liked to focus on Dale. "Olivia will be home soon."

The selfish logic hit home. "You're right. I'm bone tired. My suppliers are raising their prices double digits and requiring monthly forecasts. No matter what I do, it will force customers to shop online for a discount, regardless of how much they love me." He drew in a deep breath and sat down again. "Heavy is the burden of running a business and paying for everything around here!"

"I know you work hard," she said, offering the pacifier he never outgrew.

He cocked his head. "Yeah, while you sit around all day watching tv. I know your game. One hour before I get home, you run the vacuum and cook something, so it appears you're fulfilling your responsibilities."

Ignore the landmine, a small voice inside pleaded, but she told it to go to hell. "You see me on your day off to know that's a lie. I go from morning to night around here!"

He waved her off. "Because you slack off all week and then try to impress me when I'm home."

A familiar sensation rose from her stomach and she made two fists. "Don't take the crappy day you've had out on me! I would love to get a job and help with the bills."

His neck fell backwards, and he laughed at the ceiling. "So, you can do even less around here? But who would hire an illegal alien?"

"I could work in the store."

"And do what besides getting in my way? I suppose you could use your experience and weed the sidewalk in summer. Other than that, you would just be another lazy slug like the rest of my employees that need watching." He looked her up and down. "But that reminds me. I could use Sockeye for inventory this weekend. Look at it as a math lesson. Maybe she can stop counting on her fingers."

Minus the insult, it was the second time he mentioned getting Olivia involved in the business and away from her watchful eyes. The fear led her to move up Rezi's visit.

The back door opened and Sonny came moping in, his long brown hair covering his eyes.

"I just washed the floor, so take your shoes off," she said, glancing at Dale's work boots he refused to take off no matter how dirty. *My mother thought cleanliness was next to godliness, but why do I bother?*

The teen looked at his father for help.

Dale shrugged and stared at the spotless linoleum floor. "You heard your mother."

Gabrielle eyed him. He nearly matched Dale's height and shared his long nose. They also had the same mannerisms that led her to believe they were twins. She cherished his consistent kindness and moments when he went the extra mile. How would he take it when she left?

"Where's Liv?" Sonny asked, slipping off a sneaker.

"I'm told at the library," Dale replied.

"Wow that's a new one!" their son mumbled.

Such a tattle-tail! She always covered for Roberto when they were growing up. Sonny was aware of the consequences when he threw Liv under the bus.

Before she could make peace, Dale headed for the door.

CHAPTER FIVE

Olivia killed time by counting the exits and noticed the grass becoming greener the further south they traveled. The nerves on the ends of her fingers tingled like they did during her swimming adventures in the quarry. A gaggle of boys were always on hand, daring her to jump off the twenty-foot cliff and hoping she would lose her top when she hit the water. Teenage hormones aside, she learned hesitation is Fear's big brother and courage waited to be claimed twenty feet below the surface. Yet, there was no simple way out of this predicament. The highway's monotony and the tires' hum caused her eyes to grow heavy. Suddenly, her mother was running alongside the car carrying a slim suitcase and wearing no shoes. Before she could roll down the window, the car hit a bump and Mama disappeared into the pavement.

Blinking, she realized she wasn't home or in the back of the Catalina, but on a dirt road with a humanoid that had all the windows down. The chilly night air was like a slap in the face.

She rubbed sleep out of one eye. "Where are we?"

Rezi took a sharp right and continued down a long driveway, but the pavement was now so smooth that the tires went silent. "Welcome to the New Roswell's guest house," she announced.

"Where's that?"

"Like I said in Salem. Seth bought a farm. This is where humanity will make a new beginning."

She rolled her eyes in the dark. "That's a bold goal for a commune." She checked the buttons on her shirt as she expected everyone here would walk around naked and pretend not to know, like isolated tribes in *National Geographic.* She could still hear the boys giggling in fifth grade.

"Communes get a bad rap. If you research it, it's a community of people cohabitating and sharing possessions and responsibilities. I think we can agree that given the crazy world we live in, that's a good starting place," Rezi instructed in a teacher's voice.

"Why call it New Roswell? Does it have something to do with aliens?"

"That's the best question you asked all day. Do you find it strange how settlers named towns and cities after their homelands, adding 'new' as if to signify a fresh beginning? But nothing changes and the same discrimination…sickness…and death follows. We plan something different here. That's why we don't carry the baggage of last names. As far as aliens are concerned, all I will say is we need a fresh start from the past."

"I'm too tired to unravel any of this." It crossed her mind that the split-level, with no lights on, resembled a haunted house amidst the towering pines. "Is this where I'm staying until my mother comes for me?" she asked pointing.

"Yes and no," Rezi replied, shutting off the car. "This is the guest house. You will stay here for now."

She jumped out and retrieved the suitcase from the trunk, and followed Rezi up the short brick walkway, wet with dew. The house looked legit enough with light blue vinyl siding and black shutters. But when they reached the front door, she noticed a black symbol that resembled a figure-eight lying on its side, tattooed on the wood.

Having seen plenty of horror flicks, both she and Mama knew this was foreshadowing. She backed up and glanced up at the canopy of pine trees overshadowing the house.

Rezi sensed the hesitation and swung around. "What's the matter?"

She pointed at the door. "What does that symbol mean?"

Rezi looked and smiled. "Infinity."

"What?"

She opened the glass storm door and fingered the strange sign on the wood. "Look at how the lines turn in on itself. Reflect on it enough and you will get a sense of how the past, present, and future are one. Seth says it provides more clarity than a circle because..." she stopped and turned around. "I'm getting ahead of myself. You must feel like I started telling a story in the middle. Seth will explain everything."

"Who is this Seth guy? The Wizard of Oz?"

"That charlatan hid behind a curtain, but Seth welcomes all to see. You're his guest," she replied, unlocking the front door, "and so am I."

She followed the strange woman into the house and held the suitcase handle tight so she could clock anyone that jumped out of the darkness. When Rezi put the lights on, the terror evaporated as it reminded her of Martha's house with a spacious living room that led to the kitchen with an intersecting hallway for the bathroom and bedrooms. House design aside, the furniture looked very odd, with twin couches wrapped in white leather and fur on the armrests. More than the material, she wondered how anyone sat in them, as the seats were a good two feet wide and three feet deep. *Do you lay on them instead of sitting?* she wondered. Whatever their purpose, six dark monitors hung on the wall between them.

Rezi watched her, taking it all in. "Amazing, isn't it? Let's get you something to eat."

She led her to the modern kitchen with a palette limited to white and stainless steel. Rezi opened the fridge and Olivia noticed the shelves were empty, except for a paper plate with a cheeseburger. It looked like a quarter pounder from McDonald's with limp lettuce hanging out the side.

"What if I told you I'm a vegetarian?" she asked.

"Then I would say your mother is quite the jokester because she told me this is your favorite treat." She transported the plate to the microwave. "But if you decide to become vegetarian, that will serve you well as we limit meat here. Seth realizes it will be a transition."

She watched the burger slowly spin. The thought of the wilted tomato and lettuce being zapped was almost enough to take a pass. But she had eaten nothing but a bowl of cornflakes for breakfast. When the microwave chimed, she retrieved the burger and sat down at the industrial steel table and took a bite. It was juicy and the combo of meat, pickles, and ketchup overwhelmed the beat-up vegetables. Halfway through, she noticed Rezi leaning against the counter watching her eat.

"Aren't you going to have something?" she asked.

"Perhaps later," she responded and continued watching like she expected her to bolt for the door.

Olivia pushed the plate away. "My mother told me the key to understanding anything is through observation. Today, I failed her." She pointed at Rezi's coat. "You don't have a gun and acted tough because you thought I might run."

Rezi's face did not change one iota.

Olivia tried looking out a slider door on the far side of the room, but the harsh kitchen light reflected, making it feel like a cell. She noticed a monitor in the ceiling pointed at the table. A red light blinked.

"I don't understand. Why put yourself through this for my mother? You just met her," she said, looking at the device.

The words unlocked Rezi's ambivalence, and she took a seat beside her. "Because someone did the same for me."

The revelation made the grease from the hamburger irritate her esophagus. "I don't understand."

"Seth is the reason … but you're tired of hearing about him. You'll understand soon enough. In the meantime, let's get you settled."

She hesitated, wanting to hold on to the moment. "Are you happy living here, or is this just a big act for me?"

Rezi glanced at the monitor on the ceiling. "Happy is such a fleeting word. Hope is a better foundation for what we have planned."

She bit her lip to keep from repeating Papa Dale's quote from Mike Tyson: "everyone has a plan until they get punched in the mouth." She thought of her mother back home alone. How did she explain the dent in the car?

The sound of keys in the front door startled them both. Rezi gestured to remain quiet and tiptoed into the living room. Olivia wondered how Papa Dale tracked them down so fast. *It's possible that he became so enraged about the dent in the trunk, he assaulted Mama until she provided him with the address!* She had no desire to spend the rest of her life in the Catalina and inched toward the back door. With any luck, Papa Dale's bum knee would slow him down.

"Who's there?" Rezi yelled as the door opened.

"Good evening!" a smooth voice replied.

"You nearly scared me half to death!" the hybrid kidnapper-protector said.

The air went silent for a moment, followed by a smooth laugh. "My dear, we banished scared and death from our vocabulary years ago."

"True...forgive me."

Olivia rushed to the hall and saw a tall, white-haired man bent over hugging Rezi. Given their height difference, it looked like his back might snap.

"I wanted to see how you made out," he said, letting go.

"When haven't I delivered for you?" Rezi replied in that flat, no-nonsense tone of hers.

Olivia held her breath as Rezi led the tall stranger into the kitchen. She found his clothes amusing for a cool April evening: dark t-shirt a size too small, dungaree cutoffs, brown sandals, no socks. His skin was ghostly white and combined with light blue eyes that reminded her of a rabbit she had as a child. The humor disappeared when she noticed the infinity tattoo on the right forearm.

She was still staring at the horizontal figure eight when he extended his hand. "You must be Olivia!" he said, like she was a Hollywood starlet. But what impressed her most was his voice, which sounded smoother than maples syrup running down a stack of Mama's pancakes.

All she could do was nod as her face grew hot. Underestimating Rezi's description of their leader was a mistake.

The man smiled with the innocence of a young child before discovering the power of deception. His teeth were so straight and white she wondered if they were real.

"I'm Seth," he continued and squeezed her hand. "I've heard a lot about you and your family. Welcome."

She glanced at Rezi. "I'm sure you will hear some more."

He laughed like he was in on the joke. "Sounds like an interesting ride from Maine?" He put his arm around Rezi and pulled her in. "I'm fascinated to hear more, but from you. I stopped by this evening to check on my sister and also meet you."

"Rezi is your sister?" she asked.

He laughed again, but this time she got the sense it was the grownup type to put an exclamation mark on what came after. "Not biologically, but on a deeper level." He cocked his head and pointed at her. "Your aura is extraordinary. Has anyone ever told you that?"

Olivia looked at his tattoo again and sensed she made a mistake in not escaping. The back door was unguarded and she could have taken off when Rezi greeted Seth.

Seth appeared to read her mind because he opened his mouth and then hesitated like he swallowed the words instead. "I apologize. You've had a hard day and must be exhausted. Let's talk more tomorrow." He took a step closer and scanned her face with those icy blue eyes. Like Rezi, his eyes could not remain still and roamed her face.

"Olivia. Such a beautiful name."

"Thanks," she half-whispered and looked away.

"Your name stands for olive tree and in Greek mythology a symbol of peace and friendship." He looked at Rezi and sighed. "In this outpost of humanity, we're relearning the meaning of both."

She listened to the lilt of his voice and it sounded strong...soft...safe. Most people in her life only barked like the incoherent teacher in *Charlie Brown.*

"Olivia," he called as his eyes drilled into hers. The tone felt hypnotic, and she could not look away. "I know what he calls you.... how he punishes. It breaks my heart."

The hunger, tiredness, and nerves were too much and tears welled up.

He took a tissue out of his pocket and handed it to her. "You're valued here."

The day was one long chain of words, some angry, others desperate, most trying to make sense of this odyssey. It made her wish again for the trunk of the Catalina, where there was honesty in the silent darkness.

Olivia began moving away to find space to regroup when Seth grabbed her hand and put something in it. When she looked at the object, she lost her breath.

It was the same turquoise necklace she eyed at Pete's Roadside Extravaganza.

CHAPTER SIX

Gabrielle opened the back door and filled her lungs with the young spring air. It was a moonless night and made for easy pickings for the bug zapper on the corner of the house. The purple light crackled every few seconds, drowning out the cricket and peeper duet. She watched a few of the electrocutions, which seemed similar to shooting fish in a barrel. Not that she gave much thought to the life cycle of a bug, but it seemed cruel to use light on a dark night to fry anything but a mosquito. As it was, life was brief for bugs in Maine. Why not let them enjoy a few dawns? It made her think of being pregnant and alone after losing Luis and Roberto. She might as well have been dead too when she called Papa. He did not care about her predicament or grief, only that she was to blame for a hole in his heart and she would pay by being banished. After wandering in the dark, the neon lights of Atlantic City drew her in. Working under the table as a chambermaid proved to be the worse wager she ever made. She was vacuuming the stained carpet in the lobby when she noticed a sad-looking guest watching. The encounter made her worry the man had a disturbing attraction to pregnant women or awareness of her undocumented status. After discovering Dale had a room on the second floor by the ice machine, she avoided the area. Now she appreciated how the bug zapper might be cruel, but it was quick; unlike being bled to death for sixteen years.

Familiar headlights appeared coming up the driveway fast, and she shut the door and headed for the living room where his recliner overshadowed a loveseat that was anything but. Pretending to be asleep would not slow the tornado, so she sat down and rubbed the arm of her robe, wishing for a cigarette.

The front door groaned open and then slammed shut, followed by heavy footsteps coming her way. A second later, Dale appeared and suddenly stopped. Gabrielle thought he was considering the best approach — probe and find a crack, or go hard and deal with the mess later. Either way, the coming flood of harsh words and fists would wash away the last remnants of the relationship.

Dale shifted out of neutral, and after collapsing in the recliner, closed his eyes. She noticed his taut jaw muscles; a terrible habit he developed when aggravated, which was most days, and he popped aspirin like peanuts to deal with the headaches. She searched his face, looking beneath the crooked lines running across the forehead, the puffy sacks under both eyes, even the new age spot on his right temple for a remnant of the vulnerability that attracted her to the false light.

Taking a deep breath, she remembered how her perception of him changed. *She had just finished cleaning up a room after an ugly stag party that sprayed a keg of beer on everything when he flagged her down. The tall thin stranger looked like he just stepped out of a Walmart flyer wearing new blue jeans, a red flannel shirt and white sneakers that would glow in the dark.*

"You gotta help me!" he half shouted. "I locked my wallet in the safe and forgot the combination." He punctuated the plea with so many curse words she did not know whether to laugh or call a priest for an exorcism. When she returned with the hotel manager, Dale looked like a little boy that lost a puppy.

The pissed off dragon opened his eyes and gave her a tired look. "Did she call?"

She shook her head without blinking.

"I went to the library." He drew in a long breath and let the drama build.

"And?"

He leaned forward, eyes squinting. "It's not open."

She nodded. "I think it closes at seven."

He thrust an index finger toward her. "The sign on the door said it was closed for the day because a pipe burst in the bathroom!"

She briefly glanced at the wall clock over his shoulder. Even if they stopped for something to eat, they were in New Hampshire by now.

"She must have gone to Martha's house."

"Then she should have called."

"How can she? You won't let her have a cell phone," she replied, channeling her daughter's frustration.

"That's no excuse!" he yelled back. "She could have borrowed Martha's and called you. If you ask me…" He stopped mid-sentence and pulled on his chin. "Why am I the one freaking out about this? You're her mother and look bored by it all."

She thought of the movies and marveled at how actors not only memorize their lines but took on the character. "Because Olivia has a good head on her shoulders. Martha has been helping her with her studies like algebra. I can't!"

"But you sure understand subtraction," he said with a sarcastic laugh.

"What does that mean?"

"That I pay for everything around here." He catapulted out of the recliner. "She hasn't come home, so I don't understand how you can be so blase. Pick up the phone and call her friend's house."

Gabrielle headed for the kitchen, and Dale followed close behind. It was a profound mystery why he never allowed her to use his cell phone. The harvest gold rotary phone with the twisted cord hung on the wall next to the refrigerator. She dialed nine of the ten numbers hoping Dale would buy the improvisation.

She pretended to hear it ring. "No one is picking up."

Sonny came in through the back door with flushed cheeks and enormous eyes. She braced herself and hung up the phone.

As usual, Sonny ignored her and looked at his father.

"What happened to your car?" he asked, like the sky had fallen into the sea.

"Huh?"

"The trunk... it has a huge dent."

They hurried out, and she stayed in place and wrestled what to do. If she remained indoors, it would look like she knew. But if she stepped outside and things took a turn for the worse, he might not allow her back in. It would be a long, frosty night.

She took her chances. When she joined them, father and son huddled over the trunk of the Pontiac. After the incident, she dug a hole in the backyard and buried the rock like a murder weapon.

Dale spun around and pointed at the trunk. "Come clean before I send you back to Mexico in a taco shell."

She practiced expressing surprise in the mirror for an hour. "What are you talking about? I know nothing!"

"I know nothing," he repeated in a mocking tone. "Well, the car was sitting here all day! What happened?"

Her mind replayed Olivia smashing the rock a half dozen times before she could intercede. "Nothing! You drove to the library. It's possible something hit it."

"Like what? A meteor?" he asked.

Sonny approached her. "I told Papa I stopped at the store. Martha was there, hanging out with her friends. No one has seen Liv today."

Dale stared at her, gauging her reaction, and she heard the bug zapper fry another.

CHAPTER SEVEN

Rezi led her down a narrow and dimly lit hall. The procession stopped in front of a closed white door.

"This is your room," Rezi said, opening the door and flipping on an overhead light.

Olivia looked in and took in the double bed, cherry nightstand, and dresser. A burgundy area rug covered most of the hardwood floor.

"I'm across the hall if you need anything," Rezi said, and then gestured towards the bathroom ahead. "Settle in and I'll get cleaned up. Give me ten minutes and the bathroom will be yours."

She nodded, and after entering the room, closed the door. Placing the suitcase on the bed, she stared at its banged-up skin before popping the latch. They had both been through a lot today. The contents remained the same as last week, but they gave the impression that someone had hastily thrown everything in: a small bag of toiletries, underwear, socks, three t-shirts, two flannel shirts, a pair of blue jeans, cutoffs, and a gray sweatshirt. The sweatshirt was a last-minute replacement for the ratty-looking robe.

Papa Dale would come home exhausted from the auto parts store during the run-up to Christmas or before the first snowstorm of the season, claiming he couldn't sleep. She never grasped the sensation until now. Exhausted yet hyper. The day felt a month long, and every muscle in her body ached. She glanced at the digital watch Mama gave her at Christmas. Eight o'clock. Any other weeknight, she would be doing homework or begging Sonny to borrow his tablet to check social media or watch videos. Now she was in a strange house and eyed the accommodations again. The room reminded her of the HGTV show where a designer remodels a house and, before putting it on the market, has it staged with furniture and incidentals to make it feel like home. Examining the furnishings, they addressed the essentials, but no other details provided clues about the owner.

Her eyes focused on an empty hanger on the opposite wall, along with the outline of the missing frame. Taking a quick look around the room, she spotted another hook above the bed.

The missing artwork intrigued her, and she got on her knees and looked under the bed. Nothing. Before standing, she pulled back the corner of the area rug, half expecting a price tag, but it was clean. She made her way over to the dresser and looked in the drawers for clues. The total of her effort was a paperclip. A sudden wave of weakness hit and she put the shade up on the window and tried to open it, but it would not budge. Overwhelmed by dizziness, she settled onto the bed and contemplated Papa Dale's reaction to her being gone.

She looked at the suitcase and realized she did not bring any pajamas. Mama warned her to check everything and somehow, she did not think of that, maybe because when you're on the run, sleep is the last thing you consider. Since she lacked certainty about this being home until Mama arrived, she was unsure whether to unpack. She did not want to trip over the suitcase in the wee hours and looked at the closet. *Maybe the missing pictures are in there?* she thought.

She jumped up, but found the door locked. Before she had the chance to retract her foot, she kicked the door, causing both a loud rattling sound and an object to collide with her head. Looking down, she found a silver key. The kick dislodged it from its resting place on the trim board.

Her fingers shook a bit as she put the key in the lock. Immediately, she came face to face with a large framed poster of a historical marker hanging on the inside of the door. Her blurry eyes scanned the text.

Betty and Barney Hill Incident. On the night of September 19–20, 1961, Portsmouth, NH couple Betty and Barney Hill experienced a close encounter with an unidentified flying object and two hours of "lost" time while driving south on Route 3 near Lincoln. They filed an official Air Force Project Blue Book report of a brightly lit cigar-shaped craft the next day. The story became public after being leaked to the Boston Traveler in 1965. This was the first reported UFO abduction report in the United States.

There were no clothes or hangers in the closet but stacks of yellowed newspapers on the top shelf. She pulled out one copy, the edges of the paper curled and noticed it featured a picture of the interracial couple.

Betty and Barney Hill... What the hell has Mama gotten me mixed up in? she thought.

A knock put an end to the exploration, and she closed the closet and walked towards the door. When she opened it, Rezi was standing with a stack of clean towels. As gracious as the gesture, her eyes told a different story as she looked past her.

"The bathroom is yours," she said, handing her the towels.

"Thanks."

"I heard a bang. Is everything okay?"

She glanced behind her, buying time. "Yeah...the suitcase... it... fell off the bed."

Rezi gave her a smug smile. "I thought you might try to escape out the window."

"Not tonight," she said, still considering the possibility.

"That's good, because you wouldn't get far."

"Attack dogs?"

"No, but infrared scanners. Seth says we can never be too careful and there are high-tech countermeasures designed to stop neighbors that fear what we are building. Let's just say you wouldn't get far without us knowing."

"Good to know," she replied and thought maybe this was not all bad, since that meant Papa Dale could not get in either. *Mama should have come too*, she thought.

Suddenly, she felt the blood drain out of her legs and she grabbed the door.

Rezi noticed and for the first time, the woman's eyes softened and she helped her across the room and into the bed.

As sleep took hold, Betty and Barney Hill stared at her with sad eyes.

CHAPTER EIGHT

Gabrielle poured the last of the coffee and took a sip of the dark brew. Half a cup would be more than enough to make her heart race, plus give her a stomachache.

She shuffled back to the hard wooden chair at the kitchen table and held the mug against her forehead, hoping it would ease the headache aspirin failed to touch.

She heard footsteps and, looking up, found her son staring at her like he did when working with his father on the Catalina, or helping his buddy rebuild a motorcycle. Even if he had the tools, he would never understand her wiring, since it stretched three thousand miles to Mexico.

"Thanks for letting me sleep in today, Mama. I feel beat," he said and glanced at a ceramic clock over the sink. "I can't fathom that it's nine o'clock."

She nodded, though the clock could have read noon and she would feel the same. It had been a long night, with Dale alternating between sulking and screaming. In between, she called the few friends Olivia had and Sonny checked in with the kid she kissed. It was close to midnight when she called the hospital ER for the third time and Dale called the Chief and filled him in. Sonny monitored things from the couch and channel surfed. Around three in the morning, Dale, and Sonny headed to bed and left her sitting in the dark. As much as she planned for blowback, the intensity of this storm overwhelmed her.

Her son shuffled over to the cupboard and grabbed a box of Rice Krispies and placed it on the table.

She contemplated hearing snap, crackle, and pop as her bones broke when Dale discovered the truth. All the lying about Olivia required stamina she did not have.

Sonny retrieved a carton of milk, bowl, and tablespoon and sat down. She watched him pour the cereal and milk and begin shoveling the contents into his mouth, marveling at how the little boy she doted over was now grown up. Most of his features reflected Dale, but he had pieces of her — almond-shaped eyes, long fingers... and a tendency to keep things bottled up.

She touched his arm. "I can make you a breakfast burrito or chilaquiles instead of inhaling half a box of cereal."

He gave her a grin that mirrored his father's, but without the accompanying sarcasm. "Sure, if Papa isn't coming home soon."

"I'll take my chances," she replied and jumped up. It was one of the few secrets they shared. Dale refused to try any Mexican food and would complain it stunk up the house. Her lone victory came five years ago. Dale suffered from a terrible cold and tried a bowl of pozole and the soup made him feel better. Other than that, he avoided Mexican food, fearing that the colorful dishes from home would contaminate his Yankee genes. Sonny was a different story and inhaled everything her mother taught her to cook. The spicier the better.

She had her head in the fridge, pulling out eggs, cheese, and peppers when he dropped the bomb.

"I think Liv ran away," he said.

"Why would you say that?" she replied, turning around.

"Because I saw her packing the other day." He took another heaping tablespoon and though careful, half of the contents spilled on the worn pine top.

"Suitcase?" Coffee sloshed around in her stomach, and she had a flashback of her mother packing for the hospital stay, promising it would be short. Her father brought the suitcase home a few days later without its owner.

"Please don't get mad at me for not saying anything last night. I hoped Liv would come home by now after realizing freedom gets pretty boring when you're hiding at your friend's house."

The admission made her look at him with fresh eyes. Sonny might not be close with his half-sister, but still cared about her.

"Did you ask her about packing?"

He made half-hearted circles in the bowl with his spoon. "Kinda."

"And?" she asked and held her breath. This whole escape plan was like one giant Jenga game. All it would take would be one wrong move and everything would collapse. Olivia had to remain hidden until she left.

"She said she was sleeping at Martha's this weekend. I told her she was fibbing or dreaming because Papa would never allow that; especially after he caught her with Ricky. Liv said she didn't care what he said because he wasn't her father."

He placed the spoon on the table and glanced at her to check in. All she could do was bite her lip and nod. When her time came to leave, she would not have a suitcase to pack. Fifty-gallon trash bags would suffice.

"If she just kept her trap shut, things would go a lot easier. But she mouths off and Papa..." he stopped and looked toward the front door which led to the sidewalk and then the trunk.

She picked up an egg and examined its thin shell. "I'm glad your sister is a spitfire, even if it comes at a cost. If I were more like her, I would have been strong when Luis and Roberto...." It was her turn to stop and gauge her son's reaction.

Sonny flashed a hurt look. "Which means you wouldn't have met Papa ... and I wouldn't be sitting here." He pushed the bowl away.

She rushed forward and sat down beside him. "I didn't mean it that way! Give me some slack, as I didn't sleep a wink last night and my brain isn't matching up with my tongue." She kissed his cheek. "You are one of the greatest joys in my life," she added, running her hand through his thick mop of hair. "You and Liv make quite a combo. She's mouthy and you taste your words first."

"Maybe, but we're no Frick and Frack."

She eyed her son, the apple of Dale's eye, even if the core wasn't American pure. He allowed Sonny complete freedom, even letting him roam the store and pick out items for his projects. Then Dale would dent the box and label it damaged so he could buy it at a huge discount or get it for free. But he did not ask Sonny to help with the upcoming inventory. No, he wanted Olivia to do it after hours alone with him. It was just another trunk except he would be in there too.

Sonny cleared his throat. "I'm feeling stupid."

"Why?"

"Because I told Liv if she runs away, she better not head south, because that's where Papa will look."

"Because she's a sockeye? The biggest surprise is he's looking for her at all."

"Why would you say that?"

"Because she's not his daughter …. and worse, she's Latino." She looked down at the cereal on the table, waiting to be wiped up and discarded. After all these years, she still could not figure out why he pursued her like he did. The best she could rationalize were equal parts lust and loneliness. She hoped he would love her, but discovered he only loved himself. The bigger questions came each night as she lay in bed listening to him snore. Why did she think she could ever change him and why did she put up with it for so long?

Sonny watched her face. "I'm half Mexican too."

She smiled. "Yes, and I'll never let you forget it."

"Which is cool and I want to visit Mexico someday. Meet my relatives."

Her mind filled in a future scene; the small village with the schoolhouse in the center. Children running, laughing, playing on the swings. Old men at the table playing dominoes. The smell of roasted pig. In the next instant, her father appeared and said she was not welcome. Eden faded.

She grabbed his hand and tried smiling, but failed. "We will get through this." She wanted to say something about the future, prepare the ground for her departure.

The phone rang.

She jumped up. No doubt Dale was checking in. She readied the part of the worried mother. The role came easy.

Instead, Sonny's friend Billy said hello.

She no sooner handed him the phone when she watched his eyes grow big.

"What?" he yelled and then listened some more. She stopped breathing.

He put his hand over the receiver. "Billy spoke with his sister Lori, who was working at Humphries yesterday. Liv came in with a weird lady named Rezi. She didn't take down the plate, but can describe the car."

Gabrielle grabbed a chair and sat down. The room began spinning.

Sonny announced, "Someone has kidnapped Liv!"

CHAPTER NINE

Even before opening her eyes, Gabrielle sensed a dull pain radiating across her forehead. Sitting up only intensified the headache and brought to mind the time when she and Martha split a twelve pack of beer in Sonny's treehouse. The hangover the next day proved the buzz was not worth it.

Sunlight streamed through the window illuminating painful memories, and she felt for the turquoise necklace around her neck. She recalled Rezi assisting her to bed before everything turned dark. Looking under the blanket, she discovered she had fallen asleep in her clothes. The way she passed out together with the headache made her wonder what else was in the burger. She checked her watch and stared at the time in disbelief. Papa Dale only let her sleep until nine o'clock if she had the flu.

Squinting, she gazed through the window that overlooked a spacious backyard that stopped at a border of pine and maple trees, their arms locked together. The grass glowed shamrock green and the azure sky extended unrestricted to heaven. The scene triggered the memory of the weird poster about Barney and Betty Hill and she jumped out of bed, eager to study it again and explore the other mementoes. But the door was surprisingly locked. Frustrated, she searched the floor and door frame, but the key eluded her.

The headache beat on her temples and she retrieved the toiletry bag from the suitcase and made her way to the bathroom. There she found clean towels and a small bar of soap along with sample bottles of shampoo and conditioner.

After washing her face and brushing her teeth, she headed back to her room, when the smell of bacon and coffee made her stomach rumble.

Tiptoeing down the hall, she expected to find Rezi in the kitchen with spatula in hand, eyes darting back and forth, looking for intruders. Instead, she discovered a guy with shoulder-length wavy blond hair sitting at the kitchen table with his back to her. He wore a snug white t-shirt which accented his muscles.

"Good morning, Olivia," a smooth voice said without turning around.

"Morning," she replied, surprised he heard her.

"If you're hungry, Rezi left something for you in the fridge, but the coffee is fresh."

"Okay, thanks." She grabbed a mug on the counter, hoping the caffeine would help the headache. After taking a quick sip of the potent brew, she stole another glance at the stranger and felt her heart quicken. She guessed he was around eighteen. The sun coming in from the slider graced a thin nose, full lips, dimpled jaw. Handsome aside, she concentrated on the dark sunglasses.

The Greek god took a bite of toast. "I can't eat when I first wake up. You're welcome to join me and enjoy your coffee."

She ran her fingers through her hair on the way to the table.

He smiled as she sat down.

"I'm Luke," he said, extending a hand in her direction.

It felt so soft she had no desire to let it go. "I'm Olivia," she began, and then laughed. "Seems you already know that."

"Yes, I do."

"What did Seth do? Send my bio out to everyone?"

"Something like that." He laughed, and the way it tumbled out put her at ease. "You'll come to understand how special you are. It's a select group."

Select group? She eyed his plate. There were a few hard pebbles of scrambled egg left along with a piece of bacon that resembled charcoal. Rezi might be the gatherer, but not much of a cook. Luke reached for his coffee and his hand drifted a bit to the right before locating it. The epiphany made her inhale.

"Figure it out yet?" he asked.

Her cheeks burned. "What do you mean?"

"That I'm blind."

"No, I can see that..." Her headache spiked. "I'm sorry. I didn't mean to put it that way."

"No, I'm sure you didn't," he said with the same easy laugh.

She tasted the coffee and hid behind the mug while scanning his face, admiring how the blond locks caressed his forehead and were a shade lighter than hers. It felt wrong to stare, but he would never know.

Luke leaned toward her. "Go ahead and ask."

"Ask what?"

"You know what."

She almost dropped the mug, shocked he could read her thoughts. "I have manners even if I mess up my words sometimes. It's none of my business what happened."

"Which is admirable, but the question remains." He reached for his coffee again. "Lights out happened five years ago, but some days feels a lot longer."

"Accident?" she asked, curiosity getting the better of her.

He sighed. "I've been asking myself the same question. Accident or a revelation of sorts, the results are the same. The intense light fried my retinas."

She waited, anticipating he would comment on the light source, but he turned his head, signifying the end of the disclosure.

"Where's Rezi?" she asked, wanting to find safer ground.

"She and my dad went to a meeting. My father didn't want you waking up here alone, so he asked me to stay and watch you." He gave her a smile. "Sometimes you can't make this stuff up and yes, he put it that way without feeling guilty."

She laughed. "Seth is your father? I met him last night."

Luke cocked his head in a stiff pose, and using an index finger, traced his face. She followed the line from his forehead, down the bridge of his nose, over kissable lips and waded into the dimple on his chin. Her heart pounded and made her forget the headache.

"Don't you see the resemblance?" he asked.

"It was late and I couldn't see straight. I was so tired."

The blind hunk leaned toward her again. "It's not fair you can drink in my imperfections and I can only judge you by that velvet voice of yours."

Velvet? Papa Dale said she cawed like a crow. She thought of the red, white, and blue sneakers, which never faded, no matter what she put them through. "People are quick to judge others by their looks, so maybe—"

"You think it's an advantage being blind then?" he asked, interrupting.

The remark sucked the air out of the room. "Of course not!"

He grabbed her arm. "Then let me see you."

She hesitated to answer the trick question. "How?"

"Fair is fair. Let me read your face."

She held the air in her lungs. Diagraming the conversation to this point would be challenging. That said, she knew she would remember this moment for the rest of her life.

A million-dollar smile blocked out the sun and the rest of the world. He extended his hand. "Help me get started."

Her hand trembled as she placed his index finger at the top of her forehead. She could not determine if his touch felt soft or warm because an electric current coursed through her entire body. His finger hesitated a long moment before tracing a path down to her eyebrows, gently across her eyes, then down the bridge of her nose and slowly outlined her lips. She feared he would feel the chipped tooth, but his finger moved on to her right cheek then across to her ear and followed her hair down to her shoulder before retracing its path back up to her cheek and finished at her chin.

Luke withdrew his finger and smiled. "My father told me you were a pretty blonde, but I think he wanted to protect me. You're beautiful."

Her heart was racing, but his words frightened her because they did not sound like some smooth talker, but authentic. But vulnerability was not in her vocabulary. "I bet you say that to all the girls."

"Yeah, they line up at the door, hoping I'll read them like Braille."

"I'm sorry. It's just...." She left it there.

"Forgive me, if I come on too strong." He tapped his forehead. "Sometimes I just get lost in here."

She knew what he meant and changed the subject. "You said your father and Rezi went to a meeting?"

"Yeah, and I'm the welcome wagon."

"Where is the rest of the ...community?" she asked, not wanting to say commune.

"My father gets upset when I ruin the orientation as it pertains to your special gift. You'll see soon enough."

CHAPTER TEN

Gabrielle watched the Catalina come speeding up the driveway, careening this way and that, as Dale knew every bump and crater, except the bottomless one waiting inside the house.

She felt like she had been holding her breath since Sonny called his father at the store and between gulps of air, filled him in on Olivia's kidnapping. After hanging up, she wanted to explain everything to him before this lie continued, but he quickly left to hear the details from Lori.

Dale jumped out of his car and she could see his cheeks were beet colored fifty feet away. That was never a good sign unless the Sox were winning, and he was halfway to Blitz-Ville, which meant he would pass out in the recliner and not come looking for a midnight love fest. She considered running out and confronting him on the front lawn and take in the forsythia before he knocked her out, but preferred curling up on the loveseat when the end came. With any luck, she would not bleed on the worn cushions.

The front door flew open and an icy breeze arrived before her common-law husband.

"Where's Sonny?" he asked, rushing past her into the kitchen since that's where their son grazed 24/7.

She followed at a safe distance. "He went to see Lori to ask if she remembered anything else."

Dale opened the fridge and took out a beer. "I told that kid a million times to think with his head instead of his heart. The police will ask Lori to go over all the details." He drained half the bottle. "Ned is waiting for us at the station, so hurry and grab your coat."

Her stomach dropped to her ankles, and a flutter ran across her chest. Nothing had gone as she imagined since Olivia overreacted. The police might not bother searching for a runaway, but a kidnapped teen girl from Safe town, USA? Things like this did not happen here. The press would go nuts.

"Why the hell are you standing there?" Dale asked, cutting the air in front of her face. "Let's go!"

Her eyes followed the angry hand. Once upon a time, it held her fingers tight while saving her and tiny Olivia from homelessness. They locked hands for the first few years when they made love and she waited for a ring that would never come. Instead, his five digits transformed into an unpredictable weapon… pointing… slapping… punching. She did not recognize the man attached to the hand any longer. It took years and dozens of beatings to realize he was a monster she had to break free from.

"I'm done," she said, standing up straight and planting her feet.

Dale's head jerked back like she slapped him hard. "You're more like well-done… which I hate." His oversized head leaned toward her like a viper ready to strike. "I can't figure you out. Your Sockeye's mother and here you stand, looking bored with it all. What's the matter with you?"

Gabrielle looked past him and out the door. This time of year, the sun sprayed everything it touched with a super bright formula, unlike winter when the light came in short slanted spans and shadows reigned. She began planning the details of her escape with Rezi when the sun called it a day by midafternoon. Since then, she envisioned the added seconds of daylight as her future. Bold and bright.

"Gabrielle!" Dale yelled to get her attention. "Let's go!"

She walked to the far side of the kitchen table. The added distance would make it difficult for a sudden TKO.

"Sit down," she said firmly.

Dale hesitated, unfamiliar with the voice, before sitting in a pine chair. "This better be good or the Chief will wonder how you got such a nasty shiner."

"You have Ned so wrapped around your finger you can tell him I fell again in the upstairs bathroom. Funny how the Chief never asks how that's possible since we live in a ranch. Great police skills."

"That's because Ned and I see things the same way. Like the Good Book says. *wives, submit to your husbands.* Sometimes, we have to remind you."

"Thank you, Pastor Dale for only remembering what fits. The second part of the verse says, *husbands should love their wives as they do their own bodies.* The last time I heard it, I was nursing one of your Saturday night specials. Seems to me you owe yourself a few dozen black and blues. I'd be happy to keep count."

He eyed her like she was a giant centipede he would stomp on any second. His right leg began jerking up and down.

She swallowed, trying to find the needed saliva. "Olivia didn't run away."

His face did not change, which surprised her. "Let me guess, Sockeye ran off with that punk. I'm sure you will be a grandmother by Valentine's Day."

"For the last time, my daughter's name is Olivia. And she didn't run away. I sent her somewhere safe."

"Safe? There's no such place, sweetheart." He cocked his head. "Okay, come clean. What's this all about?"

She practiced the words so many times they should have triggered spontaneous combustion years ago. Instead, the internal fire remained hidden and her spirit turned to ash.

"I've had enough of you — of us. I'm leaving."

For years, she laughed at the weather forecast. Meteorologists would get everyone scared to death about the coming bomb cyclone, and it would turn out to be nothing but a firecracker. But she sucked at forecasts too, because Dale just yawned.

"I didn't know you won the lottery," he said without emotion. "Where's my cut?" He gave her a sarcastic smile. "Like I said, the Catalina needs a garage and a new paint job after I get the dent fixed."

Gabrielle knew words could be decoys, but the eyes were tunnels to the soul. Dale scanned the countertop and the block of knives. Next to it was a fat rolling pin. She knew he was considering the options. Cut or bludgeon?

She took a step sideways toward the back door; her only escape. When Luis, Roberto and she crossed the border the last time, the wind was at their backs and they sprinted between rocks and desert scrub. If she got a head start, Dale would never catch her.

His eyes wandered back to her. "This is the thanks I get after rescuing a pregnant woman living on the street?"

"There you go again, distorting facts." She remembered how he staggered into the hotel early one morning, half lit and bleeding after a bar fight. As she cleaned the head gash, he cried he had no one that cared. Who rescued who?

"Have you told our son?"

"Not yet. …. I thought it best we talk first." She inhaled deeply because she wanted to tell him alone. She wished she asked him to sit down after he hung up the telephone and took off to see Lori. Maybe it would have gotten ugly, but at least she could explain her reasons before Dale distorted everything.

He stood up and approached her. "Because you thought what? That I'd beg you to stay and when you said no, I'd give you a peck on the cheek? Maybe rent a U-Haul and help move you back to the land of the deplorables?" He bit his lip. "Did you expect I would have a meltdown, and that's why you sent Sockeye away? Which is it?"

"Like my father says, prepare for the worst and hope for the best."

"You're quoting the man that disowned you? That's priceless!" He came closer, and she took a step backwards. "I don't understand any of this. Why didn't you leave with Sockeye?"

"Because of Sonny," she replied and looked around the room. "I have stuff I need to take."

Dale followed her eyes and laughed. "Honey, without me, you have nothing! Everything you see here is mine. We should have talked first... but then again, you can't explain stupid to stupid."

She headed for the back door, and Dale grabbed her and spun her around.

"How long were you planning to let me run around like a fool thinking Sockeye had gone missing?"

She shoved him away, but it was like trying to move a block of cement. "Until I knew she was safe from that sick itch you get when you drink."

"So, you're psychoanalyzing me now?" He grabbed her arm. "You're the only one I ever wanted."

"Until there was a younger version of me."

He laughed. "Jealous? But now the police are involved and Sockeye wasn't in sync with your plan since she told the cashier to take down the plate. How do you explain that?"

She shrugged. "Nerves."

"Well, it will be interesting when we talk with Ned."

"I have nothing to say to him," she said walking away.

"But I do. You're undocumented!" Dale yelled after her.

She spun around. "You say that like I'm some type of ghost, but you more than anyone know I'm flesh and bone. I've been here half my life. Don't I deserve to be recognized by now?"

"Yeah, by ICE for deportation."

She raised her arms with upturned hands. "I don't think so. There are millions of us here! Why single me out?"

"Because Ned will do it for me if you leave."

She motioned for him to go away and went towards the bedroom. "I'll talk with Sonny when he comes home. I'm leaving tomorrow."

He followed close behind. "Don't count on making it until then."

CHAPTER ELEVEN

Sonny's legs ached, but he kept the bike in tenth gear and pedaled as hard as he could for downtown. Every fiber of his being fixated on finding Lori, blocking out any distractions or doubts about what the hell led to this. He looked forward to upgrading to a motorcycle once he got his license. As a steep curve neared, the bike picked up speed, and he glanced cautiously at the caliper brake assembly above the front tire. Last week, the assembly came loose and fell into the spokes. A second later, he became airborne over the handlebars. His chest still hurt.

As the bike rocketed into the town depot, he scanned the red brick buildings on both sides of Main Street and spied Lori, a black-haired beauty sitting on a cement wall outside the Community Center. He thought his heart rate was already at the max, but seeing her kicked it up the remaining notches. Seconds later, he braked hard in front of the goddess.

The girl of his dreams looked up to identify the intruder before retreating into her iPhone.

"I've been looking for you all over town!" he said, panting as he got off the bike. "I checked Buster's house… and then Kady's …" He stopped and worked on catching his breath and brushed the sweat off his forehead. "No one knew where you were!" He gave her a quick look and did not allow his eyes to linger on the face that haunted his dreams for years… the deep-set brown eyes…long eyelashes…full lips... the silky black hair that framed her face. He swallowed hard, looking at the red sweater and jeans on the petite frame. He thought, how lucky that material was. *It gets to hold her all day.*

Lori kept her eyes glued to the iPhone and pointed at a small Styrofoam cup on the wall. "It shouldn't be a mystery. Everyone knows I come here when I'm not working." She glanced at the Community Center. "I can't afford to blow money on coffee. They have AA meetings here every day and there's a nice blue-haired lady that brews gallons of dark roast and lets me take a cup. Every once in a while, she gets grandmotherly and makes me promise I will never start drinking, so I don't end up here." She let out a short laugh and fished a bent cigarette and lighter out of her jacket sitting on the wall. "Given my family history, I could run her meetings." Lighting up the cigarette, she took a drag and politely blew the smoke in the wind's direction.

Lori was the only person he knew that smoked menthol cigarettes. He got dizzy the few times he smoked with Billy and imagined the menthol variety would be like swallowing a tub of vapor rub. He speculated if he ever kissed Lori, the taste would be closer to bubble gum.

"Can I bum one?" he asked, though his lungs ached from the five-mile race.

She took another hit before shaking her head. "You're just a kid."

"You're only nineteen months older than me," he shot back.

"Well, that's over ten dog years."

He sat on the wall, trying to think of a comeback when she offered him the lit cigarette. "I only have a few left and don't get paid until Friday. You look like the top of your head will blow off any second, so I'll share."

He could hardly believe his ears and held the butt with his thumb and index finger and marveled at the red lipstick on the filter. *This is as close as I'll get to kissing her on this side of sixteen,* he thought.

"What's the matter? Afraid I have cooties?" Lori asked.

He ignored the comment and took a deeper hit than planned. The smoke raced down his throat, dragging cold spikes into his lungs. Bending over, he gagged and for a second thought he might get sick.

"What a lightweight!" she sang and grabbed the cigarette out of his hand. She took a long drag, and this time blew the smoke in his face.

"Okay, I deserve that," he said, standing up and reaching for the cigarette.

Lori moaned and handed it back to him.

Despite feeling lightheaded and queasy, he took a gentle hit, hoping to detect the flavor of her lipstick this time, but sadly unsuccessful. "My lungs are on fire, trying to track you down. No wonder I'm gagging," he said, trying to play it cool. "Why did you wait so long to tell anyone about Liv?"

"Billy would have called sooner if you had a phone!" She shook her head. "Talk about lame."

Sonny sighed. "I know. But once I save up —"

"Whatever," she said, cutting him off. She tasted a bit of the coffee and stared for a long moment into the cup. "I always thought your sister was weird."

"Half-sister," he corrected and then winced inside.

"Which means what? That you're not related to the weird half?"

"No, it isn't like that. It's just... well... she has a different father."

"Which is half the families in America today and they don't split hairs like you're doing. They would just call Olivia their sister."

He shrugged as the reel in his head replayed his father calling Luis a wetback, beaner, or spic. Mama was right. Papa's extreme prejudice influenced him, no matter how hard he tried. The gnawing pain in his stomach confirmed if Liv's dad was some white guy from Maine, he would feel different.

Lori stood up. "Call her what you want, but she's weird. I don't judge a book by its cover, but the janitor at school has nicer clothes."

He looked away and concentrated for a moment on the red brick of the Community Center. Lori might sing a different tune if she spent a few hours in the trunk. The thought prompted him to gaze upon the beautiful girl and question his feelings for her.

"Tell me more about what happened," he asked.

"She acted stuck up like she didn't know me when she came into the store." She threw the spent cigarette on the ground and stomped on it with the heel of her boot. "Then got pissed because I wouldn't let her use the bathroom unless she bought something."

"Why did you do that?"

She laughed. "Now you're sticking up for your half-sister?"

He learned from his mother not replying had more power sometimes.

Lori sighed. "Okay, it's stupid and I'm not a rule follower. As it turned out she didn't use the bathroom after the woman came in."

She let it hang there and he sensed it was the nearest she would admit to being wrong.

"No one has seen her since," he said, and felt an odd pain in his throat. He did not realize how much it hurt until now.

Lori looked at the ground.

"I told my dad everything, and he's going to the police," he said clearing his throat.

"Great! That's just what I need. My manager is already angry with me for calling out last weekend. When he gets a load of this, I'll get canned for not telling him first."

"Liv has been kidnapped and you're making your lousy job a priority?"

She took a deep breath. "No, but I screwed up bad not taking down the plate. That's why I waited telling Billy. I hoped it was just family drama."

"Remember anything else?"

"It's not like they invited me to join their road trip, but I got a good look at the Cadillac. I'm pretty sure it had New Hampshire plates."

Sonny got off the wall and picked up his bike.

"That woman really creeped me out," Lori added. "All dressed in black with spikey white hair. Reminded me of a skunk. Plus, her name is strange. Maybe that will help."

"Have you ever seen her before?" he asked.

"No, but many people come into the store. I thought she was a friend or part of your family. The way the woman escorted her out, I should have taken down the plate. What the hell was I thinking?"

Sonny thought of the way everyone treated Liv, including him. "Yeah, what the hell."

CHAPTER TWELVE

Olivia sat on the front stairs listening to the peeper and cricket duet. Their pulsating harmony sounded the same in Maine, and she wondered why there were not different dialects.

A figure came around the corner of the house, startling her.

"Didn't mean to scare you, my dear," Seth said, drowning out nature's harmony.

She tried laughing it off, but her stomach remained in knots. "Where's Rezi? She told me to get ready and meet out here. We're going into town."

He listened as the words paraded by his ears and nodded. "We have time to talk first."

Time to talk? When Rezi returned after breakfast, Luke disappeared and the rest of the day had been one long bore-fest. She watched tv, but the only thing she could access were comedy shows like *Seinfeld* and *I Love Lucy*. When she got antsy, she helped Rezi make a dozen loaves of banana bread. The bananas were black, but Rezi said they were at the height of sweetness.

He gestured towards the side of the house from where he came from. "Nothing like a spring campfire. Especially tonight with little wind. Join me."

"For the orientation?"

"The what?"

"That's what Luke calls it." She folded her arms. "But I don't see why I need it as I'm just hiding here until my mother comes." She shook her head. "I'm not joining whatever weird cult this is."

Seth's smile was brighter than the first stars. "I don't know what that boy of mine planted in your head, but he sure likes to rattle the newbies." He pointed at the border of the woods and the line of trees with their feet hiding in the dusk. "I don't see a procession of acolytes coming to sacrifice you."

She wanted to argue the point, but nodded. Sometimes the best tactic is being agreeable. It saved her a few trips to the Catalina trunk.

"I encourage you to let your curiosity guide you as you uncover the wonders of our community. There's a terrible tendency nowadays toward tribalism. The offshoot is people see conspiracy in everything...politics...religion ...medicine. It not only feeds prejudice and violence but is tearing society apart. What happened to respectful dialogue? I'm afraid we're reverting to the Dark Ages."

Olivia thought he sounded like her history teacher, Mr. Casey. He made sense of everything past and present, even if most of the other kids were not interested. However, Seth's facial expression brought to mind Sonny indulging in a sleeve of Oreo's. After unscrewing each cookie, he licked off the frosting and built a tower of chocolate wafers. More than a gross habit, his expression fascinated her — a cross between desire and smugness.

A loud bang behind her made her jump. Before she could turn around, Seth moved past her up the stairs. He halted before the storm door, which framed the peculiar infinity symbol and bent over. When he stood back up, he cradled something in his hands.

"What is it?" she asked.

Seth opened his hands, and she could make out a white head with a streak of red feathers. The rest of the body was a horizontal pattern of black and white stripes. "It's a red-bellied woodpecker," he whispered. "Poor fella flew into the glass. It happens once in a while, usually in the morning sun."

Olivia watched the bird open and close its eyes repeatedly.

Seth moaned. "Hate to say it, but I feel a broken wing."

She touched the woodpecker's head gently and the heaviness of the last day surfaced. She collided with the ugliness of her life and felt broken too. Tears welled up, and she noticed Seth looked upset as well.

"Can we bring it to a vet?" she asked in a broken voice.

He shook his head. "I'm sure there's internal damage too. All we can do is provide comfort. Let's sit at the fire and wait it out."

He led her around the side of the house to a small firepit. A couple of logs were burning. Two white plastic Adirondack chairs sat close together in a gravel circle.

"Can you hold our little friend while I tend the fire?" Seth asked.

She had never held a live bird but buried enough dead ones. Papa Dale had a nasty habit of shooting blue jays and crows out of the trees if they squawked too much on his day off. Sonny and she bet how many would meet their demise each year. Last year she won by correctly forecasting a baker's dozen.

"I don't know..." she stammered. "He looks comfortable. Why upset things?"

He stared at her intensely. "Why upset things! I'd like to burn those words instead of wood because that's why the world is such a mess. No one wants to get their hands dirty." He walked over to the chair. "Sit down and open your hands."

She experienced the coldness of the plastic chair through her jeans as she followed his orders. Before she settled in, Seth handed her the dying bird. The feathers were softer than a baby's head and its feet pinched her palm. When she first watched the bird in the front yard, it opened and closed its eyes like it was keeping time, but now the process had slowed.

"I don't think it will be long now," she whispered.

"Be still and cradle him through the end," Seth suggested, kneeling beside her. "Let it feel the connected love of the universe."

Her hands followed the directive, but not her head. "Connected love of the universe? Gag me! Ten minutes ago, the only thing it wanted was another bug or two before it got dark. That's what it loved."

"That's an ignorant and pathetic view of the world." He got up and placed a log on the fire and watched as the hungry flames embraced it.

The new log must have been cedar because it emitted a scent reminiscent of incense. She studied the poor bird; the beak stuck open; its eyes closed. "At school we follow the scientific method, not superstitions," she said in defense.

"So, you're saying it all comes back to what we can observe?" He took a seat next to her. "Can you see the wind? I have been places no human would understand. Does that make it not real?"

The poster in the closet came to mind. "Like where?"

"It will become clear in time. I'm all for logic, but it often ignores the deeper meaning." He watched the fire for a moment. "At my age, regret is like crabgrass. It found the weak spots in my spirit and threatened to overwhelm my life." He glanced at her. "I'm hoping there's enough time to rip it all out and plant seeds that will change the landscape."

"That's nice but I'm just trying to survive today," she replied.

He gifted her with that easy laugh again. She welcomed its melody and stored it away with the other treasures she mulled over when alone in the trunk. In that abyss, with focused breathing, she moved past anger, fear, frustration and limited her horizon to each moment, in a dimension beyond Papa Dale and all the stupid kids at school. She looked up at the sky and thought of the sun and stars; their light a gift from the past but felt in the now. She could hear Papa Dale opening and closing the trunk.... the past polluting the present and scarring the future.... *How damaged am I?*

"A penny for your thoughts?" Seth asked.

She blinked and cleared her throat. "I was thinking about the Benny and Betty Hill poster in the bedroom closet and how you're building New Roswell. That's pretty weird," she said, trying to lead the conversation somewhere else.

The words found its target. Seth's head jerked back, and the smile turned upside down.

She held the bird tighter and could feel the woodpecker's skeleton.

Seth reached down and picked up a small stick off the lawn. He held it in the flame until it caught and then held the burning stick between them.

"Didn't your mother teach you it's dangerous to play with matches? You shouldn't go snooping in someone's house trying to pry secrets out of a locked closet. That's the thanks I get for keeping you safe?"

She felt her cheeks burn. "You have it all wrong! I was raised properly and only opened the closet to hang up my things." She ignored the key she found.

Seth watched the burning stick and considered her defense. "Fire is a gift, isn't it? Stay a safe distance away from the source and it has many uses. But get too close … and you're consumed." He threw the branch into the pit. *"For you are dust, and to dust you shall return."* He looked up at her. "There is much to share in the days ahead."

"Are you trying to scare me?"

He shook his head. "That's a mistaken perspective. I agreed to help your mother and keep you safe. You have questions, and so do I — that's the everlasting dance of life, just like the bird you're holding. Each moment led him to dying in your hands."

"You're wrong. The bird flew into the glass and you picked him up and handed him to me. None of us had a say in any of it. All of it was random."

He smiled. "Seems like you're itching to debate free will."

Olivia leaned over and kissed the back of the woodpecker's head. *Save me from this nutty professor,* she thought. The feathers emitted an earthy fragrance. Maybe Rezi had a tissue box she could bury him in.

She felt a sudden stirring in her hands. "What the hell!"

Seth noticed and jumped up. "Hold still…Let me check," he said, taking the bird from her.

Olivia held her breath as he examined the woodpecker. A look of confusion appeared on his face, and he sat down in the chair and opened his hands. The bird sat up, skipped across his palm, and flew away.

"You said it had a broken wing and was dying!" she said.

"Affirmative." He gazed at her with a broad smile. "I rely on Rezi to find the gifted ones, and she outdid herself this time." He reached over and touched her arm. "You're a healer."

CHAPTER THIRTEEN

Gabrielle opened the closet and ran her hand over the line of hangers. The clothes she wore were sandwiched in front, and everything else served no purpose because they no longer fit, had missing buttons, or fell under the category of "what were you thinking?" It took little insight to realize the sorry-looking wardrobe summed up her life. She grabbed a few items and threw them on the bed to shove into a garbage bag valise. The rest Dale could burn.

The sound of approaching footsteps interrupted her thoughts, and she spun around. Given the last couple hours, she expected to find Dale on a blitzkrieg operation. Her father used to sing gospel songs about turning swords into plowshares, but her significant other liked to repurpose items from the kitchen drawer into weapons. But instead of Dale, her son came barreling in, his eyes bulging like his father's but without the evil intent.

She exhaled, not realizing she had been holding her breath, and pointed at his boots. "How many times do I have to—"

He held his arms out wide. "C'mon Mama!" he pleaded. "We have more important things to worry about right now!" He looked toward the bathroom. "Where's Papa?"

The simple question made her want to ask him to be more specific, as her father was missing, too. "He's not here...." she got out and left it at that.

It must have been the brief reply, because he stopped and stared at her. She walked over to the bureau before he could see all the brokenness. Maintaining a routine was her best defense, so she opened a drawer and began refolding the small assortment of t-shirts she possessed. In the drawer's corner, she eyed a small gold cross she received from Abuela on her first Communion. She had little else from home, but she hid what she had throughout the house like water stations in a never-ending desert marathon.

"I found Lori," Sonny proclaimed, like he located a lost treasure. "I told her the police will interview her. Still can't believe she didn't get a look at the plate." He rubbed his forehead. "Maybe Lori can help the police sketch the woman."

She let out a deep sigh in acknowledgement, but knew it would not take much artistic skill to realize Rezi did not blend in with folks around here. She recalled the first time she met the odd-looking woman at the hole in the wall bar. Rezi was sipping a glass of white wine surrounded by a gang of bearded hunters dressed in camouflage, curling cans of Budweiser. From time to time, one of them would gaze at the lady dressed entirely in black, with that voluminous mass of white hair frozen in the crest of a wave. What proved more impressive than her appearance was her radar. The moment she entered the bar, Rezi motioned to the empty seat beside her. It would take many shots of tequila for her to bare her soul, but as she stared at the older woman's high cheekbones and flawless skin, the confession poured out to a face that never felt a fist. Rezi's dark eyes took in all she had to dish out and never flinched.

"Did you hear what I said?" her son asked in a high-pitched tone he only used with her and his sister.

Gabrielle looked at him but did not reply. An internal voice echoed advice: *disclose everything to Sonny before Dale returns and makes you a criminal!*

After shuffling to the foot of the bed, she reached for her son's hand. "Come sit so we can talk."

He looked at her and snickered. "The last time I sat on that spread, you yelled at me for a week."

The comment caused her to have an unusual sensation of laughter, given the circumstances. "You take after me and forget nothing, which can be a curse sometimes, but cut me some slack. You were eight years old and thought the crocheted spread that took me a year to finish was the best place in the house to eat your Halloween stash of peanut butter cups."

Her son shrugged. "It was Liv's fault. She tried to steal them."

She bit her lip. Her daughter was always to blame.

"And besides, I had no intention of getting chocolate on *my* bed!" he said with a smirk and plopped down so hard she tumbled into him. Embarrassed, he tried to move away, but she held onto his arm.

"There's something I have to tell you and…" she paused halfway through the sentence as she smelled tobacco on her son. She filed it away for later.

He pulled his arm away. "Is it about Olivia? Did something else happen?"

She vigorously shook her head, but the look on his face broke her heart. He cared for her, no matter how much they argued.

"Then what is it?"

Her father often quoted Miguel de Cervantes Saavedra, *the truth may be stretched thin, but it never breaks.* "You're old enough to talk about things that are difficult. Like the ugly secrets in our family."

She looked in his eyes for acknowledgement, but all she saw was the little boy that always needed things spelled out for him.

"You and Olivia are bones of my bones…flesh of my flesh… and I love you more than life itself." Her voice began breaking as the tears flowed, but she lived long enough to categorize them as joy, heartbreak, or pain. These felt new, like a pressure relief valve, and she let them roll down her cheeks.

"I always hoped the four of us could be an actual family… and it felt that way when you and your sister were very young." She sighed. "I don't know if we were stronger or just tried harder back then. But your father… it's no secret he's always struggled with my status and Olivia not being his biological daughter."

Sonny jumped up and stomped his work boots on the solid wood surface. "You're wrong! Papa's been going nuts looking for Liv." He pointed a finger at her. "You're the one acting all weird, like you don't care. Why are we here instead of camping out at the police station or putting posters up?"

Her heart's sandbags were breached. "Because your sister isn't missing."

She watched his face collapse and his shoulder slump like a balloon losing air. "What are you talking about? Lori told me she saw the weirdo take Olivia."

"No, everyone has it wrong. Rezi is a friend of mine."

Sonny rubbed his forehead. "Then why did Liv tell Lori to write down the plate?"

Gabrielle paused, wanting to slow down the conversation because she knew what followed would haunt him for the rest of his life. "Because she must have had second thoughts after I put her in the car."

With the remaining air gone, he fell to his knees in front of her. They were on the same level and he searched her face. "Why did you send her away?"

Nothing she said would make it right. The answer had to come from his heart. "Do I have to say it? You know why."

He screwed up his face. "Olivia has been doing her chores and hasn't got into trouble at school for a while. I don't understand."

She held her breath for a moment and watched the disgust begin at the corners of his mouth. "Okay, she gets a timeout now and then."

"Don't sugarcoat it."

He looked away. "Papa was pretty pissed last time when she …. ah, took a leak in the Catalina."

"And you think that's okay?" she asked.

He shrugged. "I've been in the trunk too, you know."

"Yeah, but how many times?"

"Enough to know it sucks. When you go on a rollercoaster, it's scary whether you ride it one time or fifty." He screwed up his face. "So, that's what's behind this?"

"That's one reason." She put her finger to her tongue to wet it and then dabbed the makeup off her cheek. "I have a few more."

He watched as the bruise came to life and looked away again.

"I've had enough too, Sonny. I'm moving out and want you to come with me."

His mouth fell open like she tasered him. "Papa says you're always scheming how to take away everything he worked so hard for. Were you and Liv just going to disappear and leave me here?"

Before she could respond, the sound of a siren filled the room.

CHAPTER FOURTEEN

As usual, Rezi drove with two hands on the wheel, eyes glued to the road and her jaw muscles flexing every few seconds. Since leaving the house ten minutes ago, they hadn't spoken a word, and that was okay. The scent of smoke on her clothes intensified Olivia's memories of the peculiar encounter with Seth. Whenever Mr. Driscoll caught her meandering in the halls between classes, he would scowl and say the shortest distance between two points was a straight line. But no matter how many times she asked Rezi and Seth for straight answers, she wandered in a corn maze with nothing but dead ends, and tonight's dreams would feature a dying woodpecker. *What should I make of that campfire?* It was beyond preposterous to believe she healed the bird. If anything, Seth just sucked as a medical examiner.

The air in the car still had a musty odor, but now also felt suffocating and brought back too many memories of the Catalina. Her fingers fumbled with the window controls and roused Rezi from her catatonic state.

"Don't worry about me jumping out the window. I haven't been able to do that stunt since I was five when I rolled myself in toilet paper pretending to be a mummy that could fly," she said before the warning came.

Rezi let out a small squeak, which she interpreted as the woman's laugh. Something like that would usually make her giggle, but there was no room in that beat up valise to pack her humor. "Are we headed to some big meeting in the woods?" she asked instead. "I hope so, because I can't wait to see you dancing around the campfire while I roast marshmallows."

"Your mother lets you watch way too much tv," Rezi replied before checking the rearview mirror, like she had every thirty seconds since leaving. "We're headed to Tuscan Village."

"Where?"

"It's sort of a town within a town — and built on the grave of Rockingham Park. Once upon a time, people said it was the finest track in the world for horse racing. But nothing lasts forever. The recent development has all the amenities: housing, stores, restaurants, movie theater, even a hospital. They say if you live there, you never have to leave."

"So, it's like *Hotel California*?" she asked as her spirits brightened. "Back home, we only have a couple of shops and a Walmart." She rolled her eyes. "There aren't too many places where you can try on jeans and do your grocery shopping all under one roof."

"Well, we won't have any time for that," Rezi replied.

"Can we see a movie, then?" Olivia asked, scanning the road for the theater.

"Negative."

"Then why are we going there?"

"It's our community event night."

She sighed. "They do that sort of thing back home at the Senior Citizen Center. Papa Dale makes me hand out discount coupons for the store. Sometimes, my mother comes along and serves coffee. I'll never forget the time Papa Dale almost poked out the eyes of some old guy with a walker that flirted with her."

"The more I hear, the more I wish your mother would let me take care of him. As far as these community events go… well, that's a good example where words aren't specific enough. Our gatherings are more of an unearthing, though Seth doesn't like the term. He prefers farming."

"To what? Cultivate desperadoes like me and my mother?"

"That's uncalled for, especially after everything we've done for you."

"None of which I wanted. And when I ask what is going on here, everyone talks in circles."

Rezi shot her a glance and then pointed at a long line of cars stopped ahead, their red taillights resembling a string of rubies. "Looks like we have a good crowd tonight." She pulled over and stopped in front of a display of manufactured homes.

"Now what?"

"We walk," Rezi replied, opening the car door. "Is that concrete enough for you?"

"Yeah, but where's Seth and the others?"

Rezi pointed at a parade of people walking by the car on both sides. "Enough with the questions. We have to get a move on or we'll be late."

Olivia got out of the car and noticed they started a trend as an army of headlights were pulling off the road, too

They joined the migration into Tuscan Village, and she studied the people they passed. Papa Dale liked to throw fancy words around the dinner table and impress Mama. While she ignored most of it, she enjoyed when he talked about studying people. He called it store demographics. Ninety percent of his customers were male. While he catered to their wants, he knew he could increase sales by getting women into the store, so he sent out targeted mailers offering holiday and birthday discounts. Using the same logic, she assessed the crowd and determined the majority were men and women younger than thirty years of age. Some carried beach chairs like they were going to a concert. But the target audience also captured a good population of older people, many limping and in wheelchairs. What did that mean? She wondered what happened at these community events.

They walked for a good half mile, but she did not mind as her eyes took in more brightly lit stores and restaurants than she had ever seen. The aroma of pizza drifted through the air and she could almost taste the tantalizing combination of cheese and tomato when a black SUV approached.

The driver's side window lowered and Seth greeted them with a frown.

"Get in quick," he ordered.

They climbed into the back seat and Olivia looked at a twenty something year old guy hunched over a laptop riding shotgun with Seth. She could not see his face because of his long and stringy brown hair.

Rezi touched the stranger's thin arm. "Good to see you Liam." She did not wait for a reply, but craned her neck and made eye contact with Seth. "More souls here than last month!"

Olivia noticed the mysterious leader traded in the tight shirt and running pants for a white robe.

"Well, you can thank Liam for that," Seth replied and put the vehicle in drive and edged out into the stop and go traffic. "The post from last month spread like wildfire and now everyone is buzzing about the unbelievable find."

Papa Dale said she was born without a governor on her tongue. It was the one thing Mama agreed with him about. "Why? What did they find?" she asked loudly.

Seth peered at her in the car's rear-view mirror like he just noticed she was there.

Liam swiveled in his seat too and shot her a look. "Who are you?"

"Olivia and I'm from—"

"Maine," he said, finishing the sentence. "I know all about you."

"Huh?"

Liam glanced at Seth and then slouched in the seat and studied the computer screen again. "No time to explain, Olivia. But to answer your first question, last month Ruth pulled a piece of Amelia Earhart's plane out of the retention pond here." He looked at Seth. "The video has two million views."

Seth nodded and everyone fell silent, processing the comment.

Students at school teased her for raising her hand to ask for clarification, but she did not care. "Who is Amelia?"

"Hmmm…. not a lover of history, I take it?" Liam asked without looking up. "Only the first woman to fly solo across the Atlantic in 1932. A genuine hero."

Hero? Worry filled her mind as she contemplated her mother's long-awaited confrontation with Papa Dale. If she could have given her one present before leaving, it would have been a one-way bus ticket here.

"I'll have to look her up," she replied to be polite.

Liam pecked away on his keyboard for a long moment. "Yeah, you should. Amelia and her copilot attempted to fly around the world and almost made it until they disappeared in the North Pacific. There have been a ton of theories about what happened, and no one ever found the plane… until Ruth brought up a piece of an aluminum panel with markings."

Rezi looked like she was experiencing it again for the first time.

"How would it show up in New Hampshire?" she asked. "I mean, it must be a fake."

Rezi moaned. "Our guest is the ultimate doubting Thomas."

Seth took a sharp right and followed a dirt road lined with construction equipment before pulling over. "Olivia, I know you have many questions, and this must sound like some sick dream of grandeur. All I can promise is it will become clear to you shortly. For now, just be open to the possibility of secrets beyond your comprehension and enjoy the wonder." He glanced at Liam and then at Rezi. "We are all seekers and my friends here assist with my efforts. Rezi gathers those that are unaware of being touched and receiving special gifts. Liam is sharing what people have seen, heard, and sensed." He turned in his seat and looked her in the eye. "Until tonight, I thought you would only be a benefactor of the coming revelation, but I was mistaken. No one is here by accident. Your gift plays a central role in the coming age."

CHAPTER FIFTEEN

Gabrielle stood at the front window and watched the patrol car come to a stop next to the Catalina. She figured Dale requested the siren, hoping the noise would be as powerful as the horns that brought down Jericho. The thought made her glance at the dark paneled walls and recall a different Bible story. She wanted nothing more than to bring the entire house down like Samson. *Maybe she could if Dale had not made her cut her hair.*

When she looked out the window again, Dale was leading Chief Ned Warner up the sidewalk. Her stomach did not have eyes, but it ached as they approached. The two looked like brothers with rosy cheeks and protruding bellies from guzzling beer and devouring rare meat like Neanderthals.

Polite to a fault, she rushed to open the door, and the Chief touched his hat before entering. "Evening," he said as his eyes searched the perimeter of the room like it was harboring a nest of migrant farmers.

"Nice to see you, Ned. How's Shirley doing?" she replied with fake enthusiasm and repeating the opening line from the worn script. In reality, she met Shirley ten years ago, and they never spoke again once she learned her last name was Ruiz.

"Wife is good. Getting the garden ready."

"I read there is a frost warning later this week, so better not plant anything until Memorial Day," she offered.

"We were born and raised here so know the seasons well." He eyed the braided rug like he was standing on a landmine located somewhere beneath the alternating brown and yellow weave.

Dale touched his buddy's arm. "Would you be more comfortable doing this in the kitchen?"

Ned gave her a quick once over. "I believe a good cook experiences a greater sense of ease near the stove. Don't you agree, Gabby?"

She responded with half a smile. At least she would be closer to the knives if he called her that nickname again.

Dale led them into the kitchen, where Sonny was waiting and leaning against the fridge. His eyes and cheeks were red.

"Hey buddy!" the Chief called out.

Sonny ignored the greeting and eyed his father. "Papa, we need to talk."

"Later," Dale dismissed and sat down at the head of the table.

The Chief followed and took a seat next to his pal and then motioned to the chair across from him. "Have a seat, hon."

The last time someone called her "hon" was two years ago when a sour-looking teller refused to cash in ten dollars in coins because she did not have an account there. If the bank manager had not intervened, she would have pelted the lady with the dimes and nickels.

"Can I get you gentleman something? A cup of coffee or tea?" she asked, hoping to stall being strapped in for the cross examination.

Dale did not respond, and the Chief let out a smile shaved extra thin. "That's mighty gracious, given the reason for my visit, but no thank-you."

Sonny hurried across the kitchen and pulled out a chair at the end of the table, and sat down.

Dale looked surprised and pointed at the hall. "Go to your room."

"Why?" he asked in disbelief.

"Because this doesn't concern you. We need to have a serious conversation with your mother."

"But I know everything!" he said jumping up. "I headed over to see Lori about the kidnapping, but…" he hesitated like his insides were being shredded as he glanced at her, "Mama told me she sent Liv away with that woman!"

The air was sucked out of the room, and Gabrielle pondered how everyone interprets reality differently. Sonny experienced this as rejection, Dale perceived betrayal, and the Chief saw an opportunity to use the law to assist his friend. But no one cared she was just trying to survive.

Dale inhaled deeply and pointed at his son. "Did you hear me, boy?" he whispered, which he always did before going thermonuclear. "We'll talk everything through later. Now go to your room!"

Sonny stood motionless for a moment, no doubt considering pushing the matter as the Chief would not let his father beat him. But he must have realized the cease fire would end once the peacekeeper left and stormed out of the room.

Dale watched him leave and then looked at her and pointed at the chair.

She was eight years old again and Miss Castillo told her to stop whining about the pain in her stomach and take a seat. Ten minutes later, the entire class witnessed the gross eruption. She wished she could repeat the performance and let her alien germs defile them. *But what good would that do? I would have to clean it up. Then when Ned leaves, he'll give me a fat lip and then expect dinner.*

Taking a seat, she gazed at the worn pine surface and touched the nicks and scratches. Every few years, she would drag the table outside and erase the damage with a palm sander and apply multiple coats of poly. No amount of sandpaper would eliminate the scars inside her. For a brief moment, she shut her eyes and saw her father shaking his head. *How could he leave me in this darkness?*

She looked up and found Dale's face even more flushed, but it was his mouth that looked peculiar, like he tasted something disgusting and wanted nothing more than to spit it out.

The Chief let out an exaggerated sigh. "Gabrielle, how long have we known each other?"

"Who says we don't live forever?" she replied and then added, "because the last sixteen years sure feels that way."

He replied with a knowing laugh. "Some days feel that way, but when I have a beer with my buddies and discuss the foolish things we did in our younger days, it seems like it was only yesterday. Don't you agree?"

She saw a trap in the chitchat and just shrugged. He would have to use a pickaxe for her to say more.

"Which makes this visit all the more...difficult," he continued and glanced at the unstable volcano sitting next to him. "When Dale called and told me Olivia was missing, I dedicated all my resources to finding her."

"All three cruisers?" she asked with a straight face.

The Chief stared at her like he did not understand what happened to the docile live in that provided all the grub during football season. He laughed when his buddy boasted how he banned taco chips from the house.

She turned her attention to Dale. He still looked like he was ready to spit something out.

"Well then..." the Chief continued, "I told the State Police we're not dealing with a runaway after what took place at Humphries. Since it's a kidnapping, the FBI is also involved. So, you can imagine my heartburn when Dale told me all of this is your doing?"

Careful, she thought. "I'm sorry about how things got mixed up and misinterpreted. My daughter is fine. I sent her away with a friend."

The Chief frowned. "You know what they say: with friends like that.... What is the woman's name?"

She loved this country for its freedom. "If you will excuse me, I rather not say."

"See what I mean!" Dale said and pushed his chair back so fast the table rattled.

The Chief touched his buddy's arm. "Try to stay calm," he said soothingly and returned his focus to her. "Why didn't you tell Dale or Sonny about your daughter leaving?"

She nodded. "That was wrong of me. I should have told my son."

The Chief pointed at his friend. "Aren't you forgetting someone?"

She read the conflict on Dale's face. His mouth quivered holding back enough four-letter expletives to wallpaper the house, but his eyes looked like when his dad died. Angry and hurt were fighting for dominance.

"That's between Dale and I."

"Drop the holier-than-thou act. Ned knows you're a schemer!" Dale spit out.

She could have predicted which side of Dale would win out and looked at the Chief. "I sent Olivia away because I'm leaving too. I thought it better if I sent her somewhere safe so she didn't have to deal with Dale's temper."

The Chief leaned toward her and she smelled the onions he must have eaten. "But not Sonny?" he asked.

She nodded. "That's different. Dale is his father. We need to have a discussion about joint custody."

"Like hell!" Dale yelled.

The Chief ignored his friend. "Then why did Olivia ask the clerk to take down the license plate? Sounds like she was afraid of what you define as a friend."

"You're wrong! We planned this for months."

Dale punched the table and she could feel his fist hitting her cheek.

"Then why was she scared?" the Chief continued.

"She wasn't, and if it came off that way, it was probably nerves."

Ned sat forward in the chair and pointed a finger at her. "I should warn you that Maine takes child endangerment seriously. The penalty is harsh with the possibility of a long prison sentence."

She pointed back at him. "Like I said, Olivia is with a friend."

"Call her now so she can assure me."

"I can't. Dale won't let me have a cell phone," she said to rub it in.

"Then use mine!" the Chief said with his voice rising.

She eyed both men absorbed in their safe pompous world. They did not know what she had endured. "There's no need. I'm her mother and I'm telling you she's fine." She pointed at Dale. "I don't know why he's so distraught. He can't stand her and only happy when he's locked her in the car's trunk."

Dale shook his head. "These Mexicans sure have a temper and know how to twist things, so they look like the victims. All I can say in defense is I demand a little respect from those that live under my roof."

The Chief nodded in agreement and slapped the table to make a point. "I have a busy afternoon, so let me sum it up so even a migrant farmer like the rest of your clan understands. We can do this my way and everything goes back to being nice or it can get Maine ugly. Where is your daughter?"

She kept her hands clenched, so she did not flip him a universal sign that might get her arrested.

The Chief pushed back his chair and sighed. "That's a big mistake Gabby, and sure hope you come to your senses tonight. We have an excellent description of the vehicle, plus the woman's odd first name. We'll find her. In the meantime, like I explained, you're facing serious charges." He stood up and looked down at her. "Piss me off some more, and I don't care if you're shacked up with my Daddy, I will refer you to Immigration."

When her father came home after being gone for months, they would sit in front of the fire and talk about farm life in the States with his fellow countrymen. *Papa would light his pipe and stare at the flames. The words sometimes came quick or loud depending on his mood. They talked about low pay, loneliness, sickness, the raw politics about immigration and how Mexico and the U. S share democratic ideals. Inevitably, he would recite the words on the Statue of Liberty and say it summed up the idea of America. "Give me your tired... your poor... your huddled masses yearning to breathe free...." His voice usually broke, reciting the last sentence. "I lift my lamp beside the golden door."*

As Papa spoke, she pictured him in the sun... his hands working the soil... planting ... weeding ...picking, while his mind harvested weightier topics. That was the thing she noticed about wisdom. It passed over inflated egos and degrees in favor of those willing to admit ignorance. Papa was well read. He traveled light but always brought the Bible and a history book.

"From that invitation, people responded from the four corners of the world to build something extraordinary," Papa explained like he had given it considerable thought. "Yes, terrible mistakes were made, but time after time when the weeds threatened to snuff out its ideals, a leader would emerge and inspire the country to examine its conscience. Reforms would follow, some painfully. The thing that inspires an old man like me is realizing one's station in life was not a limiting factor. Abraham Lincoln, Rosa Parks, Cesar Chavez did not lead with their heads or hearts, but with their souls." The last time they spoke of such things, he was not feeling hopeful. "But my dear, sweet child," he warned, "I see nothing ahead, but a country wrapped in barbed wire and no genuine desire to fix the border or deal with the people living there now. I am fine with an agricultural visa, even if it feels like being directed around back for janitorial duties no one else wants. But those that enter on their own face a life in the shadows. There has to be a better way."

She and Luis did not consider the risks when they got on that bus for Brooklyn and ignored all the immigration rules. They simply wanted something better for their child and did not consider the repercussions. But she had been in the States for almost half her life now, and all she had was a harvest of pain. Looking at the two slugs in front of her, more blessed by chance than they would ever realize, she understood why the golden door remained locked.

CHAPTER SIXTEEN

Seth stopped the SUV in front of the entrance to the Artisan Hotel and glanced at Rezi in the rear-view mirror.

"Luke and Ruth are waiting in the lobby. Get everyone over to the pond. I'll meet you there."

Rezi nodded and opened the door.

Olivia wondered if that included her too, and Seth read her thoughts. "Go with Rezi, Olivia. Just remember, no matter what happens tonight, keep an open mind."

They barely got out of the car before Seth sped away.

"We have to hurry," Rezi said leading her into the crowded lobby. She believed there was some sort of convention going on until she noticed some people with figure eight tattoos on their arms and legs. Studying the assembly, they resembled all the people walking in from the main road: young men and women, along with a significant number of individuals with physical disabilities.

While Rezi looked for Luke and Ruth, Olivia searched for a face that looked friendly and found a candidate — a twenty-something with short blonde hair and sporting a red flannel shirt and jeans.

"Are you going to the..." she began and then hesitated not knowing what to call this strange assembly.

The girl gifted her with a warm smile and nodded. "A few months ago, I made fun of these events. The videos on *YouTube* were pretty lame. A few flashing lights, and then somebody would pull a dead tadpole out of the water and claim it came from the Amazon. But after last month, this is where worlds collide. I had to come and see it for myself."

Olivia was still pondering a follow-up question about colliding worlds when Rezi pulled her away. "Follow me and stay close. If I lose you, Seth will be furious."

She followed the cotton headed disciple as they maneuvered through the crowd like minnows, darting this way and that. They almost completed the circuit when Rezi pointed at a table over by the windows. Luke was sitting there with some girl.

After navigating around a group of wheelchairs, they stopped in front of a thin teenage girl with a huge mane of red hair. Rezi bent over and hugged her.

While they embraced, Olivia glanced down at Luke. Her heart quickened, taking in the chiseled face and blond locks. Tonight, the form fitting t-shirt hid under a denim jacket.

She was still trying to think of a cool way to say hello when Rezi pulled her over. "Olivia, I want you to meet Ruth."

It took a second to peel her eyes away from the guy of her dreams. When she did, the redhead was waiting. Ruth possessed natural beauty that did not require makeup. But it was her eyes that stole the show. Sonny used to collect cobalt blue marbles in grammar school. Apparently, he missed two.

The girl grasped her hand, and it had a warm sensation similar to her mother's. She missed her touch so much.

"Nice to meet you. I've heard a lot!"

She smiled, but this was getting weird.

"May I ask where Rezi found you?" Ruth asked.

You mean where she abducted me from? she wanted to say. "Maine."

"That's cool. I'm from Montreal and drifted down with the smoke from the wildfires," she offered and grabbed Rezi's hand. "This kind woman rescued me on the side of the road. I had a dollar to my name and planned on buying a candy bar before I..." She stopped and closed her eyes.

"And the rest is history," Luke added, pointing at them. "We should put a book together on everyone's sad state of affairs before the infamous Gatherer appeared."

"Infamous sums it up," Rezi commented and glanced at her watch. "We're running late. Seth wants us to head over and meet him at the water."

Ruth jumped up, smiling. "Showtime!"

Olivia gave her another once over. Nothing about the girl seemed extraordinary or peculiar. Yet, several bystanders were pointing at her and whispering.

Luke stood up. "Let's go. You don't want to see my father unhappy."

Unhappy? Back home unhappy was the daily darkness suffocating the light, Olivia thought.

"Can someone guide me over there?" Luke asked, the corners of those kissable lips suddenly looking uncertain.

Hard cobalt eyes suddenly found hers and Olivia realized that Ruth's milquetoast face could darken quicker than New England weather.

She hesitated hoping to buy goodwill, but in the next instant, Luke reached for her hand. She took it, planning on transferring it to her arm. Instead, he held her hand tight and came closer.

As they began inching toward the door, the crowd parted in front of them like the Red Sea. When they got outside, she glanced behind and could not believe her eyes. The crowd poured out of the hotel.

"This is crazy. Everyone is following us!" she said.

Luke laughed. "Crazy doesn't cover it anymore. I call it berserk."

"Huh?" she asked and looked ahead at Rezi and Ruth walking close together in deep conversation.

"Just a fancy word for frenzied," he explained and slowed their stride like they were out for an evening stroll.

He squeezed her hand and leaned toward her. "Your hand is much softer than Ruth's. To be honest, she scares me a bit," he said in a low voice.

"Why would you say that?" she asked, amazed she won the blindfold beauty contest.

"Because she's all unicorns and rainbows with me, but another side of her emerges at these events. My father calls her down to the water and all hell breaks loose. She's only been with us a few months and each time she reaches into the retention pond, something unreal comes out. I'm afraid what she may pull out of me if I piss her off!"

"I heard she found a piece of a special plane."

"Yeah, and the time before that, the skeleton remains of a homeless guy who disappeared at Canobie Lake three years ago."

She glanced at the line of stores they were passing and noticed clerks handing out discount coupons.

"I heard about you healing the bird," Luke said.

She looked up at his dark sunglasses, and she was the one that felt blind. The eyes tell all, and he hid his. "How could you know? That just happened."

He chuckled. "Cell phones are amazing devices."

She let out a moan. "I wouldn't know. But your father is wrong. The woodpecker was just stunned after hitting the glass."

Luke shook his head. "Listen to me. I may joke around a lot, but what you did is a sign. Ruth said the same thing when she pulled a diamond ring out of the water the first time." He winced. "I just wished the finger wasn't still attached."

"Are you kidding me?"

He put his head back and laughed. "Maybe. But what isn't a joke is your gift. You have been touched."

"Touched? What does that mean?"

He squeezed her hand. "There you go again, trying to pump me, but I respect my father's process. You'll find out."

She put the comment out of her mind and relished for a moment the simple joy of holding hands. *What a strange couple of days!* she thought. Gazing upward, she observed the first stars and hoped her mother could see them too.

CHAPTER SEVENTEEN

Hand in hand with Luke, Olivia followed Rezi through a rotary and then down a long curving sidewalk. People kept rushing by them and every ten yards, Rezi would turn around and motion for her to hurry.

After what felt like crawling a mile, Rezi stopped under a streetlight and waited for her and Luke to catch up. She pointed across a small body of water. "Now, that's what I call a following!"

Olivia sucked in her breath as she eyed hundreds of people pressed around a retention pond outside LL Bean. A haunting flute echoed from speakers and flashing lights scanned the crowd. As they made their way closer, she could feel anticipation building like the countdown to the fourth of July fireworks. Vendors selling drinks and sandwiches completed the party atmosphere, juxtaposed with dozens of wheelchairs lining an orange barrier fence at the water's edge. Two police officers walked up and down the small beach.

Fully engrossed, she watched as a dozen men and women maneuvered through the crowd. Clad in black hoodies, they held bamboo collection buckets. She watched one man throw in multiple bills. Another woman removed her earrings and deposited them.

"I don't understand any of this," she whispered.

"Recognize this tune?" Luke asked.

She shook her head and then realized the gaffe. "No, but it sounds eerie."

"It's *Close Encounters of the Third Kind.* Tell me what you see."

"Everyone's crammed together like it's a sold-out concert and some weird-looking people are collecting money."

"Don't be so harsh. To know them is to love them."

She saw a man take off his watch and throw it in the bucket. "Some are contributing jewelry. What are they doing?"

Luke shot her a knowing smile. "My father's message has that effect. People want to support building the settlement. Besides the infrastructure, it will need a lot of security."

"What do you mean?"

Before he could answer, Ruth and Rezi came rushing up.

"Things are about to get underway. I need to take Luke to the safe zone," Rezi said.

"Safe zone?"

Rezi shrugged. "Sometimes people get excited and begin running around."

"Yeah, last time I almost got trampled," Luke added.

"Just remember what Seth said." Rezi touched her forehead. "Open your eyes."

Rezi escorted Luke away, leaving Ruth to lead her through a human wall and, after some pushing, reach a temporary orange fence surrounding a short beach. Ruth motioned to a muscular bald guy guarding a makeshift gate and he let them into the restricted area.

They took their place behind a mobile spotlight that illuminated the water. Olivia scanned the crowd lined up against the plastic fence and could see why Luke did not belong here. While most people looked like they were in Times Square counting down the last seconds of the year, there were a few pockets where anticipation had soured into restlessness.

Suddenly, the music stopped, and the crowd fell silent. Ruth nudged her, and she looked up and saw a white light approaching from the east. Initially, she guessed it was a small plane or drone, yet it made no sound and the light was too bright to discern its form. It stopped high above the water.

So mesmerized by the craft, she ignored the faint humming noise at first. More than background noise, it washed over her in waves and made her skin feel prickly. She hoped Ruth could explain, but her new companion had her eyes closed and arms extended heavenward. A few in the crowd had similar reactions, including some in the wheelchair section.

The object in the sky seemed in sync with the strange noise and began circling the area like a high-powered mixer. She could smell incense and inched toward the gate. The logical part of her knew it would be easy to slip away and blend in with the crowd, but curiosity got the better of her.

The humming stopped, and the light disappeared like someone flipped a giant switch. A floodlight from the rooftop of LL Bean came on and, after sweeping over the crowd, stopped on a man wearing a white tunic and standing knee deep in the water.

Olivia came closer and recognized Seth. He sauntered out of the water and when he reached the sand, a figure in a black hoodie handed him a microphone.

"Good evening, friends," Seth began softly.

A few clapped, others whistled, but the majority remained silent.

Seth walked along the fence, taking in the crowd before returning to the center of the beach. "I am pleased to see many familiar faces and delighted on the number of new seekers tonight," he began. "To my new friends, I am Seth. Many ask about my family name, but extraordinary events rendered it meaningless. My mission is to reveal something so fantastic it will change the fabric of our lives, and set a course for a better tomorrow. A tomorrow where there is no pain, no disease but peace and prosperity." He let the message sink in. "I can go on and on about the potential, but will sum it up in two words. Abundant life."

Applause filled the air. When it died down, Seth smiled and repeated, "Abundant life," and the clapping and whistling grew louder. After multiple iterations, he raised his hands for silence.

"History teaches that digesting revolutionary thought requires an open mind to push back against the programming we receive from our first breath. Consequently, I must share what I offer in small doses so not to overwhelm or face rejection. The biggest secret of the ages must be revealed. That is what this series of events represents, a slow climb up the mountain." He raised his hands and pointed at the sky and a disk appeared bathed in white light. "All I ask is an open heart. If you doubt like I did for most of my life, then..." He looked up and the disk sped away as if insulted. "Everything that has been determined will come to pass in a more painful way. I will work tirelessly to prevent that."

Olivia looked around, and everyone was in rapture, hanging on each word. The humming noise began again and wrapped itself around her.

Seth began pacing along the beach. "We are on the cusp of a great recognition. There have been so many points of contact that even our government can no longer deny that forces beyond our comprehension are in our midst, monitoring our nuclear weapon sites, frustrating our military pilots, making their presence known."

Olivia perceived a commotion and, upon looking, noticed a group of men in the distance laughing. Some in the crowd yelled back and two policemen hurried over.

Seth noticed the non-believers. "I will tell my story one day in great detail, but that is not why you are here. You want signs, so you have the courage to tell others. The number of seekers tonight speaks to the importance of supporting one another as we ascend. We will continue these events until the blind and the deaf see and hear the truth. Toward that end, we are building New Roswell, where we will harness the revelation and create a place of community, maximizing health and making death a stranger."

Intense applause broke out, and Seth smiled and relished the moment. When the noise subsided, Seth looked their way and beckoned to Ruth to join him. Olivia rubbed Ruth's arm before she ran out to him.

Seth embraced her and afterwards kept his arm around her shoulder. "I find mining for those who have been touched to be the most satisfying part of my mission. These souls possess special gifts, which will play a fundamental role in building New Roswell and additional communities on each continent." He kissed Ruth on the cheek. "My friend here has the special gift of finding lost things. Last time we were here, a piece of a very special plane became visible. But don't hold your breath waiting for confirmation. We know fake news will deny, deny, deny."

He stepped away, and Ruth waded into the pond. Periodically, she stopped and reached into the water and felt around.

Minutes elapsed as she moved back and forth in search.

The crowd grew restless, which Seth read, and he motioned for Ruth to go deeper.

"But I can't swim!" Ruth protested.

Seth did not respond but continued to point.

Ruth hesitated for a moment before walking deeper into the retention pond. When she reached chest level, she paused and searched and still found nothing.

Seth pointed toward the deeper end. Moments later, Ruth disappeared under the water.

Everyone held their breath. Seconds turned into minutes and Ruth did not appear.

"Save her!" someone yelled.

Seth ran into the water and then disappeared. People began screaming for help and a few men tried to push their way past the plastic barrier, but a line of black hoodies kept the line solid.

Seth suddenly surfaced, and the crowd gasped as he pulled a body toward the shore. But it did not take long to see it was not Ruth.

The spotlight focused on a middle-aged man with dark hair and a beard. He wore a three-piece tweed suit. A gold stop watch swung from a side pocket.

Seth led him to the beach and pulled some weeds off the shoulder of the soaked suit. An assistant rushed forward and handed the ringmaster a microphone, which he put in the stranger's face.

"Where am I mate?" the man asked in a thick English accent.

"Where do you think?" Seth replied with a smile.

The man looked at the crowd, then at the spotlight and blessed himself.

"What year is it, my friend?" Seth continued.

"Any bloke knows it's 1876!"

Seth glanced at the audience and smiled at him. "Everyone here will attest to the fact you're in the twenty-first century."

Some laughed, but it frightened the man fixated on the wild scene. He began backing into the water.

Seth tried to coax him back, but it only scared him more. Before he could reassure him, the odd-looking man swam away and disappeared.

The spotlight searched the dark water and moments later, Ruth surfaced, coughing and gagging.

Applause exploded. When it died down, someone yelled, "This con artist is nothing special, just a magician with glitz!"

Seth hung his head and then looked in the insult's direction. "My friend, what do I have to do?"

A bald elderly man waved and then pointed at the wheelchair next to him. "Unlike your actors, my friend has been holding his breath for twenty years looking for a cure."

Seth nodded. "Bring him down here."

Silence fell over the audience as the man wheeled his friend down to the beach.

Seth greeted them with a smile. "Lucky for you, we just found someone touched with the power of healing." He turned and pointed in her direction. "Olivia, please join me!"

She felt pins and needles run across her chest and turned to run. Rezi, Ruth, and Luke were waiting at the plastic gate.

"Let me out of here!" she said, trying to push past them.

Ruth grabbed her hand. "The same thing happened to me the first time. Just go with your gut."

"I am! I'm nothing special."

"But you are, or I wouldn't have risked my life getting you here!" Rezi said, as her eyes darted back and forth between her and the beach.

"Don't worry. My dad won't embarrass you," Luke insisted.

Before she could reply, Ruth led her to Seth. The blinding spotlight forced her to squint.

Seth embraced her. "Just remember what I said. Lead with your heart."

She stared at the two old guys. The one standing had a beer belly and big cheeks that would be a chipmunk's dream. His buddy was slight, and it looked like the wheelchair was devouring him.

Her hands remained frozen at her side, but Seth guided them until they were on the small man's head. His hair had a texture similar to shredded wheat cereal, and she was certain that running her fingers through it would cause it to crumble into dust. Besides contemplating whether to join the British chap at the bottom of the pond, her thoughts swayed between prayer and embarrassment as she kept her hands motionless.

She heard a few boos and realized that everyone had discovered the con. She withdrew her hands and started wandering away, aware of the mocking gazes following her.

The sound of a thousand people sucking in their breath made her turnaround.

The disabled man walked toward her as the strange humming filled her ears.

CHAPTER EIGHTEEN

When Dale stepped outside with the Chief after the painful visit, Gabrielle knew the best defense was a hasty retreat if there was any hope of avoiding the coming wrath. After hurrying to make up a plate of leftover meatloaf, mashed potatoes and green beans, she put the dinner in the fridge. She quickly scribbled a note to microwave the dish for three minutes at fifty percent power, and she had a terrible migraine and was going to bed. Going through the torment of a serial abuser for so long taught her the benefits of feigning sleep. The skill saved her from both drunken advances and scapegoat beatings when he stumbled home after playing poker with the boys. The differentiating factor between lust and fist came down to whether he won or lost. Either way, he reeked of beer and cigars, and the way he manhandled her was anything but love.

Half running down the hall, she passed Sonny's room. The door was closed and bass from heavy metal music shook the floor. When she reached the bedroom, she collapsed on the bed, her teeth chattering not from the Chief's threats, but how the next few hours would play out. After seeing Ned off, Dale would storm back into the house and drink, sulk, and guzzle some more. Somewhere between the parade of empties, he would embrace being judge, jury, and executioner. Scanning the room, her gaze fell upon the black beach rock resting on the corner of her bureau. After Dale convinced her to come north with him, they drove up Interstate 95. When they reached the Maine turnpike, he turned off and followed the ragged shoreline, pointing out where the Atlantic sometimes beats the hell out of the beach. She remembered being mesmerized and frightened by how he came alive sharing these sites of destruction. After stopping for a dinner of fried dough, they brought baby Olivia down to the water so she could feel the ocean for the first time. It was low tide, and the water was colder than melted ice cubes. On the walk back to the car, she spotted a smooth black stone in the shape of a heart. It was the perfect memento from a day of so much promise and lived on her bureau ever since. More than once, she expected Dale would stone her with it.

After getting undressed, she put the palm sized rock under her pillow. If attacked, the odds of retrieving the rock were almost nil, but God favored the prepared.

Prepared. That was the word she embraced after deciding enough was enough and began planning. But if she were honest with herself, the great escape had always been risky whether she would survive the onslaught. Convincing Olivia was easy, in contrast to dealing with Sonny. She did not want him to feel abandoned like she did, but the alternative was him visiting her at the hospital or the cemetery.

Sleep remained a stranger and the headache excuse proved true after all. Midnight came and Dale stumbled in. Any other man would sleep on the couch, but he considered this his bed and she, his worn-out mistress, an alien guest. She perceived Dale shuffling around the room, huffing and puffing as if he desired her to wake up and engage in a few rounds, but she pretended to be comatose. After listening to him pee out a good six pack, he collapsed in bed. Two minutes later, the Maine Snoring Symphony filled the room.

She inched herself into a sitting position and, using the dim light from the hall, looked around the room. One thing was certain: the longer she stayed, the greater the danger, so she would leave in the morning after Dale headed off to work. He would never expect the bold move and it would give her a good eight-hour head start.

Decision made, the execution side kicked in and she made a mental note of the things she would pack. As she warned Olivia, she would travel light and with the bare essentials. The mad dash with Luis and Roberto north taught her the definition.

When the alarm sounded at six o'clock, she jumped up and put the coffee on as usual. The key for the last hour with Dale required the usual subservience.

After three sips of coffee, Dale, with a head as heavy as an award-winning pumpkin, shuffled into the kitchen.

"Do you want scrambled or fried," she asked, hoping to outflank his defenses.

"Doesn't matter," he growled, "because I'm not going in today."

"Why? Are you sick?" she asked as her plans evaporated. Dale never missed work. Even on the day of his father's funeral, he appeared for a few hours to keep the staff alert.

"Sick is what's infecting my house," Dale replied and poured coffee into a ceramic mug.

The yellow brick road leading to a new life with Olivia and Sonny evaporated.

"Given your problems, I'm surprised you sleep like a dead woman," Dale said, shuffling to the table.

"Yeah, with my head on a beach rock," she mouthed into the mug.

"Did-you-think-about-what-the-Chief-said-last-night?" The question spilled out like one long word.

She nodded. "Ned doesn't mince words."

Dale shot her a dirty look. He hated when she did not call him the Chief, because the title made him look important and connected to power.

"Where's Sockeye?" he asked like she was late for breakfast.

She knew any response other than a full confession would bring in the artillery to soften her up, so she remained silent and took another sip of coffee.

"Look! I'm not playing this game another day," he said in a low voice and then slammed the mug down on the kitchen table. Coffee flew in every direction.

Normally, she would jump up and get a paper towel, but that was yesterday. Instead, she stared into his blood-shot eyes.

"Let me explain how this is going to play out," he continued, pointing at her. "While I take a shower and shave, you're going to make me a big breakfast. I want the works: three fried eggs, bacon, hash browns, toast, and a new pot of coffee. Then you will sit in that chair and watch me eat. If you don't tell me where Sockeye is by the time I'm finished, you're going to get dressed in those tight jeans I like and we will go for a ride. Believe me, it won't be to see the Chief or to go parking."

The coffee burned her stomach but lubricated the anger. "Sounds like you thought this through, but I don't get it. You want to know where *my* daughter is before I leave you?"

The question produced a smug laugh. "Where's a pathetic illegal alien with no skills going to go? You have no money and can't legally work!" He hit himself on the forehead. "I know what this is! You've watched the news and seen the millions pouring across the border. It's like an all you can eat buffet. Free housing, medical coverage, gift cards. What's a country if it has no border? It isn't!"

"I know you still find it hard to believe, but I can read too and seems everyone is complaining, but no one wants to fix it. I'll make my way, like I did before we met, by working and standing on my own."

He shook his head like she was an airhead and did not think through the consequences of leaving a sheltered paradise.

She watched his reaction, and it made her remember how her father loved boxing. He told her all the time how the greatest fighters were not the strongest, but the most cunning.

She wiped her eyes to get rid of the tears that were not there. After living with him for so long, she knew his entire repertoire of moves, and it presented a window of opportunity.

Dale watched and nodded like the warden of hell. "All I can say is you should get on your knees every night and give thanks. If it wasn't for me, you and Sockeye would walk the streets." He tilted his head so he could check out her profile. "And by now, your clientele would be old guys with glasses and no teeth. But Sockeye…. ah…she would do all right if she didn't smile. Shame about that chipped tooth or she would get top dollar."

She fingered her nails, ready to pluck his eyes out, but the logical voice inside told her that's what he wanted and she remained silent.

When the attack did not come, he pushed the chair back, its feet making a scratching noise. "I suggest you sit here and think over everything. Just remember, after I shower and have breakfast, I'm going to ask you again where Sockeye is and you better come clean!"

Her eyes watched him head for the hall and she listened for the shower before tiptoeing to the bedroom. The hourglass had ten minutes of sand in it and faster than any fireman could ever dress; she threw on a t-shirt, sweatshirt, jeans, socks, and sneakers. She ran to the kitchen, grabbed a fifty-gallon trash bag, and flew back to the bedroom and her bureau. The first two drawers contained underwear, t-shirts, and leggings, and she stuffed them in the bag. After a desperate look around the room, she headed for the closet and threw in a few shirts. The shower was still running and her makeup and toiletries were in the bathroom. It was unfortunate, but there was nothing that could be done.

Running back to the kitchen, she braked hard at the hall closet and retrieved a coat. She noticed the photo album on top and grabbed it and threw it in the trash bag. Dale would burn it for sure.

The last gate before freedom was a withdrawal from the kitchen desperado bank. It had been difficult, but over the past two years she skimmed a thousand dollars from the grocery money. The trick was buying "manager specials," which was code for food about to go bad. The silver lining was Dale catching the stomach flu multiple times.

She positioned herself in front of the cabinet that stored all the pots and pans. Fort Knox was not as safe as this location because cooking was below Dale's station in life, which to her consternation, rubbed off on Olivia and Sonny. Underneath the griddle was an envelope thick with bills. She stood up and threw it in the back pocket of her jeans.

The fruit bowl on the counter caught her attention, and she stuffed her coat pockets with apples and oranges. Dale would be like a mad dog on the hunt, so she planned on hiding in the woods for the day. Sonny had built a treehouse that should be safe. No doubt the Chief's three cruisers would also be on the lookout. When it got dark, she planned on heading over to Townsend and a cheap hotel. It was a ten-mile walk, but each step one toward freedom.

The roar of the shower continued, and she thought Dale was doing it on purpose to torment her. After taking one last look around, she picked up the bulging trash bag and made her way to the back door. It stuck a bit, like a rock in front of the tomb.

With a powerful pull, the door yielded, and her legs buckled. To her horror, she came face to face with Dale wearing a ratty white robe.

In the background, she could still hear the water running.

He looked at her and the trash bag stuffed with clothes. "Planning to go somewhere before cooking me breakfast?"

Before she could answer, he held up the keys to the Catalina. "I'm glad you dressed warm."

CHAPTER NINETEEN

Olivia sat next to Luke on the odd shaped couch and stared at the small mountain of paper bags, wrappers, and cardboard littering the coffee table from the super-sized McDonald's feast. She inhaled a Big Mac in record time.

She knew her stomach might rebel but took another sip of the carbonated soft drink as her mind continued processing the last few hours: the animated crowd, a weird humming invading every pore, the bright light in sync with Seth's prophetic talk, Ruth replaced momentarily by a British character out of the past. The flashback slowed as Seth called her to join him, and then the deafening roar following the disabled man's first steps.

"I'm stuffed," Luke said, throwing the remains of the fourth cheeseburger on the table, interrupting the memory.

She noticed a dot of ketchup on his cheek and wiped it off with a napkin. "I rather be full as a tick than baffled."

"Full as a tick? That's funny, but gross."

She gave him a slight push. "And you claim to be a country boy and never came across that expression?" She took another sip of Coke and the replay started again. "The thing is, you'll digest everything in the next few hours, but I never will. I can't wrap my brain around what happened tonight."

Luke adjusted his sunglasses and smiled. "I almost lost my hearing when you healed that man. I never heard such a ruckus. Rezi told me she watched the crowd throw the wheelchair in a dumpster."

"But the thing is…I don't know what happened, but I didn't make him walk!"

He waved her off. "Don't be so damn modest. It's irritating."

She wanted to rip off his sunglasses and get rid of the barrier. "Look, I will not take credit for something I didn't do. I experienced such intense embarrassment when your father called me down that if you guys hadn't intervened, I would have sprinted all the way back to Maine." She stood up and looked down at the mess on the coffee table. "The spotlights blinded me and I was unsure of how to proceed. It was just plain weird when your father had me touch the head of an old guy I didn't know from Adam." The Big Mac kicked her in the stomach as she remembered the texture of the man's hair, similar to shredded wheat. "The healings you see on TV or in a movie involve a mysterious person emitting a sense of radiating energy. I felt nothing except for the humming that consumed me. I wanted to crawl under the nearest rock when nothing happened…. Then I heard the yelling, and turned around, and…" She touched his arm. "I'm just saying again, whatever happened wasn't from me."

"Well, keep it up and you'll never have to buy a beer in Salem when you turn twenty-one," Luke deadpanned.

"There won't be a next time," she replied and took the straw out of the Coke and chewed on it. "I'm overjoyed the man can walk, but I'm not claiming credit for the cure. It makes me feel like a fraud."

"I heard the local papers were there like always," he said ignoring the comment. "But they don't understand what's going on, so they never report it. If it were up to me, you would be on page one tomorrow. But no worries, because Liam will get the word out tonight on social media, which will make the next event even bigger. Our numbers were limited until Rezi found him. Now we have thousands of followers, and that was before tonight's performance."

"Performance? Is that what you call it?" she asked, looking at her mutilated straw.

He reached for her arm. "No...no...no...wrong word! What I meant is how the whole evening built up to that incredible moment. Some described it as a miracle. Whatever word fits best, it comes down to using your five senses to make sense of the world. Despite my blindness, I sensed the crowds, perceived the excitement, understood that something remarkable occurred. Once Liam puts it up online, it will go viral. It also provides proof of what my father has been preaching."

"Preaching?"

"Look the word up. I'm not talking about a sermon, but acceptance of a secret kept hidden for too long. That's why people share the events online. Liam will tell you, it's nice to have a live audience, but it's the clicks that will make this movement go viral."

She thought about it for a moment. "So many things today are fake or staged. How would they know it was real if they weren't there?"

He nodded. "Which also means they didn't get caught up in the crowd's euphoria and have a different perspective. Sure, there's a lot of fake stuff online, but they can verify what happened by checking with the people that were there. That's one reason, the events are growing because the converted are telling others."

"But what are they being converted to? Those jerks in the back were yelling it was nothing but a magic show."

"Until you cured that guy."

"Put that aside for a minute. I've listened to your father and not to be mean, I can't make sense of what he's saying. It's too vague. Why doesn't he just spit it out?"

Luke extended his hand and felt along the table until he found the red carton of French fries. He extracted a short, stubby one that looked burned and popped it into his mouth. "A few of us know the full story and what lies ahead. It's life altering to our very core.... but if we don't accept the message, it comes with scary consequences.

You heard him explain why tonight. He's spoon feeding the revelation, so it leads to acceptance. If we go too fast, people will become overwhelmed and misinterpret the plan." He touched her arm. "You're in a different category. Things got ahead of themselves before my father could explain on a deeper level."

"He started to at the fire."

Luke smiled. "I think the dying bird stole his thunder."

"My head hurts. I just want to get some sleep," she said, though it was a bald-faced lie. She trembled at the thought of closing her eyes, fearing the torment her dreams might bring.

"I'm in a coma too from all this fast food," Luke said with a moan.

She studied the coffee table. "Rezi said you try to eat clean. I'd like to see your definition."

"Tonight was special, given what you did." He leaned toward her. "Rezi can be a bit rigid," he whispered.

She glanced at the front door. "When are they coming back?"

"Could be hours by the time they shuttle everyone home, count the donations, get the word out online."

She gazed at the monitor, longing for a mindless distraction.

As if reading her thoughts, Luke stood up. "I'll be right back."

The way he hesitated made her wonder if he was too proud to ask for help. "I can show you to the bathroom if you like."

He bit his lip for a second, like she cut his pride.

"I didn't mean it that way. I just don't want you getting hurt."

He waved her off. "No harm, no foul. I've tripped over everything in here a dozen times. I know the layout unless you moved something."

She shook her head and then winced at her stupidity. "Of course not. It's not my house."

"Your mother brought you up right," he said, walking away. Her eyes followed him as he walked about twenty feet and then made a sharp left.

"See, it's just like dancing," he said over his shoulder. "It all comes down to counting steps."

Minutes passed, and Olivia closed her tired eyes. She felt herself sink deeper into the couch and saw a bright light in the distance.

A loud thud ended the nap. When she lifted her eyelids, she observed Luke hunched over, stroking his baby toe.

"What happened?"

"Stubbed my foot on the table. I do it every time I'm here."

She noticed a small bottle in his other hand. "You're still thirsty after a liter of Coke?"

He did not reply and hurried over and held out his hand. She grabbed it and he took a seat beside her.

"When we closed on the piece of land for New Roswell, we had a party. My father doesn't drink much, but we had champagne to celebrate. I kept some of the surplus, for special occasions."

She eyed the bottle with the long neck like it was a ferocious animal at the zoo. Papa Dale chugged beer and took shots of whiskey, and Mama sipped wine when she could get her hands on a bottle. None of it made them happy, only more miserable.

"Did I say something wrong? You're pretty quiet all of a sudden."

"No," she shot back, not wanting to say something stupid but unsure if she wanted to make tonight any stranger.

"Maybe you should save it for something real to celebrate."

"There you go again." He began peeling the silver foil on the bottleneck. The way his fingers unwound the metal twist around the cork made her think he had done this many times. Before she could inquire, the cork soared across the floor.

Luke held the bottle up in front of her. "I would like to make a toast to the one and only Olivia. You stepped way outside your comfort zone tonight and the world is a better place for it."

She felt the fire in her cheeks as he tried handing her the bottle.

"No, you go first," she said.

He pushed the bottle into her hands. "I made the toast, so you have to take the first sip."

She put her lips to the bottle and took a taste. The wine had a dry flavor, and the bubbles caused a burning sensation in her throat.

He reached for the bottle. "Just drink slow, or it will go to your head. It would be unfortunate to have a Big Mac attack in reverse," he said with a laugh. Ignoring the advice, he took a long swig.

"We need music," he said, jumping up.

"How?" she asked.

He reached into his back pocket and pulled out an iPhone. "Siri play *Pretty Little Poison* by Warren Zeiders."

"Is that supposed to be me?"

"Dance with me and listen to the lyrics," he said, holding out his hand.

She stood up, and he put his hands around her waist and they began making small circles as she tuned into the song.

She's my pretty little poison...my heartache in the night...with a kiss on her lips just like cyanide...Yeah, she came with a warning...But I didn't mind...I'll go out on that high every time...

He pulled her in tight and she shut her eyes. *Who cured who?*

CHAPTER TWENTY

Gabrielle sat up in bed and listened to shards of glass pelting the house.

"I didn't hear the baby," Dale mumbled in the dark.

"No, Olivia is asleep. I fed and changed her an hour ago," she replied, thinking about the metal roof back home. Her mother said the rain used to wake her up as a baby. Now she counted on the water percussion to lull her to sleep. But the hail was rain with attitude and it sounded like Papa playing the maracas.

"I have to see," she whispered and jumping out of bed, hurried across the room to the window. The midnight landscape revealed nothing more interesting than watching the hail assault the glass, some pieces bouncing off, others establishing a crystal beach-head on the sill.

"Never thought of ice as mesmerizing. Hate to disappoint you, but it's not the horsemen of the apocalypse," Dale said, sitting up.

She glanced back at the bare-chested man in the dim light. Such a cocky American, she thought. "Mesmerizing? I don't know that word."

"Think of hypnotized." He lifted the covers as an open invitation and she recognized the mix of need and want, which sometimes alarmed her. She and Luis gave each other all they had with love. This relationship felt more lopsided, like he rescued her and Olivia and there was an enormous debt to be paid. And no matter how much

she cooked and cleaned and gave in to his wants in the middle of the night, the principal remained the same. Perhaps, with time, things will change, she hoped. The cold hardwood floor made her shiver, and she hurried back to bed and Dale wrapped his muscular arms around her. His body was a pellet stove and most nights he kicked the covers off and she begged him not to open the window. She was a child from the equator and felt forever frozen since arriving at this northern outpost of humanity.

"If you enjoy Mother Nature spitting ice in November, you won't sleep a wink when we get a nor'easter."

"Nor'easter? Why don't you just call it a blizzard?"

"Because the wind..." he began and stopped. "You'll see."

"Funny, you talked little about winter when you wooed me to come north."

He laughed. "Wooed? Rednecks aren't familiar with that word."

"That's too bad. A little romance goes a long way in case you ever wanted to..." She let the unspoken word of marriage hang in the air.

Dale eased his grip and became so still she thought he either expired or was going for a world record in holding his breath. The hail had a better chance of surviving tomorrow's sun than ever getting a proposal out of him. While being very drunk in Atlantic City, he shared how his heart shattered when his fiancé ran off with his best man the day before the wedding. Closing her eyes, she saw Luis come up the dirt road with a gigantic bouquet of lilacs. The sweet fragrance met her at the same time Mrs. Gomez came running toward them with a wooden rolling pin to exact revenge for the hole Luis made in the prized bush.

She sighed and rubbed his hand. "Don't worry, babe. You wooed me plenty with your actions. If you hadn't taken me to the hospital when my water broke, I would have delivered Olivia in the laundry room of that flea-bag hotel."

Dale came back to life. "When I turned the corner and saw you like that, it terrified me."

"But then you asked how you could help. That says more than ten pounds of chocolate and cards with sweet sayings some stranger writes."

The wise guy fell silent again, and she turned over and kissed him on the lips. "None of your beer buddies are here. What made you come to the hospital the next day?"

He inhaled, and she knew he was blushing in the dark. "I wanted to see if you and the baby were okay before I headed home."

"What about the day after that?"

He chuckled. "I was making good time until I stopped for gas. The rest is history."

"What made you turnaround? Curious about what I looked like without the baby bump?"

He stroked her cheek for a moment. "Much more than that. When I first laid eyes on you, you were mopping the floor in the lobby. You were pregnant as all hell and so beautiful it made my eyes hurt. I didn't see a wedding ring and watching you dance with that mop touched me. I don't know how to explain it other than the time I shot a deer and then saw a fawn hiding in the pines. It looked lost and scared, and made me remember the day my mother died when I was nine. My old man left me in the backyard and disappeared with a fifth of Jack… No one should go through that type of stuff alone. It made me want to…" his voice trailed off.

"Rescue me?"

Dale backed away a bit. She knew he hated feeling vulnerable and would make some wise ass comment and this special moment would be lost.

"Olivia and I don't need rescuing, just someone to love us."

He pulled her in. "And I need someone to keep me warm." He stroked her shoulder. "Your skin reminds me of mocha coffee. Earthy with a hint of spice."

A loud whimper echoed in the hall, from someone not concerned about the time of night or the weather. Any moment now, Olivia would let out the full bellied cry demanding immediate satisfaction.

She felt the two-day stubble on Dale's cheek and kissed him softly. "I know you act all macho, but I see through it. You not only visited me at the hospital, but you also took me back to the hotel when we were released and waited on us. I'll never forget that," she whispered.

"Yeah, I was on a first name basis with that lady at the Pharmacy."

"Poor Olivia with all that colic! Thank heavens it didn't last long."

"Or she would sleep in the shed by now," he replied matter of fact.

"Not funny." She drew a long breath before bridging a topic best discussed in the dark. Dale bragged how he knew every inch and curve of her body, but did not seem interested in what existed between her ears.

"I want us to be a family… and that means being honest with one another. I know you don't like my status," she said, searching his face.

"Don't sugarcoat it. You're here illegally." He kissed her on the cheek. "I can't say it doesn't eat at me."

"I never understood Americans. You bitch we take your jobs, but none of you want to work in the fields. This country would starve if it wasn't for migrant workers. All I know is Olivia won't be invisible like me, because she's a citizen. This is her forever home."

Dale pulled away. "Drop the woe is me routine. Why should crawling across the border before giving birth, baptize the baby in red, white, and blue? If that's the case, when I die, I'll just park a double-wide trailer outside the pearly gate and when St. Peter isn't looking, I'll sneak in and tell all the saints I'm born again. Give me a break! Olivia is Mexican."

"Like hell, she's just as American as you. I get you don't like my status, but that didn't stop you from turning around and coming back for me and her. Right?"

He did not reply.

"Look, I wish things were different, but if they were, I wouldn't be here."

"What do you mean?"

"Because I had good grades and my father wanted me to teach English. But my mother, she got cancer from working in the fields. The doctor said it was from all the pesticides. She passed when I was eleven and my father left me with my aunt. She was the opposite of my mother, very bossy, and we fought a lot. At fifteen, I couldn't take it any longer and told my father to get me a job on a farm or I would run away. A job came up and there was no time for a visa."

"So, you gave my country the middle finger and came thinking we would support you?"

"No! I came to pick vegetables and mop floors, and didn't ask the government for a dime."

"Because you're expecting me to bankroll you."

"You're the one that begged me to move up here!" She rolled over to get up and sleep on the couch.

Dale grabbed her arm. "But you know how to dance with a mop." He stroked her hair. "Must admit, it gets me excited sleeping with a fugitive."

"Maybe I should go home and apply for a visa. You could sponsor me."

Dale laughed. "Yeah, right!"

Right on cue, the baby started howling.

Gabrielle opened her eyes. There was no pelting hail, no snuggling in bed with a stunted emotional man arguing about immigration. Time had changed everything. Now she was in a dark trunk being punished by a serial abuser. The man that saw her waltzing with a mop and wanting to rescue her had faded faster than a Maine summer.

But at least Olivia was far away and thriving. She thought of her mother and the pictures she saw of her as a young girl with dark hair and hypnotic eyes. *I never appreciated all she did for me,* she thought. Never noticed how all the farmwork drained the very life out of her. But she never complained because she wanted the best for us.

She rubbed her shoulder. It felt dislocated from being dragged while she kicked and screamed, but Dale was much stronger when sober.

When they reached the Catalina, she thought the broken lock would save her.

"Get in!" he screamed.

"This is why I sent Olivia away!"

Dale whipped her around and she saw Sonny standing fifty feet away on the grass, watching. His hair looked wild, and he was in boxer shorts and a t-shirt.

"Get me the rope from the cellar!" Dale yelled to him.

Sonny did not move.

She wanted him to intervene, but the motherly side feared if he did.

"Get it now, boy, or I'll chain you in the cellar next!" Dale screamed.

In the next moment, she became airborne and landed hard in the hole. Sonny must have carried out his father's orders because moments later, she heard the rope wrapping the trunk. Knowing Dale, he probably tied a bow.

That was six hours ago. Lucky for her, Dale would need the car to go to work tomorrow. Even luckier, she still had the thousand dollars in her pocket.

CHAPTER TWENTY-ONE

She was holding Luke close and making small circles in the living room when the roar of a vacuum cleaner catapulted her from paradise. The clock on the nightstand said it was ten, and she gazed at the glowing numbers, unable to accept them. Multiple cups of coffee would do little to erase the headache from the champagne, and she did not have the mental horsepower to ponder all the strange happenings at Tuscan Village. But what she could not get out of her head was how Luke always looked put together despite being blind. How did he pull that off? Her t-shirt smelled of his light citrus cologne and she made her way to the kitchen, expecting to find Rezi. Instead, she found a blueberry muffin next to the coffeepot. A few bites combined with the caffeine revived her a bit, and she hoped the rain showers would let up so she could take a walk. Hearing footsteps, she turned around expecting Rezi, but Seth came strolling in. His yellow rain slicker bordered on neon.

"What have you been up to this morning?" he asked, looking at her half-eaten muffin and then his watch.

The comment took her by surprise. "I rarely sleep this late… all that excitement at the event must have worn me out." She wanted to point out how unusual everything felt.

He cocked his head. "Luke said the same thing. Seems the event took a lot out of him too."

She hoped Luke also danced with her in his dreams. "I don't want to complain, but there's not much to do here but sleep. I don't have a cellphone and there's not much on tv."

Seth nodded like he expected the complaint. "Rezi can take you to the library."

He's just like Papa Dale and limits technology. She pulled on her chin. "Maybe I'll write my mother a letter. I have so much to tell her."

The frown lines on his forehead deepened.

"I know what you're thinking," she said, cutting him off before he uttered a word. "You won't mail it because of the postmark."

He nodded. "That's right, and who knows if your mother is still living there?"

She fingered a chip on the handle of the coffee mug. "I'm going to write the letter, anyway. If you can't get it mailed, I can still use it as a journal to remember every detail."

He gifted her a smile. "I see a multi-volume set in your future." He pointed outside. "Are you up for a walk? We can continue our talk."

She glanced at the window. "In the rain?"

"We won't shrink. Go get ready and I'll wait."

She threw the mug in the sink and rushed to the bedroom and grabbed a gray hoodie and the red, white, and blue sneakers. If she couldn't fade the multi-colored canvas, maybe she could ruin them in the rain.

"No rain coat?" he asked when she returned.

She shook her head. "This is all I have."

Seth walked to the hall closet and retrieved an umbrella.

"But you said we wouldn't shrink."

"Right, but I don't want you feeling miserable," he said, handing it to her.

She followed him out the front door and expected they would head for the street. Instead, Seth cut through the wet grass and headed towards the woods beside the house.

Internal bells began ringing. "Where are we going?"

He kept walking and looked over his shoulder. "Follow me. There's a path up ahead that will take us someplace special."

She considered making up an excuse, but if Seth was going to harm her, he had many opportunities before now, so kept walking.

The leaves from trees and bushes would soon hide the narrow path they entered. It was tough navigating with an umbrella and after getting entangled a half dozen times, closed it. The light rain heightened the aroma of spring and as she trailed the mysterious man, she could hear peepers from a nearby pond.

After a good ten-minute jaunt, the path widened and Seth beckoned her to walk alongside him. As she did, they came upon a break in a stone wall and a small parking lot.

"Where are we?" she asked.

"It was called Mystery Hill for many years and rebranded as America Stonehenge in the 1980s."

"What's so mysterious about it?"

"That is the million-dollar question. It's a megalith with..."

"What's a megalith?" she asked, interrupting.

"Giant stone structures — like Stonehenge in England. If you wander around the thirty acres here, you will see an odd series of rock formations and caves. Radio-carbon analysis shows human activity and they've also found tools and pottery from Native Americans. A tv program proposed this was part of a Bronze Age civilization." He cast a sidelong glance at her and smirked. "My favorite is a wild theory about Irish monks living here before Columbus."

The rain picked up a little, and she thought of opening the umbrella.

Seth paid no attention and continued up a path and stopped in front of a huge suspended rock. "This is called the sacrificial stone," he said, pointing at the grooves. "See the pathway for the blood?"

Olivia pretended to examine the channels and then glanced at the path to his left. He would never catch her. She could see herself hitchhiking back to Maine. *But then what?*

Seth continued examining the markings. "Some say it's just a cider press from colonial days." He glanced at her. "That's why I brought you here."

"To bleed me or make cider?"

He laughed and backed away from the mysterious rock. "No, to be away from all the distractions at the house and let you ask away."

Where to begin? As much as she wanted answers about last night, she decided on a different tack.

"Tell me about what's in the bedroom closet."

Seth hesitated for a moment. "What I will share is a matter of interpretation, just like this place. Besides the poster you saw in the closet, there's a collection of keepsakes in there regarding the story of Barney and Betty Hill. Do you know their story?"

"No," she replied and watched his eyes grow big.

He smiled. "It's both funny and sad how everything fades with time. Most anyone my age remembers the story. They were driving back to Portsmouth from a trip to Niagara Falls on September twenty-first, nineteen-sixty-one, when they saw what looked like a shooting star following them. They were in Lincoln — about a hundred miles north of here. Curiosity got the better of them and they stopped and got out of the car and encountered a large aircraft in the shape of a pancake. Afraid of being captured, they took off in their car but lost consciousness for two hours and woke up thirty miles away. At home, they noticed several strange things: powder covered them, Betty's dress was ripped, and the binocular strap had been torn. When they went public, all hell broke loose. Under hypnosis they told an incredible story of being probed by large eyed, gray-headed aliens."

She swallowed hard and looked at the stone, preferring cannibals.

He reached into his pocket and took out the key she recognized for the closet. "Here's a cure for your boredom when we get back," he said, extending his hand.

She reached for it, but he did not let go of the key. "But there's another chapter you won't find in those newspaper and magazine articles."

"About what?"

"My mother lived in Lincoln too and was abducted the night before they were," he said, giving her the key.

"*Your* mother?" she asked as her eyes grew as large as his.

"Yes, but she kept her mouth shut. My father was in Vietnam and Mom was eight months pregnant with me when it happened. On a warm September night, my mother sat on the patio, listening to the radio. Suddenly, the pine trees began swaying wildly. She thought it weird, as there was no wind. Then the radio cut out and bright lights appeared over the trees, followed by a gigantic flat disk that made a strange humming noise. At first, she wondered if it was some new sort of military plane out of Pease Air Force Base and walked toward it. The next thing she remembered, she was sitting in her chair and the sun was coming up."

The rain made her shiver. "What happened to her?"

He shrugged. "The better question is, what happened to me? They came back every fall and probed me when I was sleeping. When I was little, my mother said they were just nightmares, but as I got older and described the enormous heads and dark eyes, she would either laugh it off or accuse me of being a sissy and wanting attention. It didn't matter none to me. They were real. Dreams don't have smells." He took a deep breath. "They stunk like a combo of charcoal, sulfur, and urine."

"Did she ever...?"

"Come clean?" he asked, finishing the question. "Yes, a year before she passed. After watching the circus surrounding Barney and Betty, she decided not to talk about it. Worse, no matter how many times we moved, they found me every September. She was afraid if she said anything, people would think she was nuts."

"How about your dad?"

"Never met him, killed in Vietnam." He looked away.

"I'm sorry," she said, hating the overused expression.

"When I got to be about your age, the visits finally stopped." He forced a short laugh. "Maybe I wasn't as captivating as they hoped. I attended college, got married, and Luke arrived five years later. He was an angel for the first few months and then began crying every night. The doctor said it was just colic, but I had my suspicions. When he became older and the nightmares began, I spiraled out of control. My wife said I was nuts, and it led to our divorce. She made such a stink I didn't see my son for ten years."

"But he's with you now," she said, finding it strange that Luke had mentioned none of this. *Would I have trusted him if he had?*

"When he turned fifteen, he moved in with me. He doesn't like to talk about it, but they came every year until … the accident."

"He mentioned something but didn't go into it. What happened?"

Seth waved her off. "That's not my story to tell. Let's just say rebellion has a cost."

Her mind was reeling from this sci-fi story. "Is all of this related to what's going on at the events?"

"Yes, and before I proceed, reflect on all the news stories you have witnessed in the past few years. UFOs are everywhere. Even the military and federal government admit they have no answers. This is a sign the neutral time is over. The events we hold are to prepare people's minds for what's coming."

"Ready for what?"

"A choice, peace, or the end. Once New Roswell is built, people will come to realize that the future offers great promise."

Right on cue, the rain picked up. "In Salem, New Hampshire? If you're going to build heaven on earth, why not use a tropical island?"

He smiled. "That's way above my pay grade, but there's something special about this part of the world. It's possible there's a certain vibration or window into another realm. My only understanding is that it holds hope for the future… no more tears… disease …. death."

The revived bird tugged at her thoughts, but she denied it. "Yeah, right!"

"No, I'm serious. They inserted a piece of their DNA into embryos like me. It's called being touched. They need to track how much gets passed down with each generation and its impact. That's why they followed me and then Luke for years. They need confirmation the mutation took hold before the next step. Did you hear the hum at the event?"

"Sure, everyone did."

He shook his head. "Everyone hears the sound, but for the select, it's a tuning fork. It affects each person differently. Rezi has the gift of finding people who have been touched. Ruth excels at discovering lost things, and you have the ability to heal."

She backed away. "You're talking crazy. I don't have alien DNA in me!"

"I know it's hard to understand, just like the meaning of these rocks. Ask Milton Jeffrey the next time we have an event. He's a huge developer and financing the New Roswell project. After we build out that community, he says we should rehab zombie malls and expand. Milton sees the commercial ROI and, yes, he has been touched too."

This was all too much, and she began walking away.

Seth came up behind her. "Like I keep saying, have an open mind. Last night was no fluke. Did Luke share how you've affected him?"

She stopped and turned around. They slow danced for an hour and he never tried kissing her. She feared it was the onions in the Big Mac.

"He told me the nonstop headaches he suffers with have eased up since you arrived."

"That's because I have them now," she said, turning around and looking for the path. *What madness has Mama gotten me into?*

"Be serious for a second. Don't you think it strange that you haven't needed your inhaler since arriving?"

CHAPTER TWENTY-TWO

Gabrielle took another spoonful of the no-name chicken noodle soup, which required a can of water before microwaving. She despised canned anything, but the cold penetrated her bone marrow and her muscles ached from hours of shivering. The fifty-year-old cast furnace kicked on, and it sounded like a jet taking off, which is what she fantasized about for twelve hours in the Pontiac casket. Endurance does not negate tears, and she wept after a couple of hours passed. This added to the misery, as she had no tissues and had to wipe her nose on the sleeve of her sweatshirt. Exhaustion followed, and she fell asleep and dreamed of first arriving in Maine and later of being buried alive. When she woke up, she was stiff and thirsty and called for Sonny, but the desperate pleas only bounced around the small dark cabin. Then fear took hold, and she wondered if Dale might leave her in the car until she died — or if he grew impatient, drive into the boondocks and put an end to her once and for all. The idea prompted her to search the trunk for some kind of weapon, like a tire jack or wrench, but the warden removed the option. Shortly after, she experienced the warm release and the unpleasant smell. She considered Olivia's comparable struggle, which prompted fresh tears. It's possible that Dale was waiting for this ultimate humiliation, as the trunk lid suddenly flew open. The intense light surrounded a man with his arms folded, looking at her disgusted state. He led the silent parade back into the house, and she cried for a long time in the shower.

The hotness of the soup cleared her sinuses, but her digestive system sent signals it might revolt any second. Gabrielle put the spoon down and looked out the window. Dusk was settling in and she decided when Dale fell asleep, she would take off out the front door. She could outrun him and would hide in the woods. The thousand dollars would allow her to hole up in a cheap hotel and make a plan.

As if on cue, Dale sauntered into the kitchen. He looked as relaxed as he did on Sunday afternoons, reading the paper and watching NASCAR.

He hovered over her. "You can't beat soup, if you're broke, sick or have nothing in the house," he said matter of fact.

"Or after being in solitary all day. You're a monster!" she whispered, looking up into eyes she no longer recognized.

He shrugged. "While you were detained, I had an early dinner at Mabel's. The special today was pork tenderloin. It came with whipped potatoes and green beans without those Hispanic spices you sneak into everything." He shot her a fake smile, like he was posing for his driver's license. "Then for dessert, I had myself a big slice of apple pie and vanilla ice cream." He rubbed his stomach. "Man, that was tasty!"

She would have enjoyed throwing up all over him, but did not want to spend third shift in the Catalina. Instead, she got up and ran for the bathroom, and Dale followed. She looked back, expecting him to tackle her.

Dale waved his hands. "My! Aren't we jumpy tonight?"

"I have every right! You deserve to be locked up for what you did." She fell to her knees and got sick in the toilet. After finishing, she stood up and washed her face.

"I thought about our little tiff this morning and got you a gift," Dale said from the safety of the hall.

Her head jerked back. "A gift? Well, you can take it and shove it right up—"

"Wow! That's the opposite of gratitude," he said, interrupting. "Stay there and I'll get it."

Her stomach convulsing, she stumbled into the bedroom and retrieved the beach rock from under the pillow.

Hearing footsteps, she sat on the bed and hid the rock under the blanket. If she hit him hard in the face, it would give her time to run. She thought the treehouse would be a good place to hide unless Sonny found her and took sides again.

Dale came rushing in like it was Christmas morning. He placed a small cardboard box on her lap.

"Surprise!" he said.

Gabrielle noticed a long serial number printed on the box, but little else.

"Hurry and open it!" Dale gushed.

She fingered the rock, but played along and left it under the blanket. Upon closer examination of the package, she observed it was compact like a cell phone box. She prayed it was as it would help the escape plan, especially since Dale kept unplugging the land line to aggravate her. Ripping open the package, she discovered a thick strap connected to some kind of device.

She picked it up, like it was a dead snake. "What is this?"

"It's a premium ankle monitor with GPS. The Chief says it's top of the line."

Gabrielle threw it in the box. "You can't make me wear this!"

Dale smirked. "The temps are going down to the mid-twenties tonight and our bed is a lot warmer than the Catalina. I suggest you put it on."

She grabbed the rock under the cover and lunged at him. Dale made an easy target, but he moved to the right and instead of his nose, she smashed his shoulder. He counterattacked and pinned her on the bed.

"It's one size fits all," he said and grabbed her ankle.

She experienced a sensation in her anklebone as if a matchstick was being snapped in two.

After he finished kneeling on her leg, he stood up. "I was concerned you might lose this like everything else I give you, but the Chief assured me this will stay put unless you have the right tool to take it off."

"Why are you doing this?" she cried, pulling on the thick strap.

He grabbed her chin and pulled her face up toward his. "Because my momma got the seven-year itch. I watched my old man shrivel up like a weed gone to seed until she came crawling back when her boyfriend dumped her."

"But we're not married!"

"And you've been scheming about it since you moved in! Tying the knot would help your situation because you'd be entitled to half of my possessions."

"Yeah, you're a real catch! The way you treat women makes you bachelor of the year."

"Keep talking like that and I'll get a muzzle for your mouth next." He sat down beside her. "We have a son and we haven't finished raising him." He put his arm around her and she moved away. "They say the Spanish are all about family, so why are you trying to destroy what we have?"

Gabrielle jumped up. "We? It's all about what you have! An indentured servant and two abused kids. Yeah, that's something to be proud of!"

He smiled at her like he was enjoying the show. "Love and hate are two sides of the same coin. We've had a good run and I don't know what reality show put these crazy ideas in your head, but I'll wait until the fever breaks. The problem is, I have a business to run and can't be babysitting you all day, so you're going to wear that monitor until you come to your senses." He shook his head. "If I was a betting man, I'd say that will be years. But let me explain what happens if you run to a shelter or try hitchhiking back to the border. My hunting and fishing buddy will track you down and charge you with child endangerment. But forget the Chief, because you will never make the court date. I'll let your imagination take it from here. In the meantime, Ned is working on finding the car and predicts Sockeye will be home by the weekend."

Her chest caved, and she had a hard time breathing.

Dale noticed. "Now that we understand each other, I'm going to run down to 711 for a six-pack of Bud. Do you want anything?" he asked with a laugh. "By the way, I'm tired of sleeping with an ashtray, so you're giving up cigarettes. I can get you a Slushy if you like."

She ran for the bathroom and, after closing the door, listened as he stopped at the hall closet for his coat. When the back door slammed shut, she bolted for the kitchen. Not to be cornered a second time, she waited for the car to head down the driveway before opening the drawer and grabbing a pair of scissors. Lowering herself onto the floor, she scrutinized the ankle bracelet. The strap was not made of rubber but of a smooth composite material, and it hugged the skin, which prevented her from inserting the scissors underneath it. Jumping up, she retrieved a paring knife and tried cutting the strap, but it only made a slight scratch on the material. Cold sweat formed on her forehead as she examined the two odd bolts that held the unit in place.

"God help me!" she yelled and threw the knife at the wall and it bounced off and hit the kitchen table and barely missed Dale's cell phone.

She rushed forward and grabbed the phone and entered the password, which, of course, was his birthday. Dale always believed it should be a month-long celebration.

If she had her father's phone number, she would call him. He disowned her, but not his grandchildren, and would skin Dale alive. After learning about the Catalina, he might be tempted to barbecue him over an open pit too.

She glanced out the front window and dialed. It rang and rang. Finally, it connected.

"Rezi?" she asked, out of breath.

"Who is this?" came the unfriendly reply.

"It's Gabrielle."

"Who?"

"Are you kidding me? Gabrielle, Olivia's mother!" Headlights coming up the driveway beckoned. Dale must have realized he forgot his phone.

"We agreed not to talk for the child's safety," Rezi said matter of fact.

"I know, I know. But they are looking for your car."

"Do they have my plate?"

"No, but they have a description of the car and know your name from the stop at the gas station." She watched as the Pontiac came to a quick stop. "It's just a question of time before they locate your car."

"Okay, I'll take care of it," Rezi said.

"I'm not sure when I can get there. Dale is crazy and locked me up and—"

"You were afraid of that happening," she said, completing the sentence.

"Tell Olivia the plan changed and I'm coming as soon as I can. What's the address?"

The phone suddenly lost connection at the same time she saw Dale sprinting up the sidewalk. Gabrielle placed the phone on the kitchen table and rushed to the bedroom, feeling like she was now fighting a war on multiple fronts.

CHAPTER TWENTY-THREE

A loud bang startled Olivia, and she almost fell out of bed. She considered the possibility that the noise originated from a dream until another round of quick knocks on the bedroom door ensued.

Before she could speak, the door cracked open and Rezi stuck her head in. "Are you awake?"

"I am now!" She glanced at the clock on the nightstand and it read six-thirty. Since arriving in Salem, she stayed up late and slept in, so this felt like the wee hours of the morning.

"We have a … situation," Rezi explained, showing an apology would not be forthcoming.

"Don't we all," she shot back. Mama had a knack for giving only bits and pieces of a story and it drove her nuts, but this felt different. Ice water ran through Rezi's veins, so something must be wrong.

"Just hurry and get dressed! We'll meet you in the kitchen."

"We?"

"Seth's here," she replied and shut the door.

"That can't be good," she whispered and buried her head under a pillow. Their meeting ended when they came back from the field trip to Mystery Hill. Seth urged her to reflect on what he shared and then wandered back into the rain.

She threw on a sweatshirt and jeans and made her way to the kitchen. There she found Seth and Rezi huddled at the table, sipping coffee from tall Styrofoam cups. The usual put together couple looked anything but that this morning. Seth exchanged the prophet getup for a scruffy one, wearing a stained gray hoodie and torn dungarees. His white hair stuck out in the back, as if he had just gotten out of bed. Rezi looked worse. The white crest of hair had crashed on her prominent forehead and she kept brushing away the long bangs. Her flustered cheeks gave the appearance of self-strangulation as she had zipped the frumpy black top up to her throat.

Seth gave her a weak smile. "Good morning, dear."

"Is it?" she asked, thinking what could top yesterday's sci-fi tale of alien abductions and hybrid humans?

Rezi pointed toward the counter. "I got you a coffee from Dunkin'."

She feared what news might follow and, after grabbing the treat, took a seat at the end of the table. The coffee tasted hot and eased her dry throat. She learned to drink it black because attempting to secure milk and sugar proved too risky at home. Mornings belonged to Papa Dale, and he did not take lightly to anyone that got in his way. Drinking coffee at the kitchen table was a fresh experience.

Seth and Rezi watched her, and she retreated into the coffee.

"Sorry to wake you so early, but we have a challenge," Seth added.

Nothing good ever follows that word. She feared the disabled man she cured had a relapse.

"No use sugarcoating it. We heard from your mother. The police are searching for you," Seth said.

"And that surprises you?" she asked, wincing inside, imagining Mama trying to fend off a beating. "It's the reason I'm here. Papa Dale must be furious and using his buddy the Chief to make trouble."

"It wouldn't bother me none because it's a big country, but they know my name!" Rezi chimed in.

"How?" she asked, trying to bluff as her cheeks grew hot.

"When we stopped at the convenience store so you could go to the bathroom."

She heard herself begging Lori to take down the plate number. When Rezi came in, she called her by name as an added clue for Sonny. All she could do now was go on the offensive. "Why are you blaming me? You spooked the cashier when you came in the store. It looked like you had a gun in your pocket!"

Seth closed his eyes as if he had no desire to display his distress. "Rezi, please tell me our young friend is exaggerating."

"Of course she is!" Rezi responded and then pointed at her. "I told you how uncooperative she was on the way down here. She conned me to stop so she could go to the bathroom. I stepped inside the store to ensure she hadn't slipped out through the back door." She lowered her hand but followed up with an if-looks-could-kill glance. "I saw Olivia talking with the cashier and by the look on their faces, I knew what was going on."

Seth opened his eyes and took a sip of coffee. "What is done is done, but I count on you to keep your cool as things will get increasingly difficult."

Rezi pushed the bangs away from her forehead so she could feel the worry lines. For a moment, it looked like she would cry.

Seth watched and touched her arm. "Take the learnings and move on. I appreciate you calling me last night. It allowed me time to come up with a game plan to resolve this issue."

Rezi nodded. "I hid the car like you said and stayed with Ruth last night."

Seth stood up and walked over to the slider and looked outside. The morning sun highlighted the tired visionary's face. All that was needed to complete the scene was having the mother ship beam him up.

"Olivia, are you happy here with us?" Seth asked, basking in the sun.

She thought of the alternative. "Yes," she mumbled.

He turned and looked at her. "Tell me why?"

"Because you're helping so my mother and I can have a better life."

"Is that all?"

She shook her head. Maine seemed similar to the dark side of the moon compared to the last few days. Papa Dale made her feel like a beaten dog, and Mama warned things would only get worse. As much as she did not understand what happened at the event, or the weird story Seth shared, things were better here, especially with Luke.

Seth gifted her with a smile. "Rezi is a woman of few words, but I know her well. Giving me a head gesture won't be enough. It seems you're unable to comprehend the magnitude of the risk we are taking by having you here."

"I'm sorry about being difficult at first," she said, looking at Rezi and realizing how life in Salem swung between intensity and isolation.

The woman replied with a single nod but no smile.

She looked at Seth. "I'm trying to keep an open mind like you asked. It's a lot to process."

He studied her face and nodded. "That's good to hear," he replied, and came back and sat beside her.

"Your mother is depending on us. We have to do a few things to keep you safe."

Her heart quickened. "Did she say anything else? Is she okay?"

"No, we had a quick conversation," Rezi said.

Seth shrugged. "In that abusive environment, I'm sure it's day to day. I can only control what's within my sphere." He looked at her for a long uncomfortable moment. "Do you trust me?"

She settled back in the chair, wanting to distance herself from the question.

"I get it," he replied, reading her face. "We just met. If I were in your shoes, I would have doubts too."

Tears welled up, and she felt stuck on the iceberg of misfit toys.

"I'll be honest. If you and your mom were just running from your stepfather, I wouldn't feel inclined to help," Seth said as he touched her arm.

"He's not my stepfather!" she yelled.

"Fair enough. But as we've discovered, you've been touched and have a special gift." He stopped and looked into her eyes and she saw warmth and concern … like a real father would display.

"Let me explain how I want to keep you safe," he continued.

"Okay."

"Rezi is not a common name. Within a matter of days, the police will trace the car to Salem. We have to disguise you a bit. Are you okay becoming a brunette for a while?"

"Sure. Mama said blondes have more fun, but it's a lie."

Rezi laughed. "Classic marketing spin."

Seth nodded. "Good. I'll have Ruth come over with the hair dye and you can have a girl's day." He pulled on his chin. "The next step is a bit more difficult, and I need your cooperation."

She was afraid to ask the details.

CHAPTER TWENTY-FOUR

Gabrielle paced around the house, reflecting how different Saturdays were in the States. During her childhood, she and her mother dedicated the sixth morning of the week to cleaning the house and baking bread. After lunch, they would walk to the outdoor market, where the streets were a blend of colors and aromas. Her mother would smile, watching her eyes grow bigger than her stomach, and would treat her to a churro and hot chocolate. No matter how delicious the combo, she always left a bite of the fried dough and a sip of cocoa as a token of love for her father hundreds of miles away on the farm. When she first arrived in Maine, she wanted to carry on the tradition of making Saturday all about family. Cook a big breakfast before skating, sledding or going to the beach. The plan went sideways after she got pregnant with Sonny. Dale seemed overwhelmed with parental responsibilities and though he owned the store, worked most weekends and when he was home, parked the kids in front of cartoons. While God created the seventh day for rest, Dale believed every day belonged to him.

However, this Saturday had a unique atmosphere while under house arrest. The pacing stopped at Sonny's closed bedroom door. If she had given into the rage and heartache, she would have kicked it in after Dale left for work. But that was an hour ago and saw it as a test of endurance.

She knocked two times on the hollow door and held her breath.

Nothing.

Did I expect anything different? Most schooldays, Sonny slept through the alarm and she became hoarse yelling for him to get up.

She knocked again and a bit too hard as her hand ached. "Sonny, get up!"

A long silence ended with a moan. "Have you forgotten what day it is? It's Saturday!"

She swallowed the complaint, aware getting cooperation on this request did not bode well for the big ask. Who was she kidding? Sonny would back his father.

"I need you to get up because—"

The shrill ring of the phone interrupted the plea and made her wonder if the ankle monitor was working. *Why else would Dale be checking in?* Then she realized it might be Rezi with an update about Olivia. Bolting for the kitchen, she reached for the harvest gold phone on the eighth ring.

"Hello?" she asked.

"Mrs. Pearce?" a deep voice inquired.

She almost laughed. "Not quite."

"Sorry, I just assumed. Ah, …. is this Olivia's mother?"

"Yes," she replied as her stomach dropped. "Who is this?"

"Doug Jackson from the Sentinel."

A reporter? she thought.

"Can you comment about your daughter's kidnapping?"

"Where did you hear that?" Her mind went down multiple avenues and locked on Dale, ramping up the pressure by calling the paper.

"Where did I hear it?" the reporter laughed. "It's all over the news. I'd like to give you an opportunity to comment."

She heard enough, and after hanging up the phone, raced and turned on the television. The phone began ringing again, and she ignored it and watched a commercial about a terrible lung condition.

The narrator droned on, listing side effects worse than the disease. Then the screen burped and dashing anchorman Jake Willard appeared attempting to look concerned, which should have resulted in a frown, but the handsome man's forehead was frozen like a Maine lake in January from all the Botox.

"Topping local news this morning, we take you to Anne Bradley outside police headquarters regarding the disappearance of a local teen," Jake said in a serious tone.

The picture cut to a young woman with microphone in hand that looked a bit too happy given the subject. "Authorities continue to search for sixteen-year-old Olivia Ruiz. She was last seen with a middle-aged woman named Rezi at Humphries Convenience store on Monday. Chief Warner stated that cashier Lori Monroe sensed something was wrong when her classmate entered the store. After asking to use the bathroom, a stern looking middle-aged woman came in and quickly escorted her out. Ms. Monroe said the woman kept one hand in her pocket like she had a weapon. Suspicious, she took down a description of the vehicle and noted the woman's first name. Chief Warner commended her quick thinking. Authorities are looking for a 2014 Cadillac, registration number RD374-4435. Police caution if you see the vehicle, do not approach it but call 911. Olivia is five foot five with blonde hair, brown eyes, and a slim build."

"That's not how it went down," Sonny said, coming up beside her. "Lori said that Liv asked her to take down the plate, and she blew it."

"I...can't believe this ..." Her mouth refused to cooperate with her brain. "They keep saying kidnapped."

"Because she was," he replied, plopping down on the worn corduroy loveseat.

She turned the tv off and sat down next to him. "But I told you the truth."

"Yeah, your version," he said, pointing at the tv. "This isn't fake news because Lori told me the same thing. That Rezi lady is a nutcase." He ran his hand through his thick hair. "What's so important you had to get me up?"

She held up her ankle. It said more than words, and she watched her son's eyes bulge. "Your father says if I leave the house, he will track me down and I'll be...."

"Arrested?" he asked.

"Worse." A mother shields her children, but Sonny needed to know about the monster he was living with too. "The Chief threatened to charge me with child endangerment and turn me into ICE, but he won't do it unless his best buddy agrees. That's bad enough, but when your father held me down and put the monitor on my ankle, said if I left, he would track me down and take me into the woods and...." She held back the tears. "I didn't just send Olivia away because he abuses me. I'm also afraid he's going to molest her and...." She stopped as the words were too ugly to birth.

Sonny closed his eyes and rubbed his forehead. "You know Papa's bark is worse than his bite... He wouldn't touch Liv."

"You talk about fake news! What do you call being blind to what's in front of you?" she asked, pointing at her ankle. Looking at her son, she noticed how his features were transforming into a man. She longed for the days when he would follow her around the house, begging her to play LEGO's or Lincoln Logs with him. Despite carrying him for nine months, why had they grown so far apart?

He looked at her like he was reading her thoughts and was not happy with the content. "He's acting crazy because he doesn't want you leaving us. That's all."

She pulled him in for a hug, but it was one sided as his back stiffened. "I'm not leaving you. Never!"

Sonny pulled away, and she felt the brick wall rising from the floor. It was taller and more formidable than anything she ever saw at the border. She was willing to scale it, even if it meant being cut by the barbed wire on top. "Why did you help him stuff me in the trunk yesterday?"

"I didn't help him," he mumbled and looked away.

"But you got him the rope."

"Did I have a choice?" he replied and jumped up and began walking away.

She followed him. "Of course you did! When are you going to grow up?"

Sonny spun around. "Why? Because you can't stand up to him and you want me to?"

"I've tried, but look where it gets me!" She pointed at the bruise on her cheek and then at the ankle monitor. "When I worked on the farms, I didn't have to worry about some guy slapping me around or wanting something else after they drank too much on payday. Roberto looked out for me. That's what family is for!"

He shook his head hard, like he did not want to see the evidence, and headed for the hall. She followed close behind and when he got to the bedroom; he tried closing the door, but she pushed against it with all her strength and entered.

"Get out of my room!" he yelled.

"Why should I? It's my house!" she screamed back.

"Because it's not yours! It belongs to Papa!"

"There it is!" she said, nodding. "Your tongue can't hold back what your heart knows. When I met your father, I had nothing but the clothes on my back and was pregnant with your sister. I thought I hit the lottery when we first moved here. He was my hero. We fell in love and you were the blessing that came into our lives. I tried to be a good mother and …" she stopped to catch her breath, "but never his wife, because I'm not worthy, given my status." She looked down at the ankle monitor. "So, who am I besides the woman that gave him a son? Nothing but a cook, a housekeeper, a warm body to fondle when he gets drunk …a punching bag after a bad day."

Sonny began swaying from side to side. Fighting back tears, she saw her son's face change.

"Look, I could have left with Olivia, but that would have meant leaving you too," she whispered. "I'm not questioning your love for your father, and never will. But I'm asking you to judge the man. Face this darkness before it swallows both of us."

His lower lip trembled. She pulled him in and this time, he held on.

CHAPTER TWENTY-FIVE

The kitchen air reeked of ammonia.

"Hurry! I want to look!" Olivia said, ready to jump out of the chair.

"Hold your horses," Ruth replied, turning off the blow dryer. Deep blue eyes scanned her head, and a smile dawned on the redhead.

"What's the matter?" She grabbed the small mirror off the table and eyed the face looking back, framed with chestnut hair she did not recognize. The funny commercial of the man spray painting his bald spot came to mind.

"What do you think?" Ruth asked, looking in the mirror too.

"All I need is a skilled dentist to repair my chipped tooth, and I'll resemble Barbie's Latino sibling."

Ruth laughed. "I love how the color complements your eyes. Besides hiding in plain sight, you'll have all the guys lining up at the next event."

She looked away. *Mama says I'm something special, but don't all mothers? The boys at school rarely see past my second-hand clothes...except Kenny if he catches me alone and I know what he's after. Just bragging rights... It's a high price for feeling wanted.*

Ruth grabbed her pocketbook off the counter and took out a small makeup bag.

"What are you doing?"

"Stop with the questions and just shush for a minute, will you?" She leaned over and began applying mascara, blush, and lipstick. After she finished, she handed her back the mirror.

Olivia eyed herself for an extended period and Ruth let out a long whistle. "Look at you, girlfriend! I wish I could conceal my identity and appear as attractive! The others are already jealous you caught Luke's eye."

If she only knew, but chased the memories away given the opportunity to probe. "I saw some of the group at Tuscan collecting donations and keeping the crowd under control, but have met no one except you."

"You will," Ruth replied. "It's a tight group. Seth is careful choosing his disciples."

"Disciples? That sounds like a religion."

"I had that same impression, but the word fits. Look it up. Disciple means a follower or student of a teacher, leader, or philosopher. Seth embodies all three and links us to something that surpasses our comprehension."

She noticed how Ruth's eyes danced, talking about the mysterious leader. "Seth told me about what happened to his mother." She hesitated in case Ruth did not know the tall tale and, if so, hoped she would divulge more.

Ruth did not take the bait and picked up the mirror and examined her face.

"How many disciples does Seth have?" she asked, looking for safer ground.

Ruth shot her a knowing smile. "My, my, so many questions! I don't know...a few dozen. Most are active, and some Seth calls sleepers."

"What's the difference?"

"Well, the active ones manage the events. Registration, collections, crowd control. The sleepers handle the back-office duties like posting on social media, building awareness, and shall we say greasing things?"

She pondered about Betty and Barney Hill being harangued by the press regarding their encounters with gray-headed aliens. Seems they missed capitalizing on it.

Ruth shot her a plastic smile. "Things will ramp up when we break ground next week for phase two. Lucky for us, we have members in the planning department. It sure helped to get the permits," she said with a knowing laugh. "The actives and the sleepers will meet soon. That will make for some party!"

There were footsteps in the hall.

"Where are my girls?" Seth called out.

"In your new beauty parlor," Ruth yelled back.

A moment later, Seth walked in with Luke in tow. Olivia ran her hand through her hair and then sighed realizing the blind guy couldn't see the amazing makeover.

"Isn't she gorgeous?" Ruth said, pointing.

"She needs glasses," Olivia replied, as her cheeks grew hot.

Luke used her voice as a beacon and began shuffling toward her.

Seth gifted her with his charming smile. "No matter the hair color, Olivia's inner beauty always shines through."

The air turned silent for an awkward moment. Ruth must have noticed it too, because she put the makeup in the bag.

Seth noticed and walked over to Ruth. "You are a woman of many wonderful gifts. Thank you so much for your help! I hope you will understand, but I need to speak with Olivia in private for a bit. May I suggest you enjoy the beautiful spring weather for an hour and then come back?"

Ruth smiled. "No problem." She touched Luke's shoulder. "Want to go for a walk?"

"Maybe later," he replied, with a solemn face. "I'm part of the conversation, too."

The swift dismissal resulted in a confused expression on her face, but she masked it with another smile. "Okay, see you later!" She hurried out of the room.

Seth pulled out two kitchen chairs for him and Luke and placed them near her. Olivia wondered if the next installment of the fantastic story would follow.

"You know," Seth began and then stopped and filled his lungs like he was nervous. "I've only known you for about a week and already consider you like a daughter — someone I want to protect and see thrive."

She wanted to look away, but his dark eyes drew her in.

"Your gift of healing needs to be shared with our broken world," he continued.

Tingling sensations ran across her chest.

"My son is also fond of you and the kindness you have showered him with."

Luke extended his hand, and she took it. She expected it would be a slight touch, but he held it tight.

"You're freaking me out. What's this all about?" she asked.

Seth leaned forward and grabbed her other hand. "I don't know how to say this because …. there are no words."

She squeezed both their hands. "Just say it!"

Seth's eyes became glassy. "I'm afraid it's about your mother. There was a terrible car accident and…" He shook his head. "She's gone."

For a second, the words lost all meaning. They were just random letters connected to something unfathomable before they reassembled and exploded in her brain. She fell forward and Seth caught her. The tears fed the screams.

Seth and Luke took turns rubbing her back, stroking her new dark hair.

When the crying finally subsided, she sat back in the chair as an orphan. Both father and mother cut down in violent ways.

Seth left the room and returned with a box of tissues. She took the first of a million to follow and blew her nose. "What happened?" she asked with blurred vision.

"I'll tell you what I know, though it isn't much," Seth offered. "When your mother called Rezi yesterday, she said Dale was in a wild rage about you. The police were searching and—"

"Why are you going over that again?" she asked, interrupting. "That's why I colored my hair."

Seth nodded. "I'm just giving you the timeline. Your mom called Rezi again late last night and said things took a turn for the worse, and terrified what Dale would do next. For her safety, Rezi told her to drive down and join you. It would also bring an end to the entire kidnapping story."

"What do you mean, drive? My mother doesn't have a license! Ten years ago, she attempted to drive after Papa Dale was laid up with a bad back and needed pain meds. She drove to the pharmacy and almost hit a dozen mailboxes."

Seth took the story in but did not respond.

"My mother doesn't have a car either!"

"She told Rezi she would take Dale's. Figured she earned it."

"The Catalina? That car is the size of a house." She remembered the dent she put in the trunk and looked at Luke. He had his head in his hands.

"The news said she was doing seventy and missed a curve," Seth continued.

"None of this makes sense! She wouldn't take the car, never mind speed!"

"Unless she was being chased," Luke added, sitting up in the chair.

It was too much to take in. "I don't understand any of this. How did you hear about the accident?"

"When your mother didn't show up this morning, we were afraid of what happened and began checking the news. It didn't take long," Seth explained.

She stood up. "I have to go home. Can you drive me?"

Luke stroked her arm. "I understand you want to be there. But you better consider this. It's not a good idea."

She could not believe her ears. "Why not?"

"Because you're running back to the man, your mother wanted to save you from," Seth replied.

Luke's fingers found hers. "Your mother died protecting you. Honor that!"

"Then I'll live somewhere else," she said, breaking away. "But I have to say goodbye to my mother!"

"I know how you must feel, but it will be a closed casket. The car rolled over, and she got ejected and suffered massive injuries," Seth whispered.

"But I want to be there for my brother...."

"Your half-brother?" Luke corrected. "And I only say that given the risk to you."

She shot him an ugly look, but of course he was oblivious.

"Any other family?" Seth asked.

She shook her head. "Mama's family is in Mexico..... I don't even know how to contact them."

"You need time to think," Luke said in a sad whisper. "But you should consider another option."

Silence reigned for a long moment.

Seth came and wrapped his arms around her. "Everyone in our community is family. We all love you and will give you a place of honor when we build out New Roswell. In the meantime, you can go to Salem High in the fall."

Words lost their meaning again, and she rejected his embrace. "How are you going to pull that off? I'm here because Papa Dale wants to play house with me."

"By making them think you couldn't live without your mother. After that, it's just a matter of establishing a new identity." He pointed at her hair. "You're already building an alias."

Observing the two men, she realized she no longer knew who she was.

CHAPTER TWENTY-SIX

Sonny detected the scent of gasoline and exhaust, and the vice around his chest loosened as he approached the two-stall cement block garage. This place always smelled the same, regardless of the season or the crazy happenings within. From the looks of it, Lori's brother had a lot going on as usual. A Volkswagen Bug sat up on blocks and, next to it, a vintage Polaris snowmobile had its butt up in the air, exposing a torn track. In front of the year-long rehab projects sat a black Harley-Davidson Fat Boy. Heavy metal music bounced off the steel and chrome.

He spied Billy in the back corner, searching for something on the cluttered workbench. He did not want to startle his friend and waited. A minute later, Billy turned around and, seeing him, turned off the radio and shuffled over. He was a big brute, six-foot three, two hundred fifty pounds with a long ponytail and bushy black beard. Whether December or June, he wore a black t-shirt, dungarees and oil-stained work boots.

They exchanged a quick fist pound.

Sonny pointed at the Harley. "How's it running?"

Billy smiled at the motorcycle like a proud father. "Started right up after its winter nap. I'm going to change the oil in a bit and then take a ride if you're interested."

He nodded trying to play it cool even though a ride on the Harley would beat tickets to the World Series. *Billy's the best and never treats me like a dweeb,* he thought.

The hulk bent over and brushed away a cobweb from the front rim. "Any news about your sister?"

The vice tightened around his chest again. "Afraid not."

Billy took a rag out of his back pocket and worked on erasing a smudge mark on the chrome exhaust. "Funny they can't find your sis, but mine is all over the news."

He laughed, but it made him realize again how he and Olivia led separate lives. Here was a nineteen-year-old guy that was aware of what his sister was up to even if he used the information as material for jokes. Perhaps he would have a different perspective if he were the older brother.

"That's why I turned the radio off. I don't want to hear about her rapid problem-solving for the tenth time on the news. Gag me!" Billy continued.

"Say what you will, but we owe Lori a lot for what she did." He bit his lip, wishing she took down the plate. His mother's face flashed in his mind. Maybe it's better she didn't, so Liv could get faraway.

"Of course, you would say that," Billy said.

"What do you mean?"

His older buddy rolled his eyes. "Whenever you mention my sister, your voice quivers. You've been gawking at her since grade school. When are you going to move past puppy love and ask her out?"

His shoulders slumped. "I would, but she says she doesn't go out with younger guys."

He gave him a once over like it was the first time he realized he had been hanging out with a kid. "Why? How old are you?"

"Almost fifteen."

"Wow! Younger than the princess? Once you're out of high school, it won't matter. Hell, my dad was ten years older than Mom."

He wiped his leg with the rag. "Hang in there, buddy. You'll get your shot."

"Which means I'll have you on my case?"

Billy pointed at him. "You got that right. Since my old man passed, I'm the gatekeeper to your major crush." He gestured towards the injured snowmobile. "The last kid she went out with was a bear, all mouth, and claws, and acted like she belonged to him. I didn't want to waste the bullet, so I ran over him instead. The bad news is his leg will heal."

Sonny focused intently on the snowmobile. That was the thing about Billy. Given the matter-of-fact way he talked, he could never tell if he was joking. Serious or not, he filed away the comment if the chance ever came.

His buddy headed back to the workbench, and he followed at a respectable distance. "Why are you here instead of helping the cops find Olivia?" Billy asked over his shoulder.

"I can't cover much ground on my ten-speed. Plus, the highway is off limits."

Billy turned around and took a few steps toward him. The tough gear head's cockiness faded, replaced by the same sad look on everyone's face. "I don't mean to come across like a jerk. I don't know Olivia, like you do my sister," he said with a smirk, "but she seems sweet. Your mom must be beyond sick."

Sonny looked at the ground and the reel of the painful conversation with his mother replayed and the pressure headache returned.

"I wish there was something I could do to help."

He did not dare look up as the knives began slicing the insides of his throat. The gasoline-exhaust-fragrance made his stomach turn.

"I saw your father working at the store this morning," Billy continued. "If I were him, I'd be cruising every street in America. And if I found that lady Rezi," he pointed at the snowmobile, "they would never find her remains."

The words scaled his shoulders and got inside his head. There was nowhere to hide, and Billy kept talking. "Poor girl…with some sicko…everyone is praying she's okay."

"The truth is my sister isn't missing!" he blurted out.

Billy's face contorted like a shapeshifter. "What did you say?"

He wanted to retract it by devising a series of lies, but the naked truth brought satisfaction. "My mother just informed me she sent Liv off with that lady."

"I don't understand."

"I don't either, but she's leaving my father."

"That sucks but what does your sister have to do with it?" He winced. "That didn't come out right, but you know what I mean."

The answer churned in his stomach with the bowl of cornflakes he had for breakfast. It would be a shame to ruin the gear head ambience in the garage if he got sick. He looked around for a barrel and centered on the Volkswagen. No trunk space for anyone to fit.

"Because my mother believes my father will prevent her from leaving by imprisoning Liv in the trunk of the Catalina."

Billy cocked his head. "C'mon man! That's sick."

"I agree it's bad ass, but he uses the trunk like a timeout room. I've been in the hole a couple times, but for my sister, … it's her second bedroom."

Billy stared at him in disbelief, and he retreated to the front of the garage. The dark clouds shook their heads at hearing the truth, and heavy raindrops pelted the spring grass. Sonny watched an oil stain in the center of the driveway repel the spring shower. *That's how I feel. Overwhelmed.*

Billy came alongside with his hands on his hips. "Does your father know the truth?"

"He does now. My mother came clean after he got the police involved."

"Does the Chief know too?"

He nodded.

Billy let out a low whistle. "This is pretty twisted, but at least she's safe."

"I'm not sure about that. My mother fears the people she's with can't be trusted."

"Then why the hell did she...." he stopped and rubbed his forehead. "I'm sorry, man. This really sucks!"

"It gets worse. My father put an ankle monitor on my mom. If she leaves, he says she's a goner."

Billy looked him straight in the eye with the same question he asked himself every day. "What are you going to do about it?"

He looked down and watched a spider scurry across the floor.

Billy reached into his pocket and took out a set of keys and removed one and handed it to him.

"I can give you cutting pliers or a blade before you leave. If you need something else, just come back and get it any time day or night." He gestured towards the workbench. "But what you won't find here is the courage to do the right thing."

"And what's that?" he heard himself ask in a squeaky voice. "My mother did this behind my father's back... and she's not just leaving him." He wished they sold super glue that could keep the broken shards of their family together.

"Did she say she's leaving you too?"

"No, but I see how things turn out after break ups. She and Liv will end up miles away and no matter all the promises... will forget me."

"Has she favored your sister more?"

He hesitated for a moment and then decided to share the rest. "My mother's family were migrant farm workers from Mexico. When she got pregnant with Liv, she and her boyfriend took off for New York and he got killed, along with my uncle. My dad met her in Atlantic City."

Billy contemplated the news for quite some time. "So, what you're saying is she's an illegal?"

He nodded and looked away with the family secret out, certain there would be no more Harley rides, and as far as Lori went, he would plow him over next. Shunned was his new name.

The hulk pushed him hard, and he fell back a step. "I don't give a damn how she got here or her status. She's still your mother!" Billy whispered like ICE might have a drone overhead. "Your dad is twisted. Do something!"

He shrugged. "Like what? I'm fourteen!"

"Funny, minutes ago you said age didn't matter when it came to Lori. It's time you man up, buddy!"

Sonny nodded and felt the cement floor tremble.

His friend pointed at the Harley. "Don't worry man. I'll be the wind under your wings."

CHAPTER TWENTY-SEVEN

The morning arrived cold and cloudy, which might disappoint most in New England, but Olivia did not care. The last two days had been a blur. Gazing through the front window, all she could ponder were the choices she could have made. If she refused to get in Rezi's car, or told Lori at the gas station to call the police or run away when she got here, Mama would still be alive.

She saw Seth's black SUV meander up the street and ran to the kitchen. With any luck, she could get a glass of water and retreat to the bedroom. But Seth must have run up the walk too because moments later she heard the front door open and his leather sandals clapping on the hardwood floor.

"Morning," Seth said, breezing in.

She was glad he did not characterize it as a good morning, because she might have pulled a nutty and it would have scarred the vanilla greeting for the rest of his life.

Rezi played follow the leader and came bounding in too and gave her the same sad nod she had for two days, like there were no words which was the truth. She placed a large Dunkin' coffee and paper bag in front of her.

"I thought you might like a bagel and cream cheese," she whispered.

She pushed the bag away. "Thanks, but I'm not hungry."

"But you have to eat something. Keep your strength up."

She heard enough and grabbed the coffee. The bedroom, with the shades drawn, beckoned. There she could release her tears and screams in the dark cave, free from the need to pretend to be strong.

As she turned for the hall, Seth grabbed her arm.

"I know you're hurting, but we came early this morning to discuss something urgent."

She shook off his grip, and glanced back at Rezi, who looked like she rather be anywhere else than here. The ambush two days ago came to mind. "Let me guess, you're here to tell me Sonny was in the car with my mother?"

The comment sucked the air out of the room and the way they glanced at each other, she feared she guessed the news.

"No, nothing like that," Seth said and gestured toward the table. "Please sit down with us for a few minutes and then we will leave you alone." His tone did not sound like an invitation.

Olivia sighed and plopped down in the chair, and took a sip of the coffee. It had too much cream and too little sugar for her liking. But everything seemed prepackaged for her nowadays.

Seth sat down next to her and rubbed his eyes, his black t-shirt wrinkled and tiredness showing on his face, which did not reflect the picture of cool and collected he worked to portray.

"I'll be direct. We have a situation here in Salem and the surrounding towns," he began and watched Rezi take a place across from him. "Your mother is gone, but the police are still looking for you. If anything, they have increased patrols in the area, and are even using planes. It gives me the impression that they're aware of Rezi's car passing through the toll booth in Portsmouth, which leads them to think you're nearby."

"Why are they looking? I'm the orphan of an illegal." She pointed at her dyed hair and had not showered or brushed her teeth since the nightmarish news. "I'm not the same person I was a couple days ago. You mentioned they will leave me alone if they believe I'm dead. Well, I am."

Seth let out a long sigh and closed his eyes like she was easier to deal with that way. "I understand what you're saying Olivia, I do. Unfortunately, it's not that easy. Unless we do something big and graphic, they will never stop looking. You have a special gift that will benefit many, but unless we get this resolved, it's only a matter of time before they find you." He opened his eyes. "There's a special place for you here in New Roswell, but I can't risk our community by having the police going house to house searching for you."

"I should just leave then."

"And go where?" Rezi chimed in. "I talked enough with your mother to know what Dale will do if he finds you. Sick man."

She looked out the kitchen window at the gray skies. If only the fog would roll in and wrap itself around her.

Seth patted her hand. "I have to describe the challenge we face so you understand. That said, I have no intention of giving in to that evil man." His dark eyes searched hers. "But I need your full cooperation."

Papa Dale's image appeared in her thoughts and the way he leered at her. She nodded.

"We need to stage your death," Seth said slowly, so she could comprehend the mind-blowing plan.

"How do you pull that off? Bring me back to Tuscan Village and have your alien friends beam me up?" She glanced at Rezi and the sharp look on her face made her think she might get up and slap her.

"I don't appreciate you dissing everything we believe in," Rezi said.

"Sorry," she countered, more to move on than apologize.

Seth shot her a look like he was not buying it either. "Insult aside, we need a public viewing, so there's no question."

She had a taste of the coffee to keep her mouth busy.

"I'll share the plan, but you have to trust me," he continued.

Her mother taught that trust is earned, and she still had questions about whether he was the biggest nutcase on earth.

"So, do you trust me?" he asked again.

She nodded slightly.

"I'll take that as a yes because we don't have time. The key is building on what they have, which is you and Rezi in the Caddy." He stopped and looked at the woman across the table to check in. Rezi's white hair stood so tall this morning it looked like a Maine snowbank.

Seth's eyes came back to hers. "At dusk tonight, you and Rezi will drive to Haverhill and take the Basiliere Bridge, which crosses the Merrimack River. The traffic pattern is tight, but there's enough room to pull the car over on the bridge and get out."

"And then we will jump," Rezi said like they were planning to cross the street.

"What?" she asked.

Seth laughed at the look of horror on her face. "Trust me, it will only appear that way. The bridge is being replaced and there's scaffolding all over it. We scoped it out yesterday and there's a small wooden platform right below the railing. You will wait to make sure a car or two notices and then both of you will jump. After that, there are a series of ladders and ramps to the shore. A path runs along the embankment to the road and I'll be waiting for you there."

"How will people find out I drowned?"

"We will throw some of your clothes in the water along with Rezi's downstream."

She glanced across the table. "Why would she jump?"

"Because with your mother gone, there's no one to tell the truth about why I took you. I'm looking at twenty-five years to life," she said.

Seth nodded. "For a few days everyone will shake their heads at the sad story, but in this crazy world you will be off the front page quicker than ink dries. Then you'll be free and can take part in the events again. People are buzzing online about what you did at Tuscan. The world is hungry for a healer. We are having a kickoff for the first residents of New Roswell and it would be a great coming out event for you if things work out."

She looked at her fingers. The nails were longer than Papa Dale ever allowed, and she wanted to ask Ruth for some polish. That her hands held any healing power was beyond absurd.

"One question. What could go wrong?" she asked

Seth shrugged. "You could ask that about any minute of the day. We should just concentrate on putting an end to the search."

She gazed out the window and nodded. "Papa Dale can't hurt me from the grave."

CHAPTER TWENTY-EIGHT

Sonny hesitated at the back door and took a deep breath, feeling as if his body was being contorted into a T-Rex balloon. The door felt like it required extra effort to open, which he attributed to the small arms of the ferocious dinosaur.

He found Mama in the living room, vacuuming a multi-colored braided rug from the last century. She had her hair combed back and wore the same drab sweatshirt and jean cutoffs, which only made the accessory on her ankle all the more startling. He watched as she raked a small section of the area rug vertically and then horizontally. Papa said she had a touch of OCD and teased she could never scrub or vacuum away her Mexican DNA. Mama always took it on the chin and said cleanliness is next to godliness.

Afraid to startle her, he disconnected the plug from the outlet.

The vacuum moaned as it died, and she turned around. "I didn't hear you," she said without a look of surprise.

He looked past her at the ancient canister; its squat body and ribbed tubing resembling a serpent. As a kid, he used to shoot the vacuum with plastic missiles or suck up Barbie shoes, which made Liv furious. It was a wonder it still worked.

His mother took the cord out of his hand. "By the way, your father called. He's running late so I haven't started dinner yet. There's popcorn if you want a snack."

He nodded and glanced again at her ankle monitor.

She turned the vacuum back on and he started for the kitchen. Halfway there, he realized the pangs in his stomach were not from hunger and hurried back and unplugged the vacuum again. The serpent groaned for a second time.

"This isn't funny!" his mother yelled.

He looked at the cord in his hand and thought how he needed to unplug himself, too. "I want to talk about… that," he said, pointing at her ankle.

She did not follow his eyes, but shrugged. "I was wrong to put you in the middle of this mess and make you choose one of us. He's your father. I'll figure things out. All that's important is making sure Olivia's safe."

The words provided a sudden off ramp. He could hunker down in his room, eat popcorn, listen to tunes, and fantasize about cruising the streets with Lori after he got his license. Meanwhile, Mama could deal with the river of dysfunction that ran through the house. But Billy's words rang in his ears about manning up. More than the plea, it was the look that came with it, like he was a coward for not doing it already.

He kicked the vacuum out of the way and sat down in his father's recliner. If Papa were home, this infraction would guarantee a few hours in the trunk.

His mother's eyes darted to the front door, expecting Dale to come barging in any second with a giant hook to dethrone him. When he did not, she dropped the vacuum and sat down on the loveseat. Her shoulders sagged and her lips moved like she wanted to say something but had trouble forming the words.

"I'll get an Allen wrench tomorrow and take that damn thing off," he said, pointing.

She glanced at her ankle and then shook her head. "That's mighty brave, but I can't let you do that."

"You have it backwards. I'm a coward unless I do," he said, standing.

She got up and hugged him. He wondered how things got so twisted in this family. The pain in the back of his throat started again. He was seven-years old and Papa drilled a finger in his chest. "Boys don't cry!" he yelled again and again.

"Do you have any idea what your father will do if you betray him?"

"Do you have any idea what I will think of myself if I don't?" he replied. "How long can this go on? With you under house arrest?"

"Forever if necessary to get things right between us, but I made a mistake sending Olivia away and have to find her." She rubbed her forehead with both hands. "I recall my mother sharing a parable about the man who departed for a faraway land and squandered his inheritance on alcohol and women. Then a devastating famine hit and he was starving and sought employment at a farm. He watched the pigs eat, but no one offered him anything. He thought about how his father treated his servants, and headed for home to tell his father he didn't deserve to be his son anymore, but would work as a servant. That's sort of my story but without the happy ending. Luis and I had our heads in the clouds, running without planning first. After losing your father and uncle, I ended up here where the Catalina gets fed and I starve." She glanced at the window. "My father was mad when we left for Brooklyn and angrier when they died. But it's been sixteen years, and I would gladly work cleaning his house."

"But you said that door was forever closed even if you lived ten lifetimes!"

She looked at the ceiling as if in prayer. "Desperation makes you reconsider all the possibilities. Another thing I realized is that if you make bad choices, you must accept the consequences instead of blaming others. I never looked in the mirror and saw what my actions caused… to my father and Luis' family." She sighed and gazed at him. "But I still consider everything that's happened since Atlantic City a blessing because it led to you."

He looked away. "So, are we doing this or not? If we wait until things get worse, it might be too late… for you and Liv."

She walked to the front window and stared at the driveway. Sonny knew she was fearing the car that would soon carry the king home in search of food, booze and — he stopped his thoughts from going there, but the walls were paper thin. He put the pillow over his ears when she cried, telling him to stop.

"He doesn't have to know you freed me," she said, more to herself than him. "I mean, how would he know I didn't cut it off myself?"

"Because he has it on so tight, you would have to cut your foot off."

She went silent for a long moment. "I could leave the wrenches on the table and he would think I figured it out."

"You don't know the difference between a flathead and Phillip's screwdriver. He will know you had help."

She turned around, and he saw the tears in her eyes. "Then I won't do it. I will not let him beat the hell out of you, or worse."

"He won't get a chance, because I'm leaving with you," he said, experiencing a sensation similar to jumping out of a plane without a parachute. Flying is fun until you hit the ground.

She looked at him for a long moment. "You would do that for me?"

His stomach ached because words have consequences. "Yes. Papa has to understand he can't treat you or Liv like that."

"Or you."

"Me? Not so much. He lets me get away with a lot. Who knows? Maybe it will make him realize some things."

"Yeah, like how we're ganging up on him."

She wrapped her arms around him. "My dearest son. How I love you!"

His mind raced with the logistics. "Okay, tomorrow then. Where are we headed?"

"We should drive a few towns over and stay at a cheap hotel. Tonight, grab a bag, fill it with a week's worth of necessities, and stash it under the bed. After he goes to work tomorrow, we'll leave. That should give us a good head start."

"Okay. But how are we going to pay for things?"

"I have some money," she replied, sounding positive.

"Some? That won't get us far." He imagined standing at a street corner holding a cup and a cardboard sign. Trying to sum up their plight in a half dozen words with a black magic marker would be challenging.

"Let me worry about that. The first step is getting a taxi."

"That will cost way too much. I have another idea." *Billy will give us a lift. I'll ask when I get the Allen wrench set.*

"Once we're out of here, we have to get in touch with Olivia. I made a terrible mistake trusting Rezi."

CHAPTER TWENTY-NINE

The sun installed new batteries and broke through the clouds midafternoon and the temperature quickly ramped. Olivia sought freedom by walking around the yard barefoot, as the guest house felt like a high-end prison. Memories of simpler times flooded her thoughts as the grass tickled her toes. An outcrop of dandelions made her reminisce how she used to gather yellow bouquets for the kitchen table. The tenacious weed reminded her of Mama because, no matter how much Papa Dale tried to pull out her roots, she continued to flower year after year. Unexpected tears welled up and she would have sat down among the yellow tops, but a swarm of mayflies chased her inside.

The kitchen clock revealed it was zero hour, and she headed for the bedroom to pick out her suicide outfit. She doubted anyone would agree on the right combo, and the beep of a horn ended any further consideration. Looking out the bedroom window, she saw the Caddy pull into the driveway followed by Seth's SUV. Moments later, Luke popped out of the passenger seat of Seth's vehicle.

She ran down the hall and met them at the front door. Luke carried a large pizza box.

"You sure know how to spoil a girl," she said, guiding him inside and ignoring his escorts.

Luke smiled like he did in her dreams. "Have to warn you, the food won't taste great once you're dead."

They all laughed, which broke the tension. She headed for the kitchen until Seth put up his hand like a stop sign. "Let's have a picnic in the living room instead."

"Wow! This must be a special occasion. Before you arrived, we had bubble wrap on all the furniture." Luke teased.

Rezi retrieved plates and napkins from the kitchen. Olivia considered sitting on the weird couch, but nixed the idea when Luke sat on the floor. She joined him and felt surprised when Seth and Rezi followed, forming a small circle.

Rezi placed the pizza in the center and served everyone. At first, she was disappointed to find it had no toppings. But the tangy tomato sauce and stringy cheese was a heavenly marriage, and she devoured two large slices like it was her last meal. The conversation was surprising too, as they shared stories of amusement parks and favorite beach food. When the pizza was gone, Rezi disappeared and returned with a tray holding four fluted glasses. Not that she knew anything about after-dinner drinks, but the liquid looked darker than the whiskey Papa Dale guzzled. Given the amount of tea Rezi drank all day, she believed it might be a new variety, until the aroma of nail polish hit her nose. *No wonder they see little green men!*

Seth held up his glass. "I would like to toast our dear Olivia, who stands at the threshold of a new life. May the flight into eternity be as soft as the spring air tonight."

Seth, Rezi, and Luke cheered before drinking. She tried a small sip and after the initial burn, it tasted flowery before fizzling into bitterness.

Luke inched toward her and somehow found her ear. "I'd rather have champagne and a slow dance with you."

"Hey, no secrets!" Seth said, noticing.

The comment made her blush, and she took another sip of the mystery drink to hide behind. This time, it made her head heavy, and she closed her eyes. When she opened them again, Rezi and Seth were in the kitchen. *Did I black out?*

She looked in the glass and asked Luke, stretched out on the couch, "What is this?"

The blind man laughed. "Moonshine that sneaks up on you."

"Where does your father get it?"

"Doesn't matter because he doctors it up. He doesn't let me have it often. He should brand it as Seth's shot of courage."

Her tongue felt fuzzy, and the room began spinning.

Luke sat up and held out his hand, and she moved to the couch and sat beside him.

"This is killing me!" he whispered.

"Why?"

"My dad won't let me come along as moral support. He thinks I'll just be in the way." He touched her cheek.

She scanned his face and wished she could rip those dark glasses off even if it was a one-way mirror. "I don't know what the big deal is. Your father says it's nothing more than a wooden jungle gym and then a short run. Why can't you wait with him?"

He shrugged. "He's a worrywart and I don't push." His hand wandered to her chin and before she could process what was happening, he pulled her in for a kiss. His lips were soft, and she melted into them.

When he sat back, she leaned in for another.

"It's time," Seth announced with Rezi in tow.

She was still in dreamland and pointed at her t-shirt. "Should I bring along my sweatshirt and throw it over the bridge?"

Seth thought for a moment. "Better still, hurry and put it on so people will see you wearing it. I'll throw it downriver tomorrow."

She hurried to the bedroom and grabbed the gray sweatshirt. When she returned, she found the living room deserted and her adopted family in the driveway. When she joined them, Seth wrapped his arms around her and said nothing for a long, uncomfortable moment. She took in his cologne, which smelled like a mixture of burning wood and charcoal.

"I've been over this a hundred times with Rezi," he said. "Just do everything she says and you'll be fine."

His tone frightened her. *What could go wrong?* Before she could ask, Luke gave her a tight hug before Seth pulled him away and headed for the SUV.

Rezi stood beside the Caddy. "Seems like we're back where we started. Just you and me, girl."

She opened the passenger door and froze. The seat looked like a dumpster covered in Styrofoam cups and wrappers from McDonald's and Wendy's. Empty beer bottles and newspapers littered the floor. The back seat was a trash heap, too.

Rezi read her face. "Remember what I told you about perception being reality? We have to make the cops rationalize we've been on the run and living out of the car."

She brushed off the seat and got in.

Rezi followed and, reaching in the center console, pulled out a blank piece of paper and a pen.

"Write in big letters: I'm sorry but can't take it anymore. Then sign your name."

"Why would I do that? I rather it looked like I lost my balance and fell."

"We need to make an open and shut case. The note makes you look as desperate as me."

Her hand trembled holding the pen. "How about I say something about my mother's accident? That would be more believable and—"

"C'mon Olivia! We don't have time to argue about the wording!" Rezi interrupted.

Seth blew his horn to make the point. She quickly scribbled the note.

Rezi read it before placing it above the visor. "Okay, now sit back and make yourself comfortable as possible in the mess."

"How far away is the bridge?"

"Nine miles as the crow flies, but we can't chance things on the main roads, so it will take twice as long." She backed out of the driveway and followed Seth's vehicle.

"Why are you doing this for me?"

Rezi's eyes remained glued to the road, like always. "Because Seth asked me."

"I don't know if I would do something this crazy even if my mother asked. What makes you believe in him like that?"

She shot her a quick glance. "Because actions speak louder than words. Everyone said poor you and cried crocodile tears when I was homeless, hungry and sick. None of my family gave a damn if I was spending days in the library to keep warm. That is where I first met Seth. He was carrying a stack of psychology and science fiction books. He stopped where I was sitting and said hello."

"You consider saying hi a big deal?"

"I did because we never met and he knew my name. He said he had been waiting for me and when I asked why, he said he would explain in time, but we were both pioneers. You should count yourself lucky. Look at the length he's going to save you, too."

The strange liquor she had at the house made her mouth dry. She sat back and watched the passing cars, all wrapped in their own sunny stories, while they headed to stage her death. She wondered how people would react when they heard the news. The thought of Sonny grieving about Mama and then finding out she abandoned him too shredded her heart. She imagined Papa Dale would need a freezer to store all the food people would drop off. He would suck up the sympathy, hoping it would increase sales in the store. *And how will my class handle the news?* She felt as popular as the bread heels the lunch ladies left at the end of the line in the cafeteria for starving teens. Her memory would fade quicker than the time it took for the bread to grow mold.

The scenery changed as the back roads emptied onto a major thoroughfare. Seth veered left and disappeared. They continued on for a few minutes in silence.

"Are we there yet?" she asked in a squeaky voice hoping to sound like a six-year-old.

Rezi missed the joke. "Welcome to Haverhill."

"Where?"

"Haverhill, Massachusetts. Back in the day, people knew it as the Queen Slipper city."

"Did the shoe factories leave like the paper mills?"

She nodded. "*There is a time to sow and a time to reap.* But after many years, Haverhill has been undergoing a renaissance of sorts and —" She sucked in her breath and waved her arm. "Quick! Scoot down in the seat."

She obeyed and got low. "What's going on?"

"There's a cruiser up ahead!" She gripped the steering wheel at two and ten o'clock.

"Can't we take a side street?" she whispered.

Rezi shook her head. "The bridge is around the next corner."

She held her breath and watched Rezi. The driver's eyes darted from the road to the rearview mirror.

"Oh no!" Rezi moaned through a clenched jaw.

Her stomach dropped to the floor. She could sense Papa Dale's sweaty hands running down her back.

"Here he comes!" Rezi said.

She sat up and looked out the back window. The cruiser lights were visible about a dozen cars back. "What are we going to do?"

"Finish what we started," she replied, and stepped on the gas. Rezi passed three cars on the two-way street before the siren sounded.

Olivia watched the traffic behind them peel away like a giant zipper. Suddenly, the Cadillac was sliding sideways and horns blared as Rezi took a hard right. The bridge was straight ahead and lined with construction barrels.

"Get ready to run!" Rezi yelled with more excitement than she ever expressed.

The car's suspension bottomed out on a section of broken pavement before coming to a stop.

Rezi opened her door. "Let's go!" she yelled in a voice embracing both defiance and fear.

She jumped out and noticed the cars behind them stopped. The blue lights from the cruiser bathed everything.

Rezi came around and grabbed her by the arm, and pulled her toward a cement pilot's house fifty feet away. Upon arrival, she observed a slight space between the railing and the structure. Heavy orange fencing roped off the area.

Rezi moved beneath the barrier, and she followed. The blue lights from the cruiser made the scene look surreal, and Rezi took her hand and inched their way to the edge. All she saw was black water below.

"Where's the ramp?" she cried.

Rezi did not answer, but stared down at the dark abyss. Olivia looked back and saw a police officer running toward them with gun drawn.

"Remember when Seth said to trust him?" Rezi asked, panting.

"But there's no escape route like he promised!" she replied and took a step back to surrender.

"There's no future for us if we don't jump! Just have faith and trust."

Before Olivia could process the insane argument, Rezi clutched her arm, and they went airborne. She used to think before dying, your life flashes before your eyes. But the black water swallowed everything before it could.

CHAPTER THIRTY

Sleep was a stranger, and Gabrielle watched the digital clock on the nightstand strike midnight in bold numbers. She smiled in the dark, knowing this was a day of emancipation, of new beginnings, of reclaiming her heritage. The smile faded as she recalled the last escape attempt. *But this time Sonny donned a cape to save her.* She knew it was crucial to stay in the present, even if it felt like purgatory. She longed to be cleansed and free.

Dale must have read her racing thoughts because he began moving, and she ignored the urge to rake the ankle monitor against his skinny legs in defiance. She debated sleeping in the same bed as the warden, but the couch aggravated her back and playing the beaten woman part of the plan. The strategy worked as there had been no serious flare-ups in the last twenty-four hours, and tonight had been especially easy. Dale rolled in close to seven o'clock, inhaled dinner and then fell asleep in the recliner watching tv. The lack of drama allowed her time to choose underwear, t-shirts, and jeans and store them under the bed for quick retrieval. She even swung by Sonny's room and provided input on what he should bring.

Now she watched the clock tiptoe toward morning. The forecast called for a sun-filled day with temperatures in the low seventies. Nice, but it didn't matter. It could be a January blizzard and she would not postpone this momentous day.

Surprisingly, she found her eyes growing heavy and drifted off to sleep. *Dale waited in the morning light next to the Catalina. "I'm on to you," he said with the cocky smile she hated. She tried backing away, but he grabbed her and opened the trunk of the car. She looked in the hole and saw Olivia curled up in the corner, her beautiful face contorted and lifeless.*

"Look who I found!" Dale yelled in a ghoulish voice. Before she could scream, a loud bang roused her from sleep.

"Tell Sonny to turn down the damn music!" Dale yelled.

She glanced at the clock and it read one-thirty. *What is Sonny doing?* She jumped out of bed. Keep it up and he would ruin the plan.

Another loud bang followed, and she realized it came from the front door.

She shook Dale. "Someone's here!"

There was a long pause. "Tell them to go away…. I don't want solar panels on the house."

Another barrage followed, and it sounded like it would destroy the door.

"Dale, someone's breaking in!" she said, hoping to scare him.

The plan worked, and he sat up. "Stay there while I get my gun," he whispered, rolling out of bed. On the way to the closet, he glanced out the window.

"There's a police car out front." He grabbed his robe and made his way to the hall. She followed close behind.

They met Sonny standing outside his room. He was rubbing his eyes and looked confused, too.

When Dale opened the door, the trio found Chief Warner waiting on the top stair dressed in dungarees and a navy-blue hoodie. She rarely saw him out of uniform and by the uncombed hair looked like he must have thrown them on.

"Sorry to wake you folks," the Chief said.

None of them answered and stared at the man.

"Can I come in?"

"Of course!" Dale backed up, and they played follow the leader as the Chief headed for the recliner and sat down. Dale stood over his buddy looking like he had been dethroned. Olivia put her arm around Sonny and huddled in the middle of the room.

The Chief focused on Dale. "Again, I'm sorry to rouse you at this hour. I considered calling first... but given our friendship came in person."

She could not hold her tongue a second longer. "You're scaring us! What is it?"

The Chief looked at her. "It's Olivia. I want you to understand the search is still underway, but—"

Sonny rushed forward, and she followed. "Is she okay?"

The policeman stood up and the look in his eyes betrayed the calm approach. "We received a call from the police down in Massachusetts," he began. "They spotted the suspect's car in Haverhill and no sooner began the pursuit when the vehicle stopped on a bridge that crosses the Merrimack River." He stopped and let the words sink in.

"Great! So, they have them?" Dale asked.

The police officer ignored his friend and looked away. "Several witnesses observed Olivia and the other woman presumed to be Rezi Nagle. The bridge is undergoing repairs, but they got behind the construction fence. As the officer approached..." his voice trailed off like he ran out of steam.

They waited as he took a deep breath.

He finally looked her way. "I'm sorry... they jumped," he said without emotion.

The words blew her sideways into Sonny's arms before she collapsed on the braided rug. She wanted to scream, but felt as if someone kicked her in the stomach, knocking the air out of her. Her stomach revolted at the same time and thought she might be sick. Sonny wrapped his arms around her.

"Did they find ...." Dale inquired and then stopped. The man who prided himself on being a blowhard evidently ran out of words.

As the Chief shook his head, she inhaled more intensely than the ancient vacuum and released a wail that filled the room. The pain in her chest, deeper than the ocean and wider than the sky, gnawed at her. Her mind raced as it autopsied every miscalculation in the piss poor plan. It was a mistake to send Olivia away. She should have summoned her courage and protected her daughter from Dale. The right path would have been packing their bags, calling a cab and using the thousand dollars for a hotel. From there, she could have worked it out with Sonny. Dale might have come looking along with ICE, but with the millions of other illegals, the odds were low. And if he beat or killed her, at least Olivia would be alive. Now all was lost.

As the first wave of tears subsided, Dale lifted her up and deposited her on the loveseat. He sat down next to her and put his arm around her.

The Chief came and touched her hand. "Listen to me Gabrielle. Things are still very fluid at the scene. They are searching the water by boat and helicopter."

"How high is the bridge?" Sonny asked.

Dale shot him a-this-is-not-helping look. "I'm sure it's difficult to search at night."

The Chief nodded. "Yes, and will continue for as long as it takes." He looked at Sonny. "This is still a search and not a recovery operation."

"I should never have let her go with Rezi," she cried. "She must have pushed her!"

Dale nodded. "I agree. Granted, we didn't see eye to eye on much, but I chalked it up to her being a teenager with a mouth. She had a lot of spunk and I don't believe she would jump. No, she must have been pushed." He looked at his friend. "I don't know if she can swim."

The Chief looked away.

"What aren't you telling us?" Dale asked.

"Like I said, it's still early, but the authorities in Massachusetts looked through the car. As expected, they were living in it. In the visor, they found a note from Olivia."

She looked up. "What did it say?"

"Nothing that will comfort you, I'm afraid. It was a suicide note."

CHAPTER THIRTY-ONE

Olivia opened her eyes and experienced the sensation of looking through a telescope, as if her eyes had become recessed. She could not move and perceived herself as being trapped in overlooked spaces — the interval between raindrops, words on a page, the void between breaths. Silence made its kingdom there. The idea startled her because she could not identify the person conceiving it. Alarmed, she searched for something familiar, but even color now a stranger. The ceiling, walls, shades, and cotton blanket that she was tucked under gleamed stark white.

Closing her eyes, she tugged on the memory of what happened, but it evaded her. Sleep rolled in like a powerful tsunami, which swept her off the bed with icy black fingers that stung every inch of her. The current carried her under and in the madness, she lost sense of what direction led back to the surface. Exhausted, she surrendered to the blackness and there was neither regret, hope, or identity... just a watery peace. She experienced herself being lifted upwards as a dazzling white light burst forth, while the discomfort in her chest engulfed her.

When she woke up again, she rediscovered color and caressed the pale-yellow blanket. The realization something terrible occurred pulled on her thoughts, but remained missing pixels in her memory. Sleep was her only comfort, and she waited for it to come calling.

Suddenly, the bedroom door swung open. Seth walked in, followed by Rezi and Luke.

The three of them stopped at the foot of the bed and stared at her. Seth and Rezi wore thin smiles and Luke hung back, facing the window.

Her mouth was so dry she did not know if she could talk. "Water?" she whispered.

Rezi came alongside and picked up a glass on the nightstand. This led her to believe she might have had some before.

She held the cold liquid in her mouth for a minute, hoping to lubricate everything. When she finally swallowed, the middle of her chest ached, but she concentrated on Rezi. The tall white wave of hair was gone, replaced with a dixie cut and colored black, which matched her eyes. But it was the bruise on the woman's right cheek that caught her attention. It was red and purplish in the middle with a yellow tinge running along the edge. It reminded her of a diseased rainbow, and she wondered where these strange thoughts were coming from.

"More please," she asked, struggling to sit up a bit.

Rezi helped her get comfortable before sticking the straw in her mouth again. "How are you thirsty? Wasn't the Merrimack River enough?" she deadpanned and then glanced at Seth. "This one is a trip."

Seth smiled and came alongside Rezi. "You gave us quite a scare, Olivia," he said, touching her cheek.

The missing pixels remained, and pins and needles ran across her chest. "I remember the bridge…." She stopped and considered taking another mouthful of water in order to spit it at both of them. "You said there was a platform underneath!"

Seth sighed like the words cut. "I checked that morning and it was there. The workers must have removed it."

Rezi nodded. "You're not alone, Olivia. Remember, I counted on it too."

She thought the argument sounded rehearsed and stored it away. "I don't remember what happened after...."

Seth leaned in. "Don't push yourself. The jump was traumatic, both physically and emotionally."

"Jump?" she asked, sucking in her breath.

He nodded. "Considering the height, the impact was like colliding with a cement wall. It's our belief you suffered a concussion, and that's the reason for your confusion." He touched her cheek. "But don't fret. Our nurse friend checked you out and confirmed that nothing was broken. You just need to take it easy for a while."

She did not reply, because what else could she say?

Luke inched to the other side of the bed. "I wish I could see right now. This must appear similar to a scene from the *Wizard of Oz* when Dorothy awakens and sees her family gathered around the bed."

The sinkhole in her heart deepened as she remembered her mother's death and realized they were her only family now. "Does everyone believe I drowned?"

Seth pulled an iPhone out of his pocket, and after fiddling with it, showed her the screen. The front page of *the Eagle Tribune* read: *Tragic Ending for Maine Teen.*

She wanted to read the article, but Seth put the iPhone back in his pocket. "I'll save you the blah, blah, blah. It says you and Rezi jumped off the bridge and the recovery operation has been massive. Boats, helicopters, drones, and divers have taken part in the search along with teams of volunteers. But there's a lot of ground to cover. Given the fast current, you could be anywhere in the seventeen miles between Haverhill and the Atlantic."

Luke held out his hand until she touched him. "I'm blind but found you!"

Rezi moaned. "You're a real hoot. But it wasn't funny when we were in the water."

Olivia glanced at her terrible bruise again. "I...don't... remember what happened."

"It's best you don't," she replied with more attitude than usual. "But now that you're awake, I have to ask. Why didn't your mom teach you how to swim better when you were a kid?"

She shrugged. "Because the only water she felt safe in was the bathtub. I love jumping waves at the beach and swimming in the quarry."

"Well, lucky for you, Rezi was a lifeguard and on the college swim team," Seth said.

"Yeah, but never on the dive team!" Rezi replied. "We're lucky the river was running high or we wouldn't have survived the forty-foot fall." She sucked in her breath, reliving it for a moment, and then gave her a disapproving gaze. "You sank like a rock and kicked me in the face."

"I'm sorry," she offered and pulled the cover up around her arms. "I haven't been able to get warm."

"That's expected," Seth said. "We kept checking on you to monitor for dry or secondary drowning."

"What's that?"

"You took in a bunch of water. If some got in your lungs or upper airways, it puts you at risk for…." He stopped.

"For what?"

"No need to bid the devil good morning, as they say. You're awake now."

"We should have both drowned," Rezi said in a loud voice. "The water was so cold it sucked the air out of my lungs and you were deadweight." She paused for a moment, took a deep breath, and pointed at Seth. "Tell her what happened."

Seth backed away. "In time. Let the poor girl rest."

"No, please tell me now," she pleaded.

"C'mon Dad!" Luke added. "It's so cool."

Seth nodded and sat on the edge of the bed. "It would be a much richer story if your memory comes back. As we planned, I stationed myself on the rail trail about a quarter mile away. While I didn't observe you and Rezi jump, I saw the blue flashing lights. Suddenly, the air changed. I can't explain it other than say it became tranquil like it does at sunrise. Then a low-level hum echoed and seemed to penetrate everything — air, ground, even me. The intensity was greater than anything I experienced at our events. I sensed our plan had gone astray, and they knew you were in trouble. But the knowledge did not produce panic, just surety that everything would be fine. I gazed up at the first stars in the sky and witnessed a light descending fast from high above. It was small and intense and when it touched the water, it made the surface shimmer."

Rezi nodded. "A light carried us to the surface and brought us to shore. You were blue from the cold and had ingested some water, but we were saved."

"This calls for a toast!" Luke sang.

"Always the party, boy," Seth said, scowling at his son. He reached into the nightstand and pulled out a bottle and passed her a pill. "This is an antibiotic in case of infection. Who knows what was in that water?"

She looked at the oblong pill. It was small and yellow and unlike anything the doctor ever prescribed her for an infection. But Seth was big on trust, so she popped it in her mouth and took a long sip of water.

"So, what's next?" she asked.

Seth smiled and put the pill bottle in his pocket. "I brought you to my house so I can monitor your recovery. You will stay here for a few more days until you get your strength back. Like I explained, we need you to lie low for a while before you appear at an event. If I learned anything the other night, your special gift is being protected by our celestial friends."

"Can I still go to school in the Fall?"

He looked like he did not recall the promise. "Let's take one day at a time. Okay?"

Olivia looked at Seth's face and saw a blank space in one eye, like it was missing a few pixels, too. Suddenly, she was on the bridge again and glanced at Rezi. *I never jumped. She grabbed my arm and pulled me over!*

She shut her eyes before they could read them.

CHAPTER THIRTY-TWO

Gabrielle thought the weather was fitting. Gray skies and a cold steady rain made the young garden shiver in the breeze. Briefly casting her eyes out the front window, she observed the black limo progressing up the driveway, maneuvering to avoid the water-filled potholes. It reminded her of Olivia in grammar school tiptoeing to the bus stop in nasty weather, trying to protect her patent leather shoes.

"But no matter how careful, the mud always finds us," she whispered.

"Is the limo here yet?" Dale asked, coming alongside.

She cast a sidelong glance in his direction. His cheeks were red from sucking in his belly to get in a black suit a couple sizes too small. If Olivia were here, she would tell him he looked like a pig in a blanket if you replaced the hotdog with a knockwurst. The pants were especially clownish as the hem ended mid-ankle, given the amount of material required to cover the midsection.

"Why are you still in your robe?" he asked and looked at his watch. "Sonny's dragging his feet too. We're going to be late!"

She shrugged. "It's not like they can start without us. If it were up to me, we wouldn't be having a funeral. But I don't get to call the shots... even for my daughter."

Dale jerked his head. "This is the thanks I get? You have been MIA since we received the news. We need closure."

"We?" she asked, pointing. "You're playing this up to get sympathy traffic in the store."

"Are you serious?" he replied, but moved away so she could not read his face.

She retreated and looked out the window again. The limo was next to the sidewalk. Smoke from the exhaust curled up around the back of the car. The driver had his head down, either napping or passing the time on his cellphone.

Gabrielle pointed at the car. "You Americans handle death like fast food. Wake, funeral, burial, a quick mercy meal, and then everyone turns the page." She closed her eyes. "You say we need closure? For me, there will be none, because I don't have my beautiful daughter to hold and kiss."

Dale let out a heavy sigh and, surprisingly, came and wrapped his arms around her.

"I know your insides are busted up, but we've discussed this a hundred times. The police have looked in every nook and cranny in the river and haven't found her or the devil she was with. Let's take comfort in the thought that your daughter was buried at sea. When you're feeling up to it, we will take a ride to Salisbury Reservation so you can see where the Merrimack River meets the Atlantic. Seals sun themselves on rocky outcrops and people come from all around the country to camp and fish. There's even a long jetty we can walk out on and spot a whale. If you ask me, it's a better resting place than six feet under Maine tundra."

She knew he was trying and recognized remnants of the man she fell in love with before the thorns grew thick. "It's just that... I continue hoping there's a possibility they survived and are hiding somewhere."

Dale's red face got a shade darker. "Listen to yourself! They fell over forty feet into ice water that's racing toward the sea after the spring rains. The cops said there's an enormous boulder where they jumped in and Sockeye probably hit her head and the end came quick. As far as that Rezi monster is concerned, I hope she survived the seventeen-mile ride before a great white finished her."

"I wish you would finally drop the damn Sockeye! Her name is Olivia!" she yelled.

He put his hands up. "Sorry, it's a habit."

"I also think the police should admit there's a chance they could have survived!"

"That's impossible."

She pointed at her chest. "If she were not in here, I would sense it."

"I forgot you Mexicans have faith in that Day of the Dead nonsense. Do yourself a favor and face the fact she's gone," he said like it was no big thing.

She wanted to spit at him, but had no saliva. "Let's get this over with so you can get back to the store this afternoon."

"You're unbelievable! Is that your opinion?" He pointed outside. "Well, sweetheart, you're the reason the show is at a standstill. Hurry and get dressed before they tack on a late charge."

The knife penetrated her chest, and she felt it come out her back. The pain almost took her legs out and she bent over and looked at her ankle.

"Tell me, is the Warden going to make me wear the monitor to my daughter's funeral?"

Dale came at her with his fist raised and then stopped and pointed out the window again. "Lucky for you, the Chief is here."

He was the last person she wanted to see and hurried to the bedroom. Sunlight avoided this northern room, and she didn't turn on the light and showcase the black dress on the bed. Instead, she laid down beside it and stroked the material. Memories of feeling pretty when she wore it to Dale's holiday party last year bubbled up. Now grief would weave itself into the cotton fibers. No stain remover this side of heaven would help. Tears refused to come, and she decided after the funeral to throw the dress away — unless she didn't make it through the day and died of a broken heart. If so, Dale could save a few coins and use the occasion to bury her in this foreign soil, unless he and the Chief agreed corpses get deported too? She sat up and held the dress to her chest. If they found Olivia's body, she would want to jump in the grave… But if they never found her, how would she find peace? Dale's words reverberated and her defense begin to crumble. She would accept Dale's offer and visit Salisbury beach. She would head for the long jetty he described, knowing she could outrun him. One mouthful of ocean water would be enough. God's mercy could bring her back to her daughter in the deep ocean, far from the evil that caused their separation. The gnawing hole in her chest returned, knowing she did not deserve some mermaid fantasy, but severe punishment for placing her beloved daughter in the hands of a disturbed woman.

While shedding new tears, she put on the black dress, aware good intentions, and a lack of backbone paved this hellish road.

After retrieving her flat black shoes from the closet, she opened the bedroom door and found Sonny leaning against the wall in the hall. Unlike his father, he looked like he was drowning in the gray suit. Fresh pangs of guilt spiked at not cooking much since Olivia left.

Her son looked past her, uncomfortable with the mess standing in front of him. "Papa sent me for you."

She nodded and straightened his blue tie. "How are you doing?"

"Do you want me to say okay or tell you the truth?"

She pulled him in tight for a long moment and then followed him down the gangplank to the living room.

Seth and the Chief stood close in the center of the room whispering. They stopped when they saw her.

"The limo driver says he can't wait much longer," Seth said.

She ignored the Chief's stare. "Let him leave. We can drive ourselves."

Seth came at her fast. "I do a fair amount of business with Dick Mahoney and he offered the limo at half price. It would be a slap in the face to send it back now!"

She laughed. "I don't care."

"Oh no!" Sonny announced. "A tv truck is coming up the driveway."

She rushed to the window and, sure enough, a large van with a satellite dish on the roof inched up the driveway. When it got to the top, it pulled behind the limo.

Dale headed for the door, but the Chief held him back. "Let me handle this."

"I can get my shotgun and after I blow out a couple of tires, they will understand the meaning of the no trespassing sign by the mailbox!"

"They would welcome the drama for their ratings," the Chief argued and glanced at Gabrielle. "That's why I'm here. It's going to be a media circus at the church. The press started setting up hours ago. I'm here to make sure there are no shenanigans on the way. Once we arrive, I have a detail to escort you into the church."

She felt her knees weaken. "I don't understand. Why is that necessary?"

"Because people love a story and this tragedy isn't over yet," the Chief replied.

"Of course it isn't! They haven't found my daughter," she shot back.

Seth moaned. "You got it wrong, like always. He's talking about you, Gabrielle. Your legal troubles are just starting."

The words twisted her stomach. "Deport me then. I don't care."

"It's not that simple." The Chief pulled an iPhone out of his back pocket and held it in front of her face. "Before these things were invented, folks would chew the fat around the dinner table or over a beer at the bar. Now everyone is online kibitzing how Olivia's death is all your fault." He slid the phone back into his pocket. "I didn't plan on bringing this up today out of respect, but I can't control how things will play out anymore. The FBI and Maine, New Hampshire, and Massachusetts State Police are involved in this case, not to mention the District Attorney. You don't have to think too hard to expect charges being filed and politicians advancing their agendas because of what you did."

"I guess undocumented or illegal won't cut it anymore, but deplorable will," she whispered.

Sonny rushed from the corner of the room where he had been brooding. "I can't believe this! Hasn't she suffered enough?" he yelled and headed down the hall. Moments later, the door slammed shut.

She studied the two men standing in front of her — brothers from different mothers. "Bring it on then. If there's one thing I've learned, it's how to bend and not break."

CHAPTER THIRTY-THREE

Olivia finished the blueberry muffin and eyed the remaining one on the counter. Seth said he baked them himself, but the claim seemed pretty farfetched as they were in a cardboard box wrapped with the thin string bakeries used. *He's always pushing me to trust him, but lies about something stupid like this?*

She glanced at Luke sitting across the kitchen table and frowned as his fingers searched for crumbs on the plate. That was the odd thing about hanging out with him. She could put him under a microscope and he was none the wiser. Even better, she did not have to impress him with hair or makeup.

Her better angel intervened. "There's one muffin left. Want to split it?"

Luke pushed the plate away and gingerly reached for the coffee mug. "No, it's all yours."

She jumped up and retrieved the prize. She considered heating it, but the stove's microwave seemed NASA-designed. Besides, she had no desire to make the large blueberries mushy.

"How long have you lived here?" she asked, rushing back to the table.

"About ten years. I was in grammar school when we moved here."

She peeled off the paper wrapper and reached for a napkin. "Just you and your dad?" she asked.

Luke took a sip of coffee. "Yeah…and before you ask, I don't enjoy talking about my mom. The breakup was painful and the custody battle made me feel like a pawn."

"Trust me, I understand, considering the price my mother paid to give us a home. Did your dad work around here?"

"Yeah, he studied microbiology and had some jobs in life science, but my eyes glazed over whenever he tried to explain what he did. We still laugh about it. But all that's in the past." He pointed at his sunglasses. "Since this, he wants to get the Roswell project launched and hopes whatever they know will cure me."

She took a bite of the muffin. "That's weird. You have contact with these beings, but they have told no one what to call them?"

He nodded. "We struggled with that question before deciding to call them Firth. It's an old English word that means peace, protection, safety, security, refuge and seems to fit. While they didn't provide a business card, they haven't been shy in sharing what they call us."

"Humans or earthlings?"

He shook his head. "It's closer to what we really are. They call us Menace. With their help, we hope to become Menacing."

She rolled her eyes. "I don't get it."

"I had to think about it for a while too before it made sense. We have always defined ourselves by tribe or country. Add to that our self-centered and violent ways and they see little progress since we lived in caves. But technology has outpaced our evolution, and that makes us dangerous. It's like giving the car keys to a six-year-old knowing a crash is inevitable. The only question is how bad will it be? Firth did not want to interfere with our progress, but the risk is too great now. They want to move a dangerous, destructive species to one that sings in harmony, hence the progression from men-ace to men-a-sing. They have seen the best and worst of us, and focused on what's possible. After all, they have been here longer than us."

"C'mon! Here on earth? Are you joking?"

Luke adjusted his glasses. "I wish I were."

Olivia took a sip of the black coffee, wishing for milk, but Rezi explained certain foods contained ingredients that blocked the frequencies for communicating with the other realm. She believed it was nonsense until Rezi inquired if she noticed the hum before adopting their diet.

She took another bite of the muffin. "I couldn't sleep last night and wandered into your den." she paused, hoping not to come across as nosy. "I saw the collection on some guy named Jim Jones. Was he a scientist?"

Luke smiled and took a sip of his coffee. "More of a criminal psychologist of group dynamics. Whatever you do, don't drink his Kool-Aid."

"I don't get it."

"Inside joke." He sat back in his chair and laughed. It sounded as genuine as his father's.

It made her giggle even if she did not understand. She retreated into her mug, wanting his kissable lips again.

Her silence made him lean across the table. "What am I missing?"

"Absolutely nothing."

Despite his inability to see, he appeared to gaze at her. "My father won't be home for a while. Let's go into the den, and you can look over his collection again while I read you?"

The pass made her heart jump, and she froze. In the next instant, Luke reached over and brushed a crumb off her upper lift, and kissed her. It was long and passionate and she tasted crystals of sugar. When she pulled away, her heart was racing, and she was hungry for more. But the sequence of what just happened nixed the raging hormones.

Before she could say anything, he stood up. "The couch is waiting."

"Let me finish my muffin first," she replied, as calm as possible.

Luke cocked his head and sat back down. "Sure, whatever."

She eyed his dark glasses. "I noticed your dad has a ton of movies too, but most are about aliens. *ET, Close Encounters, Independence Day, Signs.*"

He let out a knowing chuckle. "And that surprises you?"

"I guess not."

"People in the know have been working for years to get our society open minded about Firth. Heck, even the government is releasing videos now. That's why New Roswell will put us on the map. It's the great awakening."

The words flew by her ears, and her lips were still buzzing from the kiss. She stared at his blond curls that were never out of place.

"You haven't told me much about yourself. Where did you go to school?"

"Right here until the accident." He pointed at the sunglasses. "Then my father hired a tutor, and I finished high school."

"Did you learn Braille?"

He looked away even though he was blind. "I struggled with dyslexia as a kid and that didn't change reading with my fingers."

She pushed the rest of the muffin away. *He has a quick answer for everything... but the emotional rollercoaster of losing his sight never comes up.*

"But I'm living the dream now," he added. "Are you almost finished? My father won't leave us alone for too long."

She contemplated her mother and how she attempted to stay a step ahead of Papa Dale to ensure their safety — which was successful until it wasn't. Mama was also resourceful. Mrs. Dickinson called her MacGyver after she used a toilet plunger to remove a dent in her passenger door.

"Thirsty?" she asked.

"No thanks," he replied and fished a peppermint lifesaver out of his pocket. "Though I hate coffee breath. Want half?"

"No thanks," and winced inside, thinking she must have tasted like coffee grinds. "I'm going to get some water."

She proceeded to the cabinet and got a tall plastic glass, then headed to the sink. The May sun streamed in and it hurt her eyes. She focused on her racing heart. It would be so easy to move on and not taint a memory of their kiss, and many more were waiting in the den. But she saw how putting things off played out for her mother.

Taking a deep breath, she spun around and began walking back to the table. The pretend trip went according to plan, and as the water cannon fired, she included an unintended yell, too. Unfortunately, she could not tell whether the water or her voice first startled the only guy in the world she wanted to make out with.

"What's going on?" he yelled, jumping up.

"Oh, my goodness!" She ran for a roll of paper towels on the counter. "I don't know what I tripped on."

"Neither do I! There's no rug on the floor!" He backed away from the table and brushed water off his white t-shirt.

"The river must have messed up my inner ear. I've been feeling dizzy on and off."

"Well, I have to change. I'll meet you in the den."

She considered the idea of asking to accompany him to inspect his room, but that posed other risks.

"Sure, I'll just finish cleaning up and meet you there."

As he headed for the hall, the iPhone in his back pant pocket rang.

Luke answered it and continued walking. She tiptoed toward the hall, and straining her ears, heard him talk in a strange language. It was unlike anything she ever heard and spoken in a high-pitched voice. It reminded her of the hum.

When the talking stopped, she heard his footsteps coming and backtracked to the sink.

"Olivia, are you still there?" Luke called out.

"Yeah, just finished cleaning up the mess."

"Change of plans," he said, followed by a wide smile.

"Oh?"

My father called. "The renovation on the barn is almost done. Dad believes it's an excellent chance to move up the rally to tomorrow night. You know, get the word out about New Roswell."

"Sounds like a plan."

"Glad you believe that, because you're going to have a significant part to play."

"Why me?"

"The video of you curing the man at Tuscan Village went viral. Do that again and we'll be able to fund the next phase. Dad has a friend in Tampa that wants us to set up a satellite community there."

"But what about the plan of me lying low for a while?"

"Dad believes it's a secure wager. Your memorial service was yesterday."

She fell back on the counter. "Yesterday? That was mighty fast!" Then it hit her. Mama was gone, so why would Papa Dale drag his feet? "Was there an obituary in the paper?"

He shrugged. "I believe you received sufficient press when you jumped, don't you?"

She bit her lip. He was right. Apart from the dramatic ending, she could summarize the rest of her life in just a couple of sentences.

"Let's put a movie on," Luke said.

She eyed those dark sunglasses again. "But how can you ..." she began and her voice trailed off.

The smile would make a star high school quarterback jealous. "Who says we will watch it?"

CHAPTER THIRTY-FOUR

"Okay, I win!" Gabrielle yelled at the afternoon sun that hung in a cloudless sky. Collapsing on the grass, she wiped sweat out of her eyes. The cotton t-shirt clung to her skin, and she attempted to disregard the unpleasant sensation by focusing on the six-foot dogwood. She planted the tree in honor of Olivia, and like her daughter, nothing had been easy completing the project. Dale balked at the price and where to locate the flowering tree, and she argued it was less expensive than an empty cemetery plot. She thought the front lawn was the ideal spot, as it would welcome visitors and provide comfort when she looked out the window. Digging the hole proved just as tough, and she fought for every inch in the rocky Maine soil. When a boulder would not budge, she relied on a long iron pole to dislodge it. After reaching the required depth, she added the special fertilizer before rolling in the root ball. Now, she would rely on sun, rain, and TLC, and look forward to a bouquet of delicate white blossoms next spring, around the anniversary of when Olivia left this broken world.

She took a drink of water from a plastic cup and looked at the shovel, rake, pickaxe lying prostrate on the ground while the iron pole rested against a half dozen unearthed rocks. The project proved tiring, yet there was satisfaction in accomplishing a worthwhile aim rather than dwelling in the house with a gloomy attitude. A warm breeze caressed her face, and she looked up at the forever free sky instead of the insulting monitor around her ankle. The irony was Dale used it now not to keep her home, but from following her daughter's watery escape.

A familiar noise caught her attention, and she turned her gaze towards the driveway, where she spotted Sonny swiftly approaching on his ten-speed. She knew once he got his license, he would never pedal again.

Her son came toward her quick, and for a second feared he would run her over or worse, take out the tree.

"What do you think?" she asked, pointing at the stick skeleton.

Sonny gave a quick glance before dismounting. "Looks good, but I told you I would help dig the hole."

"I know you did, but it felt good to get my hands in the dirt and spend some alone time with your sister." She wiped her forehead again. "Olivia probably had a good laugh watching me struggle. I was afraid Maine turned me soft."

He eyed the rocks and then her dirt-stained pants. "Looks like it took a while."

"Yeah, a couple of hours. Now I understand what your father meant that if the country had been settled from west to east, things would look quite different in New England. I never understood how people farm here. Especially in colonial times."

He pondered the comment for a moment. "I guess they had to make the best of a tough situation. All the stone walls prove that." He picked up the scattered tools and put them next to his bike.

"What are they saying at school about...." she stopped, unable to finish the question.

He kicked at the grass with the toe of one sneaker. "You don't want to know."

"Yes, I do. Your father has a lock on the cable box and canceled the paper. He says it's for my own good, but it's driving me insane."

He looked her in the eye. "I won't lie. It's not pretty. Let's put it this way, the kind one's think you should go to jail before getting deported."

She nodded. "How about your friends?"

He stretched out his right hand with swollen knuckles. "We went back and forth about things before they understood."

Gabrielle stood up and gave him a hug before remembering her sweaty clothes and moved away.

"It can't be any easier at the store. Your father must be under the gun too. I ask, but he won't say."

Sonny picked up a rock and heaved it a few feet.

She knew her son had trouble dealing with anger or frustration and channeled it into physical activities. "What is it, Sonny?"

"It's more like what it isn't. Papa says you told him you were from Texas when you first met."

She filled her lungs with a long breath. "There's the man I know. Believe me, I sugarcoated nothing."

"I think he's selling the story before you get indicted. He says he didn't know you were undocumented until you filled out my birth certificate." From his back pocket, he retrieved an iPhone. "He came in my room late last night and gave me this… Says I should own a phone because what happened to Liv haunts him. It's nothing but a payoff."

She looked at the shiny black phone and sighed. "He says he loves the flag because those colors don't run, but when it comes to his character, not so much."

Sonny rubbed the back of his neck. "Perhaps you should follow his example."

"What do you mean?"

"Run!"

"I can't do that," she replied. The sweaty clothes turned cold and her legs felt like gelatin, so she sat down on the grass.

Her son joined her and pulled a clover out, and inspected it. "This will not end well once you're arrested. I doubt Papa will even post bail."

She shrugged. "I don't care. My life ended when I lost Olivia."

"But you still have a son!" he said, throwing the clover at her. "I already lost my sister. Won't you fight to save me?"

She looked at her son and saw the little boy who followed her around the house, helping with the housework. "What do you want me to do?"

"Go back home like you planned."

"That was a crazy idea." She shook her head. "I've tried escaping twice and failed. It's not meant to be."

"Third time is the charm."

"But I have the same obstacles," she said, pointing at her leg. "The Chief should have arrested me by now, but I think your father asked him to wait until he figures out who will cook for him."

"Make jokes, but you have little time. When Papa leaves for work tomorrow, let me remove the damn monitor. Billy can give us a ride to Portsmouth or Boston, and then we can take the bus."

She stared at the dogwood for quite some time. "All right, but you can't come with me. It would cause another circus with the police. Even if I make it, my father may not let me stay."

He gave her a big smile. "I'm coming. Don't you see I'm the ace in the hole? He won't deny his grandson."

CHAPTER THIRTY-FIVE

Olivia stood behind a giant maple and watched a long line of people inch toward a makeshift plywood table manned by three women she did not recognize — though it would be hard to tell because they wore black hoodies with an image on the back of an alien with white slit eyes and a donut shaped mouth. The women worked in rapid fashion, collecting registration fees and handing out plastic ponchos. They took special care of those with walkers or in wheelchairs. Once registered, other men in hoodies directed them toward an extensive set of bleachers beside a weathered barn.

"This is unbelievable!" Ruth commented.

"More than that," she responded. "I don't understand why they're willing to shell out a hundred bucks and get eaten by mosquitoes. For what? To witness a spectacle?"

Ruth shook her head. "Just the opposite. They're disgusted by what they see every day. We're worse than ants fighting each other and destroying the planet, too." She pointed toward the half-filled bleachers. "These events give them hope that there's a plan underway that will make things right."

She watched a sizable man in a hoodie moving a box of ponchos to the registration table. "But what I've seen, Seth only feeds them small bits of information. I know more than most, and it still leaves me hungry because it's hard to fathom we're not alone."

"That's because we're hard-wired to be skeptical."

"Or because the people we depend on let us down." The image of the Catalina trunk appeared in her thoughts, mixed with stale air and the smell of sweat and urine.

The spotlights trained on the bleachers began blinking.

Ruth grabbed her by the arm. "That's our cue. The event will start soon, so we better get going."

She followed Ruth down a narrow path in the woods that ended at the back of the barn. A dozen people in black hoodies huddled near the far corner. When they got close, Rezi emerged from the cluster.

"Where the hell have you been?" Rezi yelled, with her eyes scanning them like they might be imposters.

"Just checking to see how many came tonight," Ruth replied, backing up like she expected a slap.

"It's all my fault," Olivia said, stepping between them. "I was curious and Ruth came with me, so I didn't wander away."

The alien eyes on the back of the hoodies looked friendlier than Rezi's. "Do you have any idea how much Seth is depending on you tonight?"

She wanted to say no, but learned over the last few days, silence was the best approach.

Rezi's eyebrows began twitching. "Did you get the package I sent you?"

She shook her head.

"See, this is what I'm talking about! Pay attention." She scanned the group and pointed at a skinny girl with thick red hair. "Janice! Give Olivia your hoodie and put on a poncho."

"I don't need it," Olivia protested but received no response as the girl obeyed. Rezi paid attention to the transfer and then glanced at her watch. "Okay, it's time. Line up!"

"We didn't go over what I'm supposed to do," she whispered to Ruth. The idea of repeating the Tuscan act seemed absurd.

"That's because none of this is staged, my friend. Just remain open and Seth will guide you."

She no sooner reached the back of the line when a loud drumbeat shook her insides as well as the earth.

Rezi hurried along the line and finding her at the rear, escorted her to the front.

"You're the reason for all the wheelchairs, so have some presence," she muttered, glaring at her. When she did not reply, the weird woman moaned. "Okay, just smile and follow me."

The procession made their way alongside the barn as the drumbeat quickened. On the way, she tried smiling, but it kept collapsing and hoped a smirk would do since it communicated happiness and also hid the chipped front tooth. *No one will take a healer seriously if I look like the sister of Alfred E. Neuman!*

When they reached the front of the barn, loud cheers, and applause filled the air. Because of the drama, she altered her speed and took in the view. A few hundred people wearing black ponchos filled the bleachers to capacity. Stretching out in a large semicircle with a depth of twenty people, the overflow reached the opposite end of the barn. Soft blue light from strategically positioned spotlights in the trees illuminated the entire area.

Rezi grabbed her arm. "Stay with me," she mouthed as they moved to a small fenced off area to the right side of the barn.

Olivia surveyed the crowd, and it looked similar to the Tuscan event, faces filled with a mix of expectation and happiness being with like-minded people. Most attendees looked between eighteen and thirty-five years of age except for the walker and wheelchair population, which were mostly elderly, though included a few children.

The drumbeat being piped in from loudspeakers on the barn went silent, which brought the bleacher crowd to its feet. Olivia scanned the moonless sky. There were few stars out and the mysterious light from the Tuscan event was absent. Minutes passed, and she watched the crowd grow restless as the other expected visitor — the surreal humming sound which connected her to everything and everyone, did not come rushing out of the tall pines.

The double barn doors opened and Seth came out, dressed in a long white tunic that ended at his sandals. The crowd erupted as he stood smiling and waving. Repeatedly as the cheers subsided, he would say, "Good evening!" and a fresh wave of adulation would erupt and he would hold his hand over his heart in reply. After a few minutes, he flashed a stop sign, and the cheers dissipated.

Seth waited until the silence grew to an intense focal point. "I am overjoyed to welcome you here this evening as we embark on an epic journey," he said and began walking the perimeter of the audience. "What makes it even more special is sharing this milestone with friends from our past events and fresh faces that I hope will join our ranks tonight."

Seth received more cheers as he toured the line, shaking hands and hugging wheelchair-bound individuals. Olivia observed many people were crying as he passed. In her mind, she perceived a faint hum amidst the noise, and as she glanced at the spectators in the bleachers, she noticed a few pointing at their ears. They heard it too.

Seth walked back to the front of the barn like it was a lazy Sunday afternoon. He rubbed his forehead for a moment.

"Thank-you for sharing this evening with me," he continued. "While the last two years have been intense for our movement, my personal journey began over six decades ago on a September evening near this location when my mother — while pregnant with me, was contacted by a higher lifeform. In my experience, Hollywood, and science fiction writers have done a great disservice in making interstellar species a boogeyman by naming them aliens, extraterrestrials, Martians, little green men. I refer to them as Firth since they represent all that we lack: peace, protection, safety, security, freedom, refuge. One thing is clear, they are a higher life form and were here before us, so who is the alien? They have been observing our evolution, refraining from exerting any influence, and waiting for the day when we reached a level of intelligence suitable for dialogue. However, what they have witnessed, particularly since the Industrial Revolution, is that despite the rapid advancement of technology, our growth as a species has remained stagnant, as shown by our persistent prejudice, conflicts, and cruelty towards one another, not to mention how we are destroying the climate which made earth so special." Seth took a few steps forward and pointed up at the dark sky. "They see the risks ahead, especially as we tout the benefits of artificial intelligence which, if not managed correctly, could be our undoing. For our new friends this evening, I would say: take off the blinders and see for yourself. A simple Google search will provide multiple reports of UFOs monitoring strategic military facilities and even turning off nuclear warheads. Why would they do that? Because our destructive nature impacts their multi-dimensional world, too. Think back to the reports of the UFO crash in 1947 at Roswell caused at the time by all the testing of nuclear weapons. This is an ideal example of the impact we are having on them." He stopped and scanned the crowd. "Our weapons have only grown more deadly since then. Firth can no longer tolerate the risk. Against this dark omen, Firth is planting seeds of transformation throughout the world; one of which is here in Salem, next to America's Stonehenge." He motioned toward a small group standing to the right of the barn. They took the cue and with broad smiles lined up behind him.

"This dozen men and women will be the first seeds of a hybrid community — inhabited by us and monitored by our new friends," Seth announced. "Firth have studied us for eons and together, we will test speeding up the maturation of the mind through holistic approaches. The net effect will augment intelligence and also bring physical benefits such as the eradication of disease and a two-fold increase in life expectancy." He held his hands up high. "I expect in a short amount of time to surpass the capacity of this location. We will need to police the perimeter, as our progress will anger many as they hold on to self-centered and violent ways." He shrugged. "Yet, as they observe the outcomes, these same doubters will willingly spend every cent they have to buy into this community in order to enhance their intellect... not become ill... extend their lifespans. But no amount of money will purchase the wisdom of the open-hearted! Let there be no secrets to abundant life!"

The crowd exploded and people held up their iPhones with the flashlights on. Olivia believed it was the most impressive thing she had ever witnessed, and it resembled a rock concert. Time stood still.

Suddenly, the lights dimmed, which seemed to break the crowd's connection and attention. The iPhone lights began popping off.

Seth raised his hand for silence. "At our past events, we witnessed inexplicable insights. The faithful do not need such signs. That said, my heart is full seeing so many with physical challenges here tonight. Since our mission is to serve, I would like to ask someone that has been touched to join me. Please welcome her."

I don't have a name now? she thought as Seth motioned. Olivia wished she was still treading water in the Merrimack.

She sensed someone pushing her forward, and she spun around.

Rezi's face was devoid of the joy enveloping everyone around her. "Stand up straight and don't look weak. Get out there!"

Deeply breathing, she started her approach towards Seth and watched the iPhones in the bleachers being raised to capture her.

Seth gave her a hug. "There's a woman in a wheelchair to the left of the bleacher wearing a Red Sox sweatshirt. Wheel her to me," he whispered in her ear.

She scanned the crowd. All she saw were screaming people and everyone in wheelchairs waving.

"Hurry, before they charge us!" Seth said, looking nervous.

Olivia calmed her racing gaze and located the woman in the red sweatshirt as Seth described, and ran toward her. Two men in wheelchairs came out of nowhere, and she dodged the traffic.

The Red Sox fan was a middle-aged woman with curly dark hair and a crooked smile. She looked sort of familiar, but Olivia could not place her. She wheeled her back to Seth. The yelling was deafening.

"What do I do now?" she mouthed to the leader.

The woman grabbed her arm. "Heal me!"

Seth ignored the plea and held a microphone up to the woman. "What's your name and how long have you been unable to walk?"

"My name is Tricia Hamilton," she replied and pointed at her legs. "I was in a terrible car accident twenty years ago. The doctors said I will never walk again."

Seth nodded and turned to the crowd. "Please sit down and be quiet so our friend who has been touched can concentrate."

The audience obeyed.

Seth winked at her. "Just repeat what you did at Tuscan."

Olivia nodded and put her hands on the woman's head. The curly hair had a soft and fine texture. She could detect the humming noise, but it was almost imperceptible. Nothing occurred and with a sense of being fraudulent, she closed her eyes. She had no desire to witness the disappointment on the lady's face or the anger in the crowd.

Suddenly, she realized Tricia's head was moving. Opening her eyes, she watched the woman get out of the wheelchair.

A mighty cheer shattered the silence. Tricia pulled her in and began sobbing. When she let go, she fell back and saw a line of wheelchairs coming toward her. A dozen men in hoodies stopped the advance.

The crowd booed and Seth looked perplexed as he raised his hand, attempting to control the situation, but the unity shattered. The shouts grew.

Olivia found Rezi standing beside her. "Follow me. We'll be safe in the barn until Seth gets everyone calmed down."

They began hurrying away when she heard a man yell over the speaker. "Healer! Healer! Where are you?"

Turning, she spotted Luke amidst the wheelchairs, attempting to push through. She feared he would be trampled any second, so she ran to him.

She grabbed his arm. "It's me Luke! Let's get you out of here."

He pulled away. "Why will you cure a stranger, but not me? Don't I matter to you?" he asked into the microphone.

She wrapped her arms around him. "What are you doing?" she whispered in his ear. He pushed her away and Seth came between them.

"This is my son Luke," Seth yelled to the audience. "He's been blind for years after a terrible accident damaged his retinas." He stroked his son's arm. "What none of us appreciates is how much each healing takes out of our friend since Firth is using her as a conduit." He pointed at the barn. "It's one of the key areas we plan on learning how to optimize."

"I can't take the darkness anymore!" Luke yelled into the microphone.

Seth's face dropped, and Olivia had an urge to crawl away. Luke opened his arms, and she gave him a tight hug. He hid his face in her hair and cried in great waves. When she attempted to pull away, he held her even tighter, and she believed he might break her back.

When he finally let go, Luke fell into a kneeling position, his face buried in his hands.

She kneeled down beside him. "C'mon, let's get out of here," she whispered.

Nodding, he stood up. But she noticed the dark sunglasses were gone. Deep blue eyes scanned her face.

"You're more beautiful than the angel I imagined," he said into the microphone.

The crowd rushed forward and enveloped them.

CHAPTER THIRTY-SIX

Gabrielle stood in the window and watched the Catalina disappear down the driveway. She let out a sigh of relief and noticed the sky filled with large white clouds, which reminded her of those puffy comforter's rich people buy to make their beds feel too good to leave. In the distance, the horizon looked clear and the color of orange sherbet. She sipped her coffee, knowing a new life existed at the intersection of earth and sky and she would be there soon.

It was only seven thirty, but felt like she already earned a medal in slalom skiing. The first gate was shutting off the alarm clock before it buzzed and ignited Dale's fury. Next, she feared her hands would shake, but after so many years, the automatic pilot kicked on and she made his standard breakfast: three fried eggs, six slices of bacon cooked extra crispy, wheat toast meticulously buttered into each corner, six ounces of premium orange juice and black percolated coffee. She zigzagged this way and that, each movement rapid and efficient, and plated the meal in record time. She threw a load of laundry in while Dale inhaled the breakfast and, much to her surprise, did not complain about anything. When he headed back to the bedroom, she busied herself washing dishes and prepared for the last gate. On his way through the kitchen to grab the car keys, he said he wanted steak, mashed potatoes and corn for dinner and added the usual warning not to sneak in any Mexican spices. She nodded with a submissive expression while pondering the surprise he would find coming home to a lonely house. *Would he ever mull over the pitiful end of their relationship?*

She took another sip of coffee and made it back to the kitchen before Sonny came rushing in. His wild hair looked like he stuck his finger in an outlet.

She swallowed the laugh because he got sensitive about his looks. Growing up, she never felt uncomfortable in her skin, but Olivia and Sonny did not inherit this trait. She blamed it on the crazy self-absorbed society.

"I was going to let you sleep in for a bit, as it will be a long day," she said, almost singing.

"I can sleep on the bus." He opened the fridge and took out the premium orange juice.

By habit, she sucked in her breath. "Any other day, drinking an ounce of Papa's orange juice would get you grounded for a week."

"Well, I'm sick of the frozen concentrate he makes you buy us." He poured a tall glass and took a huge gulp.

"So, what do you think?" she asked.

He shrugged. "Not worth the hype."

"Back home, my mother made juice by squeezing oranges." She waved him away. "Go get ready and I'll make us breakfast."

He headed for his room, but a minute later, came rushing back. He had a set of Allen wrenches in his hand.

"Okay, let's do this. I don't want to eat another meal with an inmate."

She abandoned the stove and rushed to the kitchen chair. Sonny kneeled down beside her and started working on the lock.

"Talk about feeling like Cinderella," she said, watching.

He moaned in reply. "They must have a special tool, but I think this will work. Just hold steady." She shut her eyes and prayed. A moment later, she felt the strap fall away.

Sonny cradled the device in his hands and smiled. "You're a free woman."

As she jumped up, the sound of a car outside made her freeze. Sonny heard it too, and his smile vanished. She looked around the kitchen. *Had Dale installed a hidden camera? What would he do if he sees the ankle monitor off, not to mention the missing orange juice?*

Before she could get her feet moving, Sonny ran to the window and let out a giant sigh. "No worries. It's just Billy." He grabbed his iPhone out of his pocket and frowned. "He wasn't supposed to come until ten."

Sonny raced to open the front door, and she followed close behind.

Billy wiped his work boots on the outside mat before entering. Gabrielle sensed that heaven had sent a guardian angel to protect them when she noticed his enormous frame filling the doorway.

"Mama, this is Billy," Sonny said, pointing.

His friend nodded and wore a shy smile. "Hello Mrs....." he stopped, unsure what to call her.

"Please call me Gabrielle," she replied. Tears welled up and while intending to shake his hand, gave him a hug, although it seemed like embracing a redwood tree. "I can't thank you enough for helping us like this."

The embarrassed giant nodded.

"Let's go in the kitchen and talk," she said. "Your timing is perfect as I was going to make breakfast."

She led them to the kitchen and offered Billy the chair at the head of the table reserved for Dale. His enormous frame overwhelmed the pine chair. Sonny sat down beside him.

"Can I get you some coffee?" she asked.

He took a deep breath. "Sure, but I think we need to talk first."

Her stomach did flips as her thoughts raced. If he backed out, she would have to call a taxi and get out of town. Then they could figure out how to get to the bus station.

Sonny ran his hand through his wild locks. "Is everything okay? You're over two hours early."

Billy pulled out the adjacent chair. "Gabrielle, please sit down so I can show you something."

She locked eyes with Sonny and obeyed.

Billy looked at her, and his shyness vanished. "You don't know me, but I think Sonny can vouch I'm a pretty level-headed guy."

She nodded, wondering what was coming next.

"Sonny told me a little of what you've been through, and I'm sorry." He smiled. "To be honest, if you weren't a lady, I'd say something that would peel the paint off the walls. While none of this is my business, Sonny asked for help and in these parts, that makes me feel obliged."

"Thank you," she whispered.

"I'm saying all this because I need to share something and ...." He winced. "I don't know if it's true because you can't believe anything you see nowadays without confirmation. But it will change your plans."

"C'mon man! Spit it out!" Sonny said.

Billy shot him a surprised look and then reached in his pocket and took out an iPhone that looked like it got run over a few times. The screen had two cracks and the plastic casing smudged with grease.

"This morning, Lori woke me up real early, which she knows is dangerous." He looked down and began working the phone. "She's a social media junkie, and when they have brain implants, will be first in line. She was getting ready for school and came across a weird video about some .... ah, I don't know how to describe them other than a strange group in New Hampshire. The video quality sucks but I fast forwarded it to the spot…Take a look."

She and Sonny drew close and Billy hit play. The video showed a teenage girl in a black hoodie hugging a young man with blond hair. The background noise was extremely loud, but a deep voiced yelled, "She cured him! He can see!" The video then zoomed in on the girl much too fast and became lost in her dark hair. A moment later, the image refocused, and the girl was crying and laughing at the same time. The video zoomed in on her smile and highlighted a chipped front tooth.

Gabrielle jumped up fast enough to put a skylight in the kitchen ceiling if Sonny had not grabbed her.

CHAPTER THIRTY-SEVEN

The kink in her back jolted her awake. As her eyes fluttered open, Olivia's gaze landed on a pile of pizza boxes, paper plates, napkins, and two-liter bottles of Coke on the coffee table. The memories of last night came rushing back; the woman getting out of the wheelchair; Luke looking at her for the first time; the crowd rushing them. When they broke free, they ran down the dirt path, past the plywood registration table, and then up the hill to the house. They hardly made it through the front door before Luke picked her up and deposited her on the couch. Silent tears flowed down his cheeks as he tenderly kissed every inch of her face. She sensed an internal barrier shatter, causing her to both laugh and cry, desiring only to halt time and live in the present. But minutes later, Seth burst in, followed by a hundred others in black hoodies. They lifted her off the couch and she crowd-surfed the living room and kitchen before making it back to earth on the porch. After too many hugs to count, she made a beeline for the living room and discovered, to her dismay, that Seth and Luke were gone. Rezi must have seen the look on her face, because she explained how the evening had sapped their energy and they went back to the barn to sleep. Before she could probe more, a hulk of a man picked her up, and she crowd-surfed again. The party lasted until the wee hours of the morning and she collapsed on the couch.

Raising her head, she glanced between the pizza boxes and discovered Ruth asleep on another couch. Her face looked more peaceful than the angel statutes at church.

The aroma of coffee provided the needed incentive. When she got to the kitchen, she spotted Luke going through a cabinet. The scene looked so unreal that she became motionless watching the attractive guy no longer blind.

"Good morning!" she practically sang coming up behind him.

He turned around and gifted her with a smile that could make the cover of *GQ.* "No, it's a splendid morning!" he replied. "It's so nice to see you!"

She reached up and gave him a kiss. "I don't believe I will ever grow weary of hearing that."

The smile grew brighter and his blue eyes twinkled. "Want coffee or something to eat?"

"Coffee sounds great," she replied, controlling her face as the dark thoughts she obsessed about in the pizza coma last night returned. As they ran away from the barn, he didn't waste a moment deciding which direction to go. His sense of direction was too good for someone that just reclaimed his sight.

"I must say you're pretty impressive. Blind yesterday and this morning a short-order cook?" she said first with a smile until realizing he could see her chipped tooth and looked away.

He kissed her forehead. "It's like riding a bike, babe. Everything comes back quick. It's not like I was blind since birth."

She sat down at the table and watched him pour her coffee. "Do you take it with cream and sugar?" he asked, looking her way.

I thought milk and sugar blocked the transmissions? "Black is fine," she replied, even though she could use some sweetener to neutralize the next question.

"What happened last night?"

He sat down beside her. "I got my life back, thanks to you."

"No, after everyone showed up, you and your father disappeared."

He bit his lip for a second. "Given how I lost my sight in the first place, my father believed it was appropriate to express our gratitude."

"You never explained what happened exactly," she asked, seizing the opportunity.

He took a deep breath. "I resisted when they came to probe me. They had an instrument up my nose and I swung my fist. I hit the thing in the eye and the next second, I was blind. Tough payback."

She examined his eyes again. There were no scars.

"It's not like we can drop in on Firth, but in the right place and state of mind my dad knows how to … shall we say, send a message. I promised not to say anything, but owe you an explanation. We were planning on coming back before the pizza got cold, but I felt exhausted. I hope you understand."

What can I say? Before she could reply, Luke stood up.

"I have to meet my dad at the site. He wants to review the next phase with me, as I can take on a more active role now. Stay here or you can go back to the guest house." He gave her a quick peck on the cheek. "I'll be back this afternoon."

"I'll hang out with Ruth. Maybe we'll take a walk," she said as cheerful as possible despite the pang in her stomach. She expected he would want to spend the day with her and marvel at God's creation.

He gave her a quick kiss and headed for the hall. She retreated into her coffee and when she looked up, Ruth came shuffling in, her hair so tangled it looked like a rat nest.

"Grab some coffee," she said, pointing at the pot.

"Yuk," she whispered and headed for the sink and got a glass of water before collapsing in the chair Luke vacated.

Olivia admired the line of freckles running from cheek to cheek. "Don't feel well?"

"The pizza and champagne conspired against me."

"Champagne?"

She smirked. "Girlfriend, you need to hang with me if you want to have a good time. The actual party was on the back deck. Jimmy found a stash of bubbly in the basement and we toasted your success a few dozen times." She took a quick sip of water. "What you did was amazing. I saw the woman you cured doing an Irish jig with her family, never mind Luke regaining his sight. You'll never surpass that!"

"I can mull it over for the rest of my life and it still won't make sense." She looked at Ruth and wondered how she could take all of this in and not question it. It was one thing to put her hands on some stranger's head and wait for the buzz that flowed through her body to do something. It was another thing to see her search the waters at Tuscan, not knowing what she might find.

"You never told me how you ended up here?" she asked.

"Like I said, Rezi picked me up on the side of the road. I had a buck to my name and was pretty depressed. She drove me to work." Ruth took another sip of water. "After breaking up with my boyfriend, I was couch-surfing at a friend's house and working at a dive bar. She came back just before closing one night and ordered a Manhattan."

"What's that?"

"Rocket fuel," she said with a laugh. "I found out Rezi's a killer sales pro — and sure knows how to close."

And fearless. She jumped off a bridge. "Did you know you had a gift of finding lost things?"

Ruth rubbed the glass. "Are you kidding me? I'm the poster child for the saying I'd lose my head if it weren't attached. When Seth told me I would uncover what the universe hides, I thought my ex put him up to it. We had fights over all the things I put in a safe but forgotten place."

Olivia took another sip of coffee and knew the pangs in her stomach were not from the powerful brew. It was time to address her doubts. "You look exhausted."

"The couch is a lump fest. I'm supposed to stay in the barn from here on out, but who can nap with all the construction going on?"

Olivia reached for her hand. "Tell you what. I moved back to the guest house yesterday. I just changed the sheets, and the blanket is extra soft. Go take a nap and I'll clean up around here. I'll wake you up in a couple of hours."

Ruth kissed her hand. "You're the best!"

She walked her to the door and watched until she was out of sight before heading for the hall.

Both bedroom doors were locked. She searched the top of the doorframes, hoping against hope the key would be there, but all she felt was dust.

Not stopping for shoes, she flew out the front door. The spring morning came with a soft breeze and a Blue Jay squawked somewhere nearby. She ran around the house, examining all the windows, and found one unlocked in the back. It took all her upper strength to wrestle it open and climb in.

Noticing the messy double bed, she concluded it belonged to Luke. Overhead was a framed picture of the *Pale Blue Dot,* which she remembered learning about in school. In that moment, she perceived herself as Voyager 1, billions of miles away and looking back at the earth bathed in a ray of sunlight that somehow missed 107 Pleasant Street. Considering the image from Luke's perspective, it no doubt served as a reminder of Firth. The other walls in the room were bare, but Olivia observed abandoned picture hangers like in the guest house.

The cherry bureau beckoned. When she explored the drawers, she came across neatly folded underwear, socks, shirts, and sweaters, but nothing extraordinary.

Guilt welled up unannounced. As she turned to leave, the closet door beckoned. Before she could question herself, she opened it and moved her hand over a long line of starched shirts and pressed pants. The blue denim shirt caught her attention, the same one he wore when they slow danced. She held the sleeve to her face, remembering the small circles they repeated for an hour. With a sigh, she let it go and, looking up, saw several small frames nestled beside a pile of sweatshirts.

She gently took them down and sat on the bed. The first picture captured Luke as a youngster running with a black and white sheltie on the beach. The love between boy and dog made her smile. Next was a family portrait. Luke looked about ten and wore a button-down white shirt and blue blazer, with the killer smile already on display. Seth stood to the right of his son dressed in the same colors, with a serious look that began with his eyes and kept the rest of his face under control. A woman with blonde hair in a yellow dress stood on the other side of Luke wearing a thin, forced-looking smile. There was something about the mother that gave her stomach a jolt, and she rushed to the window and, studying the picture in the sunlight, discovered a younger Rezi. She glanced back at the bed, which cradled another frame. As she lifted it, she discovered a photo of Luke wearing a graduation cap and gown, clenching his high school diploma. Seth was beaming and had his arm around him.

She collapsed on the bed. Papa Dale liked to grill Mama and say, "let's throw some spaghetti at the wall and see what sticks." But nothing in this tangled mess did. The coffee made her feel nauseous, and she misjudged rolling off the bed and ended up on the hardwood floor. Her eyes caught sight of a pile of magazines under the bed, and pulling them out, found a dozen *Playboy's.*

The memory of the Catalina's trunk came rushing back… air alternating between cold and sticky and smelling of sweat and urine. But at least everything in that dark place located somewhere on the Pale Blue Dot was real.

She found enough saliva to spit on Miss January and ran for the door.

CHAPTER THIRTY-EIGHT

Sonny felt conflicted about sitting in the front seat of the truck. After his mother jumped in the back, that left the front passenger seat open which he likened to middle school. As a baby, he worked his way up from car seat to booster to an occasional seatbelt. But in another year, he would graduate and take the wheel. In the meantime, he hated when his older buddies offered him the wingman position. It was a meaningless role.

The sun played hide and seek by using the clouds which matched the theme of this road trip. From the beginning, the conversation between Billy and Mama had been tense, centering more on the quickest way to New Hampshire rather than the dangerous adventure they were embarking on. In between the stilted words, there were long periods of silence that emphasized every noise. He wished Billy would put on some tunes and camouflage their nerves for the daring mission, but the cool, confident motor head was MIA and the replacement kept his eyes glued on the highway. In order to deal with the anxiety, he watched the mile markers speed by, aware they were making good time by staying in that sweet spot of exceeding the speed limit, but not so much to attract the police on the Maine Turnpike.

He wished the wingman seat had its own rear-view mirror, so he could spy on Mama and make sure she had not imploded. As a workaround, every few miles he redirected his gaze to the left, feigning interest in a passing car, so that he could use his peripheral vision and monitor the silent person in the back seat. For the first fifty miles, she hovered over his iPhone and he thought she was catching up on all the news she never read about Liv's kidnapping. But the last time he checked; she sat upright with eyes closed. He figured she must have read what the authorities said about the coming charges.

Suddenly, she tapped him on the shoulder and handed back the small device that connected the world as much as tore it apart.

"Read enough?" he asked, looking for confirmation on her tired face.

She gave him a sad smile. "I lost the signal a couple of minutes after we left the house."

"Why didn't you say something?" he blurted out like she was an idiot. "Ah, …I mean, perhaps I could have found a hotspot to use."

She shook her head. "I'm not sure what hotspot means, but I kept my eyes on the blank screen and replayed everything that's happened. What a sickening story."

He looked at her again. "Do you want us to stop so you can get some cigarettes?"

"No, those are part of my old life. All I want is my little girl back."

Billy exhaled a deep breath, and Sonny glanced at his friend's face, which resembled a stone dam holding back the rising waters. He imagined Billy must be thinking, how did I go from giving Sonny's mom a ride to the bus station to looking for a dead girl in some weird cult?

"We need to talk about where we're headed," he announced.

Billy gave him a quick glance. "If the traffic holds, we'll be there in an hour."

"That's not what I mean. We can't make this up as we go along."

"Why not? It's worked so far." Billy replied, sounding chipper. "Case in point — your father is chasing a FedEx truck all over town."

A laugh came from the back seat. "I would love to see Dale's face when he finds the ankle monitor attached to the truck's grill. Hopefully, the Chief sent a cruiser too."

The laughs were a relief valve, but the painful silence returned until Billy cleared his throat. "Lori blew me away when she showed me the video, but the more I think about it, I'm afraid someone is setting us up for heartbreak."

"Why would you say that?" he asked.

"Because the quality of the video sucks and the girl's hair was a different color than Olivia's." He looked in the rear-view mirror at Gabrielle. "Many people have chipped teeth."

"But I noticed her eyes," she replied. "Olivia has her father's almond nuggets. A mother knows her child. It's her."

Sonny watched and his mother's words did not erase the doubt on Billy's face. "The healings have weirded me out," he said, changing the subject. "Think they're real?"

"Can't say. I used to believe it when a magician sawed a lady in half," Billy snickered.

"You might believe it again if you stayed at our house for a while," Mama replied.

Sonny turned around and winked at his mother. "Look at you! Free from house arrest and you're already making jokes."

Billy changed lanes and sped up. "Call my sister. Maybe she found more videos."

Sonny sucked in his breath. "Uh, I don't know her number."

The driver shook his head. "And you never will, acting like that." He picked up his iPhone from the cup holder and hit a couple of buttons.

"I was going to call you," Lori said, skipping the greeting.

"Then why didn't you?" Billy replied with attitude. "By the way, you're on speaker, so watch your language."

A short pause followed. "Not funny."

"Find anything else?"

Lori sighed. "Just content and marketing crap about wanting to build a better world. Yada, yada, yada. Seems they broke ground on a new community in Salem called New Roswell."

Billy slapped the steering wheel. "New Roswell? Are you kidding me!"

"I don't understand," Gabrielle called out from the back seat.

Billy glanced in the rearview mirror. "It's a play on Roswell, which is in New Mexico and the site of a UFO crash back in the 1940s. There are a lot of conspiracy theories about the place."

"I also found some posts about their leader named Seth, who has no last name," Lori continued. "The guy claims he's linked to the Betty and Barney Hill abductions that took place sixty years ago in New Hampshire. Seems his mother was pregnant with him and abducted the night before the Hill's.

"Sounds like a crackpot," Sonny said with a laugh. "Why would anyone fall for it?"

"With all the fake stuff we see online these days, I'd agree," Lori replied, "but then I found a video taken a few days before Olivia ended up on the bridge. It shows a huge gathering at a pond in front of LL Bean at Tuscan Village in Salem. There's a bright light in the sky and people are yelling at some guy in a tunic. Minutes later he calls Olivia over and she puts her hand on the man in a wheelchair and the guy gets up."

"That makes three people she healed!" Sonny said.

"Anything else, Lori?" Billy asked.

"No, and I have to go to work."

"Which means you will continue surfing," her brother said. "Call me back if you find anything else."

"You can scroll just as well as me," she shot back.

"This means a lot to us. I can't thank you enough," Sonny said and noticed the funny look on her brother's face.

She hung up without replying, and the silence descended again, but this time because everyone was processing what they heard.

A few minutes later, Billy put the radio on. Sonny expected some hard-edge stuff, but out of respect for his mother, he found a station playing soft rock.

The music carried them down Route 495 to exit 108. Ten minutes later, they pulled into Tuscan Village.

Sonny pointed to a building a half mile away. "I see LL Bean!" *Maybe there is something to this wingman thing after all,* he thought.

Billy navigated around a series of rotaries before stopping in front.

"Now what?" Sonny asked.

Billy bit his lip and scanned the area.

"Look at that guy handing out flyers," his mother commented. "The back of his hoodie has an alien on it."

Billy pulled into a parking space. "Wait here while I go talk to him. If they beam me up, you're on your own."

CHAPTER THIRTY-NINE

With her departure from the fraudulent alien hideout, Olivia began her journey eastward, assured that she had enough spirit and determination to walk back to Maine and then some. The way she looked at it, Papa Dale could lock her up every day, but at least she knew the devil she was dealing with instead of the handsome one that broke her heart. If there were an ounce of hope left in the universe, perhaps Mama's death mellowed Papa Dale and made him regret the cruel things he had done — or planned to do when he got her alone. If not, she and Sonny would figure out a way and break free. The argument held as she traversed several streets, most without sidewalks. But after a couple hours, her feet ached and reality set in on how ill prepared she was with only the clothes on her back and no money. Mama warned her about the risk of not thinking things through. She regretted not keeping the secret and stealing the resources needed to hide. But there was no turning back now, and she picked up the pace and noticed how the spacious single-family homes and renovated farmhouses on the country road were giving way to a mixture of condominiums and three tenements.

The traffic continued to build as the road ran downhill, and she noticed a magnificent church perched high above on a pedestal of land. A long line of cars snaked from an adjoining street through the church parking lot and stopped in front of a large sign in blue letters that read St. Vincent de Paul Food Pantry. Her feet turned on their own. Though she left her stomach on the floor next to Luke's bed, a terrible thirst nagged at her.

Slowly shuffling up the hill, she followed the line of cars around the front of the church to an adjacent brick building. She stopped and watched an older gentleman with a clipboard check in a car at the front of the line and then direct it toward a small maroon canopy. A half-dozen men and women were waiting, and they deposited bags in the car's trunk. It looked like a well-oiled operation and everyone was smiling.

The man with the clipboard looked her way and waved and then motioned to the team. Immediately, a thin middle-aged woman with gray hair and a smile that looked like it never aged made her way over.

"Are you here for the food pantry, my dear?" she asked.

She pointed at the cars. "Should I get in line for a bottle of water?"

"That's unnecessary, but it reminds me of a funny story. Last year, my husband and I were on vacation and had the munchies, so we walked to a nearby McDonald's. It was almost midnight and only the drive-up window was open and they wouldn't serve us unless we were in a car." She glanced at the vehicles and laughed. "Don't worry, we don't discriminate like that here. Walk or drive up, it doesn't matter. You came on a good day too. We stocked up at the Boston food bank yesterday. Fantini's bakery is also very generous and donates bread fresh out of the oven. It was still warm when I picked it up an hour ago."

She attempted a smile but failed. "That sounds good, but I'm just thirsty."

A motherly look came over the woman's face, and she gave her a subtle once over. "What's your name, dear?"

"Olivia."

She extended her hand. "Nice to meet you. I'm Nancy. Live around here?"

She did not answer, afraid if she opened her mouth, her eyes would flood.

Nancy read her face and returned a warm smile. "Well, let's get you something to drink! Follow me."

The woman led her past the worker bees under the canopy and down a flight of stairs where she saw a half dozen others filling plastic bags with canned goods, cereals, and toiletries.

They continued down a narrow hall that emptied into a room featuring a large conference table with piles of food on top.

Nancy sighed. "This is supposed to be our meeting room, but we had a food drive yesterday and this is the overflow."

She cleared a section and offered her a chair. "You can rest here for a bit. Besides some water, are you hungry?"

The pizza she had last night was the last thing she ate, and she felt nauseous from the upset. "I'm okay. I don't want to be a bother."

The woman's head jerked back. "Bother?" She pointed at a frame on the wall. "Truth is, we see the face of Jesus in everyone we serve. I'll be right back."

She collapsed in the cushioned chair and felt a blister beginning on the back of one ankle. Closing her eyes, she pictured Luke twirling black sunglasses in his hand. *I'm such a fool!* The thought catapulted her out of the chair and the muscles in both legs protested. She looked around the room, trying to erase Luke from mocking her. The frame Nancy pointed out caught her attention.

After the love of God, your principal concern must be to serve the poor with great gentleness and cordiality, sympathizing with them in their ailments and listening to their little complaints ... for they look on you as people sent by God to help them. You are therefore intended to represent the goodness of God in the eyes of the poor. (St. Vincent de Paul)

Olivia sat back down and compared these genuine words of help to her experience. Mama sent her away thinking Rezi was a savior, when in fact it was all a sham. *Why did they want me?* She studied her hands. They healed no one. The spikes in her throat dug in and she stood up, ready to run away from the mental torture.

As though on cue, Nancy came rushing in carrying a tray loaded with a ham and cheese sandwich, a bowl of chicken soup, chips, cookies, a green apple, and two bottles of water. "I made you up a little something."

"This is all for me?" she asked, wiping her eyes with the sleeve of her sweatshirt. She opened a bottle of water and gulped half and afterwards pointed at the wall. "What is this charity about that helps people like me?"

"Have a bite of your sandwich and I'll give you my thirty-second elevator speech," Nancy replied and waited until she obeyed. "As with many things in life, the right question can challenge what you believe and inspire action. That's what happened back in 1833, for a group of Catholic students from the University of Paris. A question challenged them — sure, your church did a lot of good in the past, but what is it doing now? The accusation cut the students to the heart, and they moved to respond, including Frederic Ozanam, the principal founder of the Society of St. Vincent de Paul. They needed help to get started and looked to Sister Rosalie Rendu from the Daughters of Charity. She assigned families for them to visit, explained how to assist, and taught them to go out in pairs. After home visits, they would meet with Sister Rosalie and talk about what they had seen. She taught them to see the face of Christ in the poor, in the tradition of St. Vincent de Paul. From that mustard seed, the Society grew to be global and operates in 150 countries, 5 continents and has over 800,000 members. In the United States, we have been helping people in need for 175 years." She pointed at the frame on the wall. "Our mission statement is a network of friends, inspired by Gospel values, growing in holiness and building a more just world through personal relationships and service to people in need. Many have faced difficulty in the last few years because of the rising cost of everything, or encountered a sudden crisis such as a serious health issue, loss of a job, divorce, or a death in the family. The line of cars outside shows the level of food insecurity in the city. While the list of requests is endless — help with rent, utilities, medical bills, a bed for a child, no act of charity is outside our ministry."

Olivia contemplated the high-powered events Seth and his minions orchestrated for attention. "You do all this without blowing your horn?"

Nancy nodded. "Our most basic activity is meeting people in their homes, so we are the guest. We listen to their needs and provide material and spiritual help and everything we do is confidential." She pointed at her sandwich. "I'm convinced what D. T Niles said is true. Christianity is one beggar telling another where he found bread."

"I saw the line of cars outside. How can you afford all this?"

"Our funding comes primarily from generous parishioners that sustain our work. There are also programs from the Boston Council that target specific needs. We also apply for private foundation and city grants. It seems like whenever we are about to run out of funds, something happens in the nick of time. It makes me think a lot about the story of Jesus feeding five thousand with two fish and five loaves of bread."

She noticed how Nancy's green eyes danced as she talked about the organization. When her mother talked about faith, she dismissed it as old-fogey stuff she dragged here from Mexico. *But maybe I have it all wrong. If more people embraced this type of faith in action, the world would be a significantly different place. What a difference to hear how fish were central to a miracle that has been remembered for over two thousand years. I wish Papa Dale could see me in that light instead of a salmon driven to spawn!* She also thought what Seth and Luke said about Firth growing tired of humans and their destructive ways. This charity was goodness in action and underscored the lie.

Nancy looked at her watch. "I've gone on long enough. Enjoy your lunch and I'll check back soon."

She had a sudden idea. "Could I borrow your phone?"

Without hesitation, Nancy reached in her back pocket and took out an iPhone and typed in her password. "Calling someone to pick you up?"

The pain in her throat repeated. "No. I need to check an obituary."

The woman's head jerked. "I'm sorry! Did you lose someone close?"

"Yes," she replied. *I could rock this kind woman's world if I said I wanted to read mine too.*

Nancy handed her the phone. "Take your time."

Olivia took another bite of the sandwich and typed in her mother's name, expecting the obituary to pop up. Instead, dozens of articles from multiple news organizations came back about Gabrielle Ruiz facing charges of child endangerment after her daughter's kidnapping and presumed drowning. Her eyes scanned the long list, looking for something about her mother's death, but none appeared. She sat back in the chair with a handful of chips. *Poor Mama, she went through hell protecting me to the end, but no one cares about her death? It makes little sense!*

Setting aside the phone, she concentrated on the lunch. The food tasted delicious and revived her spirits. *Maybe Nancy and the organization can help me with bus money back to Maine?* She picked up the phone again and noticed that many articles had been updated yesterday. *How can they bring charges against a dead woman?* The thought shot a bolt of electricity through her.

She jumped up and began pacing around the table, ecstatic that maybe Mama might be alive, but fearful she might be mistaken. It came down to how big a lie did Seth tell her?

Nancy came rushing into the room with a big smile on her face. "Look who I found!" she sang.

Olivia froze as Luke followed the good Samaritan.

CHAPTER FORTY

"Slow down, or you're going to miss it!" Sonny said, scanning the road for the next driveway. The foliage was a good two weeks ahead of Maine and camouflaged many of the properties on the country road.

The truck took the next curve much too fast and Sonny pulled his head in before a branch sucker punched him. He glanced at the driver, expecting a devious grin, but Billy stared straight ahead like he was in a trance.

"What's eating you, man?" he asked.

The question was like a hot poker, and Billy shot him a gimme-a-break look. "I don't get this macho act of yours! You're aching to take on Darth Vader and his creeps, but afraid of Lori?"

He tried to look offended. "That's not true!"

"Sure, it is. The second I asked you to call my sister, you started clucking like a chicken," he replied, jerking his neck back and forth.

"That's enough!" his mother barked from the back seat. "We don't have time for bickering over this nonsense."

"Is that what you call it?" Billy asked in a strained voice, looking in the rear-view mirror. "We're being set-up for a big letdown and I'm not crazy about showing up unannounced at some cult commune."

"What choice do we have but to see if Olivia is there?" She leaned forward and hovered in the space between the front seats. "The skinny kid you talked with looked high as a kite. I think he got a kick out of watching the color drain from your face."

"Like you could see that from fifty feet away?" He snickered. "Plus, my beard hides a lot."

"My mother survived the last sixteen years by watching my father's moods," Sonny chimed in.

Billy shrugged. "I agree that kid sure loves his weed. But even stoned, he verified what Lori saw online. No doubt about it. This Seth guy is leading one crazy cult."

"It says they're a community of like-minded people," Sonny said, reading from his iPhone.

"Whatever. He has my daughter. That's the only thing that matters," his mother whispered.

Billy pulled over and put the truck in park. "All I know is we're flying by the seat of our pants and going in there is risky. I'll admit there's a tiny chance Olivia's alive, but we have to be honest and admit she's more likely in the river." He took a deep breath and sighed. "The problem is we don't have time to do a thorough search of ET headquarters." He checked his watch and glanced at Gabrielle. "We have an hour and then need to head for Boston. The police may search the airport, train, and bus stations for you."

"Well, I'm not going anywhere until I find her."

Sonny sensed a change in the air in the truck cabin, as if it became colder. He studied his friend's face and the strange combination. Billy clenched his jaw, but his eyes were glistening.

He touched his arm. "I can't thank you enough for this and know it puts you in a difficult position. You're helping your mom make ends meet and looking after Lori and can't afford to get caught up in this. It's risky enough you offered to drive us to Boston." He looked back at his mother, who was nodding. "If you want to stay out here while we check out the place, I understand."

Billy put the truck in drive. "You don't know me very well, if you think I'd be fine with that. Let's check out the site and see what happens. But I doubt they'll be glad we stopped by to pick her up."

"Don't be so sure. After Seth sees the size of you and the tough woman in the backseat, he will cave or face a tornado."

"And the other hundred goonies? I'm thinking you must have smoked some weed too," Billy said, eying his phone. "Maps says the address is nine-hundred feet away." He slowed down to a crawl.

"I see the barn through the trees," Mama said.

"The driveway is straight ahead," Sonny added, pointing.

Billy pulled in and followed a dirt road a good quarter mile to a large red barn.

He turned the truck around before coming to a stop. "Just in case we need to leave fast," he said matter of fact.

They got out of the truck and Billy wandered over to the bleachers to the right of the barn. "This is the place on the video!" he said, looking back before walking to the top and surveying the land behind the barn. "They're building a road back there."

He no sooner came down, when a short plump woman in a business suit came out of nowhere. Sonny looked for antennae to match the stern face, but her dark curls were too thick.

"Can I help you?" she asked, directing the question to his mother.

"Yeah, bring us to your leader," Sonny whispered loud enough for Billy to hear and receive an ugly glance in reply.

"We've heard a lot about this place and hoping we could get a tour if possible?" his mother asked in a sweet voice.

The woman replied with a forced smile. It reminded Sonny of the lunch lady whenever he asked for a larger portion. "Welcome then to New Roswell. My name is Amanda. Are you interested in joining our community?"

The three glanced at each other.

"What does joining mean?" Sonny asked, taking the lead.

Amanda shot him a puzzled look. "Well, we just completed phase one through a lottery process and selected a dozen from our group to live in a quintessential but modern New England facility. Phase two is underway." She stopped and put her hand to her ear. "You can hear the construction out back. We broke ground on seven hundred apartments, which will include several exciting possibilities. We have a few units left and taking deposits."

"I saw some of the … possibilities online," Billy said. "My question is—"

Amanda held up her hand. "Why don't we hold questions until the end?" She pointed at the door. "Shall we?"

They played follow the leader into the barn and entered a large spacious area featuring a massive fieldstone fireplace with a bank of chairs arranged in a semi-circle.

Amanda let her eyes wander over the room like a proud mother. "A couple years ago, this was nothing but a sad looking hundred-year-old barn with half the roof missing and weeds growing where you're standing. We purchased the property and worked with some of the area's leading architects on an extensive renovation, preserving most of the original timbers and highlighting the fieldstone foundation." She pointed at a hall to the right. "Seth envisions a vibrant community living in the shared kitchen, living room and library. In here we will hold small group sessions." She looked up at the thick wooden beams overhead. "To me, this is like Noah's Ark."

"What do you mean?" Sonny asked, gazing upwards.

"Because unless we change, the flood is coming," a man's voice boomed behind them.

Turning around, they discovered the star of the videos. Seth's white hair looked more like snow in person. He wore a t-shirt, jeans, and sandals.

Sonny exchanged looks with Billy, and their eyes said the same thing. *Where did he come from?*

"What brings you here, my friends? In pursuit of a better life?" he asked.

"We saw the videos and thought we would check it out," Billy replied loudly like he hoped the police were monitoring and they would rush in now.

Seth smiled. "I noticed the plates on the truck. From Maine?"

Billy nodded.

"Whereabouts?"

Before he could reply, his mother stepped forward.

"Enough with the small talk. Where's my Olivia?" she yelled.

Amanda rushed forward, but Billy blocked her.

Seth flashed them a puzzled look. "I lead this community and pride myself on knowing everyone. I can assure you no one by that name is here."

"Let's try this again," she said, pointing her finger at the man. "We're talking about my sixteen-year-old daughter, Olivia. I made the mistake of trusting Rezi to look after her for a while until I got things straightened out. She said she worked for you. But you brainwashed her because she jumped off the bridge and..." she stopped and began crying.

Sonny rushed forward and put his arm around her.

Seth watched and sighed. "Yes, I know the tragic story and am so very sorry for your loss. You have to understand every movement attracts a fringe. I refrain from calling them disturbed, but they pervert the message and sad consequences follow. If you attended our events, you would see we talk of peace and the dawn of a new age in the universe."

"So, you're telling me the woman I gave my daughter to...the one that promised me you would safeguard her, you don't know?" Gabrielle asked regaining her indignation.

"I don't and it pains me."

"Liar!" she yelled, and lunged at him, but Seth sidestepped her.

"We saw the video of Olivia curing a blind man," Billy said, hovering over him with clenched fists.

Seth looked away for a moment, like he was rewinding the tape, and then shrugged. "I can see why you would think that. I recall the pictures of your daughter in the papers and on tv. Grief colors one's perception and the healer last night had some of the same features."

"Where is she now?" Billy asked.

Seth shrugged. "In the wind. The magic that occurs at these events is not pre-planned. Everything is spontaneous."

"Olivia is also on another video in front of LL Bean and made a man walk again," Sonny argued.

Seth pulled on his lip in thought. "Hundreds show up at our events. That said, I remember the recent meeting at Tuscan and a blonde girl coming out of the crowd and healing that gentleman. As I told the police after the tragic drowning, I did not know her or the woman she was traveling with." He glanced at the grieving mother. "I also read about your legal troubles, and surprised you can leave the State."

The air went quiet.

Seth began walking away. "Amanda will show you out. I hope you find peace."

"Go to hell," Mama yelled after him.

They walked back to the truck in silence. Light rain began falling, which made the depression more intense.

"He's a liar!" his mother said over and over.

"Did you expect the Welcome Wagon?" Billy asked.

No one answered, and Billy started the truck. Five minutes later, he pulled into Dunkin' and, seeing a half dozen cars in the drive-thru, swung into a parking space and handed Sonny a twenty-dollar bill.

"Get you and your mother something. I want a large black coffee."

Sonny took the money and got out without saying a word.

Inside the store, he waited behind a lady ordering for a dozen children. Ten minutes later, the overworked teen looked at him. "What would you like?"

Before he could reply, a voice behind him boomed. "A regular coffee, heavy on the cream."

He turned around to find his father glaring at him.

CHAPTER FORTY-ONE

Sonny said she had a wicked fastball for a girl, so Olivia picked up the green apple off the tray and hurled it at Luke's head.

The throw was high, but the demon still caught it.

"Let me guess, you were an all-star in Little League?"

He nodded. "And made the varsity team as a freshman." He took a bite of the apple. "Granny Smith is my favorite. Been so busy chasing you, I haven't eaten."

She looked at the remains of her lunch and regretted finishing the chicken soup. Watching him try to catch that would have been worth the cleanup. The only ammo left on the plastic tray was the chocolate chip cookies, and he wasn't worth it.

"How did you find me?" she asked.

He finished chewing before replying. "The bigger question is, why did you leave?"

The handsome features she drooled over since setting eyes on him now repulsed her. "How can you ask me that with a straight face? This whole thing has been a sham!"

He came toward her and she backed up and looked toward the hall, ready to scream for help. Instead, he pulled out a chair and sat on the opposite side of the table. "Sit down so we can talk."

"Why? So, you can lie to me some more?"

Luke took another bite of the apple. "You're a smart girl and know the truth can be nuanced."

"Where I come from, we don't use big words like that to hide behind and deceive people."

He pointed at the chair across the table. "Please! Just give me a few minutes."

Hurt and curiosity welled up, and she sat down.

Luke placed the apple on the tray and gestured as if preparing to lead them in prayer. "When I left you this morning, everything was fine. Then I come home and find you're gone. I was afraid that monster Papa Dale found you, but a neighbor told me he saw you walking up the street. I'm the one hurt and angry, but open to giving you an opportunity to explain instead of reacting harshly."

"Once again, you're twisting things, so I'm the guilty one. Why don't we start instead with you admitting you were never blind!" she yelled.

Luke glanced at the hall to see if the outburst attracted attention. "That's true. I'm no longer blind because of you."

She jumped up and would have hit him if the table did not separate them. "I had my suspicions a few times. It was all an act! Then last night, after you regained your sight, you ran up the street to your house with no hesitation."

He held up his hand. "Stop! I can explain—"

"With some other made-up story?" she asked, interrupting. "Save it, because pictures don't lie!"

"What pictures?"

"The ones in your bedroom closet," she said sarcastically. "Besides the graduation picture, I saw the family portrait. I also found your stash of *Playboy's.* Do you have a twin brother.... or did Firth provide a body double?"

It was his turn to jump up. "You broke into my room?"

"That's going to be your defense?"

Luke sighed. "Okay, let's take things one at a time," he said, as his shoulders sagged. "I may not have been physically blind, but was metaphysically. My father made me realize that."

"I don't know what the hell that means. Why did you fake it? I thought you liked me more...." Her tongue froze.

"I do, but you need to understand the context."

"Here you go again, hiding behind words. That's the thing I love about Maine. We recognize BS no matter the pretty wrapping paper."

He sighed. "Then let me tell you what isn't in question. We need you."

"More spin? I'm getting dizzy."

He shook his head. "Listen to me! You've been to our events, seen the guiding light, felt the buzz drill into your very core and healed people that have given up hope."

"But it's all fake! Just a big show, so all the hoodies can collect money." She pointed at the donated food on the table. "You should volunteer here for a while and see what giving people hope is all about."

Luke's face hardened. "You're embracing ignorance. I'm here to tell you Firth means business. A few years ago, I was skeptical too because the events only drew a few people. But my father was patient. He said the timing wasn't up to us, and the key was pushing forward with an open mind. Fast forward to today, and our story is gaining traction and people are lining up to hear the message. The number of UFO sightings is off the charts. Let me tell you why. If you study mythology or listen to tales around the campfire, you discover Firth has always been here in the shadows. But we created a massive problem for them when we developed a nuclear bomb. Each detonation creates not only an electromagnetic but also a scaler pulse that impacts interstellar travel and communication. Who knows what else it affects? I think we risk blowing up their world along with ours. It's too late to put the genie back in the bottle, so they are interceding."

She cocked her head and studied the guy standing there. It was like he swapped out his brain with someone else. The Luke she was familiar with had a fondness for music and goofing off. "This sounds like *Stranger Things* meets *War of the Worlds*. If this is true, why don't they just come forward? Why all the secrecy?"

He reached across the table and picked up a chocolate cookie and broke it in half. "They did years ago, and how do you think the world responded? With hubris."

She rolled her eyes. "Hubris?"

"I mean with excessive pride. Multiple governments saw it as the ultimate way to remain or become a superpower. They kept the contacts secret and reverse engineered whatever they could get their hands on." He took a bite of the cookie. "Firth became disillusioned watching the arms race and decided on another approach... a grassroots campaign of sorts. But the Barney and Betty Hill encounter became a circus. Then, years later, they tried working with the Heavens Gate gang, but that became a nightmare when they believed Firth would transport them to another world. Luckily, my mother kept quiet. Now it's up to my dad, and he's determined to seed an enlightened hybrid society."

"You're talking crazy!"

"No, just listen! It takes several generations for their DNA to strengthen in human form. My mother—"

"You mean Rezi! I saw the family pic and don't understand why you don't call her Mom?"

He shook his head. "Rezi is more like a surrogate mother because they implanted their genetic material in me."

"C'mon. You can't think I will believe a lie that big!"

"Like I said, I was blind for years. I denied it even after lab work showed weird abnormalities. But enough about me. You're in on this special experiment too. We know Firth monitors the population for special sensitivity and chooses carefully. We think it comes from a combination of nature and some other stress factor. You should ask your mother if anything weird happened when she was carrying you."

"Leave my mother out of this! You're insane. And I didn't heal anyone. It was just part of the show."

He shrugged. "Okay, I'll admit you didn't cure me, but the others really couldn't walk. That wasn't fake. Honest!"

"Honest coming from you? That's rich. If I have this incredible gift, I'll visit the nearest hospital and heal everyone."

"It doesn't work that way. Firth is sick and tired of people going rogue. It has to be done in coordination with them. You said it yourself. The buzz and the pulse of energy came before they healed."

She backed up to put more space between them, afraid his darkness would infect her. "Then why did you pretend to be blind?"

"I did that before you joined us... and yes, I regret it, especially after meeting you. We were not drawing the numbers and afraid Firth would become impatient. Being blind was proactive marketing to pull a rabbit out of the hat to grow our base if needed. What we didn't understand was Rezi's gift of finding those who had been touched. Ruth is a gem, but nothing compared to you. The healing last night broke the internet. Who knows what other people with special gifts may still be out there?"

She reached for the other cookie and took a small bite.

Luke came around the table. "My dad has been working for years trying to define the formula for getting the message out and capturing hearts. He even ran it through AI and it doesn't tell us anymore than what history shows: have a good story with a hero." He flashed her a killer smile. "We have all the pieces here for a blockbuster: poor girl meets blind boy, they fall in love, she discovers her special gifts and cures him only to find out he is more than he seems. Their love changes two worlds."

"But back on earth, it's a story about a desperate mom attempting to hide her daughter and a group of sickos exploiting her."

He lightly touched her arm. "I'm telling you as sincerely as I can, that you're wrong. Together, we possess the ability to be part of something special that will not only save the world, but transform it. I know your mother has difficulties affording the basics. Money will never be an issue again."

"Before we follow that yellow brick road… why did your father lie to me and say my mother died?"

He held out his hand. "Because you have a special mission and that life in Maine is beneath you."

"So, you made me an orphan? Besides all the lies, what upsets me the most is messing with who I am. That makes you no different from my mother's boyfriend, who's been screwing with my identity for as long as I remember. But you know what? This sick ride makes me realize no one gets to define me. I'm going home."

"Home is with us. In Maine, they will taunt and reject you," he laughed.

"No, they will sit spellbound when I tell them about the likes of you and Seth." She looked down at her feet. "They may even see past my ugly sneakers."

His smile disappeared. "You can stop with the tough talk, as it looks pathetic on you. Like most things in life, we can use the carrot or the stick. I'm doing my best to explain the possibilities if we collaborate. Firth won't let you fade into the pine trees of Maine. The stakes are too high. Do you consider it by accident that I found you here?"

She began for the hall. "All I can say is I question their superior intelligence if they pinned the hope of the universe on your sick gang."

CHAPTER FORTY-TWO

Sonny enjoyed pushing the boundaries in video games, recognizing that the only risk he faced was a bruised ego. This experience, however, felt more like jumping on a grenade to protect Mama and Billy. Papa did not say a word at the coffee shop, just grabbed him by the arm and marched him outside. His instinct took control, eyes locked on the ground to conceal the truck's location. When they reached the Catalina, he expected Papa would open the trunk for the long ride back to Maine, but instead unlocked the passenger door. As he bent over to get in, he looked through the driver side window to where Billy's truck sat minutes ago. The space sat empty.

Papa started up the car and sped out of the lot. The four-lane road threaded through a chain of retail stores, restaurants, and gas stations. Every traffic signal remained green and the way he weaved in and out of traffic, he got the sense his father knew the area. When he sped up toward Interstate 93, they passed Tuscan Village and he glimpsed LL Bean in the distance. *Where's a UFO when you need one?*

The highway brought more road noise and only amplified the angry look on his father's face. Bad enough, Papa had to take time out from work for this manhunt, but he was putting unnecessary miles on his pride and joy. The penalty for both would be painful. Dozens of thoughts competed for attention and made him nauseous.

He closed his eyes, hoping not to be sick, when Billy's voice cut through the fear and yelled, "Man up!"

His dry mouth made swallowing difficult, and he regretted leaving the coffee behind. "How did you find me?" he asked, his voice sounding small and strained.

Papa kept his eyes on the road, but the corners of his mouth curled with a smug smile. "Better keep your grades up, boy, because you suck as a fugitive. I tracked your phone."

"I will not lose you like your sister," Papa said, when handing him the new iPhone. Now it seemed like thirty pieces of silver. He believed it would put an end to all the teasing at school that he was saving up for a Blackberry. He thought Papa gave it out of fatherly concern and was so enamored with the gift, he never considered the secret agenda.

His father cleared his throat. "Okay, where is she?"

He bit his lip, not knowing if he was talking about Mama or Olivia? He shrugged, still reflecting on the vagueness of the question, and knowing anything he said could be used against him.

Papa responded with his fist coming fast toward him. Sonny braced for the punch, but it moved past his face and opened the glove compartment instead. A breakfast bar of nips arranged neater than candlepins was on display.

He grabbed two Jack Daniels and drained one.

"I should change your name to Mommy Junior, because you don't have my back when it counts. Tell me, after all I've done for you, including that fancy new phone you bitched and bitched about getting, why would you stab me in the back and undo the ankle monitor?"

The smell of whiskey overwhelmed the new car air freshener. Last summer, he found half a bottle of Jack Daniels under a pile of towels in the hall closet. He took it and he and Mike had a wild night camping in the tree fort he built in the woods behind the house. It was a wonder no one heard them laughing and hollering or getting sick.

"Answer me, boy. Why did you do it?"

"That's the wrong question. Why did you trap her like an animal?" he asked instead. They had a long drive ahead, and he positioned himself against the door to repel any of Papa's punches. If he stopped the car, all bets were off.

"Better watch your mouth, or you'll be sucking your next meal through a straw. You can't imagine the sinkhole I rescued your mother from. Things were all lovey-dovey for a while, but now we're like black beans in the fridge. One day they're good, and the next stink to high heaven." Papa took another sip. "But I haven't changed, she has! I'm the same man that saved her and Sockeye from a shelter."

"And you believe an ankle monitor will make her want to stay?" He intended to end it there, but could not dam the words. "You're always putting her down... and when you drink, knock her around... I hear the crying during the night coming through my wall. Yeah, you've done a lot for her, and don't get me started about Liv. I'm surprised she didn't run off from all the times you locked her in the trunk."

A fist came fast for his face and, ducking it, only caught the top of his head.

"Just wait until I get you home, Mommy Junior. You're picking the wrong side and will find out what it costs to cross me. It will be a painful lesson."

"You treat me like gold compared to them. Why do you want them to stay?"

"Your mother owes me, and I'm determined to work it out. As for Sockeye..." He let out a heavy sigh. "No matter how much I've tried to bring her up the right way, it's clear she won't be able to overcome what's in her genes. She will end up shacking up with some lazy loser and have a dozen kids. I can see it now: welfare, food stamps and all the freebies she can get. Of course, by then she will dye her hair red! I just hope Sockeye swims south before she spawns, because I'm not giving her a dime." He glanced at him for a moment, like he was planning the location of the next punch. "But I still have a few years to straighten you out, and believe me, I will."

"I'll call the police if you touch me," he replied, rubbing the top of his head.

"You mean my buddy the Chief? He isn't afraid to use the belt on his kids either."

"And it shows. Tim and Jane are mutes at school." Sonny looked at the breakdown lane whizzing by. "I'll just run away."

"You're a minor, so the police will drag your ass home. What do I have to do, put a monitor on you too?" He finished the second nip. "So where is she?"

"I don't know."

A long skinny finger came toward his face. "You won't be able to sit for a month if you don't tell me right now."

With a deep breath, he directed his gaze towards his father. They shared the same long, thin nose and coarse hair, but Sonny hoped the gray matter between his ears was more like Mama's. No matter what he said, the gallows would be waiting. *Jumping on a grenade sure sucks.*

"I have no idea!" he yelled, hoping the lie would fly. "As soon as I got the monitor off, Mama ran. I knew you would be furious, so I headed for Salem."

He eyed him for a long moment. "How did you get down here?"

"Hitchhiked. Met a trucker headed to Boston."

Papa fell silent, evaluating the alibi. After a few minutes, he let out a long sigh. "I know why you flew to Salem. I saw the video about Sockeye."

Sonny hesitated, but had to probe. "You mean at LL Bean after Rezi took her?"

Papa waved him off. "No, I'm talking about some video last night where a teenage girl healed a blind guy. The Chief said he received many reports the healer looks like your sister."

"Did you look for her too?" he asked.

"No. I'll leave that to the Chief."

"It's all fake news. You can't believe anything you see," he replied, and looked away, hoping Papa would abandon the idea.

"Well, if it turns out to be true, I wouldn't have to work another day in my life. People would line up to be healed, and I'd collect a service fee." He nodded, weighing the opportunity. "Better still, maybe I would have her come to the store. Spend five hundred and get your arthritis cured!" He laughed and pointed to the glove compartment. "Give me another."

He handed him a nip. "Even if she's alive, she won't come home."

"Sockeye will to help her Mama, who's in a world of legal hurt. That's the other reason I had the monitor on her. Keep her from running so the Chief can arrest her. Now you're in trouble too, aiding her."

He looked away again, wishing he could jump out.

"Soon they will add attempted murder to the list of charges."

"Of who?" he asked without turning his head.

Papa smiled. "Watch and learn, boy." He drained the bottle.

Sonny sat back and closed his eyes. When he woke up, it was dark, and they were in front of the house. Exiting the car, he was immediately intercepted by Papa, who took hold of his arm and directed him towards the trunk.

He tried resisting, but his father held a tire iron in his face.

"Get in right now or I'll hit you so hard you may never wake up."

CHAPTER FORTY-THREE

The smell of something burning filled the cabin and Gabrielle rolled the window down to keep from gagging.

"We're almost there, just another mile," Billy said, glancing at the illuminated temperature gauge for the hundredth time. "I despise the odor of antifreeze. It makes me nauseous."

Her stomach churned, too. "Sorry about pushing your truck so hard on account of us," she said into the breeze.

"It's all good," he replied, patting the dash. "She's great around town, but too old for marathons like this. You can tell from the glaze on the headlights. She doesn't see in the dark well either."

"Instead of overheating, I just shut down." She looked out the window so he would not see her face.

"After what happened in Salem, I understand. I'm at a loss for words myself."

She ran her hand through her hair. "It's a wonder I'm not bleeding from my ears from all the internal voices screaming at me. I should have told Seth I wasn't leaving until I got answers about Olivia, and sure as hell should have rescued Sonny instead of leaving him to face his father." She sniffed the air. "The burning smell isn't the truck. It's my soul."

Billy rubbed the back of his neck. "We've gone over this for hours before heading home. The only play was to leave Sonny. If you intervened, there would have been a commotion. Dale would have called the police and you would be in jail."

She listened and envisioned it playing out as Billy described. "Yeah, and Dale would dial the Chief so I got a cell mate with lice."

"Look, I don't mean to pry, but why did you wait so long to—"

"Leave him?"

"Yeah. Sonny told me a little of what's been happening. After watching you handle that Seth character, I have a hard time believing you would put up with that garbage."

She sighed. "Did he also tell you about my status?"

He nodded. "I told Sonny, I would not judge. I can't say the same about the guy you're living with."

"If I could go back, I would have stuck it out living with my difficult aunt and become a teacher. After losing Olivia's father and my brother, Dale became a life preserver. Things happened really fast and before thinking it through, I was living with him. I thought I could smooth out Dale's rough edges that give people splinters. A partner does that — loves them enough to help them become a better version of themselves. But he wanted no part of that. Instead, he tried sanding away my heritage, which made me insecure and dependent. The weird thing was I was tough enough to take everything he dished out, but didn't want to see what it was doing to my children. It took years to confront the darkness and see it blink. I thought back to how my father raised me, encouraging me to read classics like Pedro Paramo to inspire my dreams. I realized I had given up on hope, not just for me but also for Olivia and Sonny." She looked at the young hero. "Enough about me. I admire how you're holding your family together."

Billy pulled on his beard. "Still can't believe my father is gone. The man was an ox and could bench press three hundred pounds. It made little sense that he would have a massive heart attack bringing in the groceries. Two years in, and my mom still can't accept the fact and having a hard time finding more than part-time work."

"And your sister?"

"Acts tough and keeps things bottled up like my mom." He smiled. "Sonny does his best to make her smile."

"You think I didn't know about that?"

"Good, then we can both tease him until he does something about it."

The headlights illuminated the white mailbox with the post leaning after getting struck by a snowplow. She sensed a kindred spirit with the combo wood and metal contraption. It was a symbol to remain upright, no matter the hit.

"Please pull over here, Billy," she whispered.

He slowed down, but kept coasting. "Here? Why?"

She gave him a look to clarify that it was not open for discussion.

The truck came to a stop at the center of the dark road. The aroma of antifreeze intermingled with exhaust fumes filled the cabin.

Opening the door, she looked at Billy in the harsh dome light and saw a man not afraid to put on a homemade cape to make a difference. Bending forward, she planted a kiss on his bearded cheek. "You have a giant heart, and I can't thank you enough. You're a role model for all of us."

He smiled for a second and then looked past her at the long driveway leading up to the house. "What are you going to do?"

"What I should have done a long time ago."

"Wait!" he said in a rush. "Why don't you come back to our house and get a little sleep? Like my mother says, nothing good happens after midnight. All your problems will still be there come morning but you won't have to deal with the shadows."

She shook her head. "Thank-you but putting things off is one of my biggest faults." She got out of the truck and closed the door.

"Promise me if you need help, you will call," he said through the open window.

"Of course. Besides my son, you're the only other superhero I know."

He smiled and put the truck in drive. "Too bad you need a landline to reach me."

She waved as the truck rolled away and then steadied herself by admiring the crescent moon and listening to the raucous crickets. The driveway began its steep ascent to the left of the mailbox. Filling her lungs, she took the first step, which is the most difficult in every journey.

Smelling pine made her reminisce about her first days here. Dale warned her in advance that he worked insane hours and the house was a disaster. She was ill prepared for the dirty windows with no curtains, mice droppings in the pantry and cobwebs in the oven. Dale watched her face after the tour and, holding her tight, said she could make it their home, which she did. Shortly after, they were blessed with Sonny. Now, walking up the driveway, it looked like a haunted house from the movies — dark and dangerous. The Catalina sat in its usual spot in front and positioned so Dale could monitor it.

After making her way up the sidewalk, she found the front door unlocked, which was a hoot since the key part of the evening ritual was making sure the doors and windows were secure.

Sneaking in, she noticed the living room was devoid of light and noise, which was odd, as Dale drifted off in the recliner with the television turned on. Recognizing the immense effort, he must have put into searching for Sonny, she assumed he called it a night. Billy was right. She should have left this for the morning. But motherly instinct overrode self-preservation. She needed to find her son.

The dark hall beckoned, and as she shuffled forward, the floorboards squeaked.

Sonny's door was closed, which was a good sign, she told herself. Turning the door handle, she looked in the room but it was too dark to see much and tiptoed in. *Get him up, run for the door and hide in the woods,* she thought, constructing the plan. Sonny could use his iPhone and call Billy for a ride.

She realized it was a trap when she touched a soft lump in the bed.

The overhead light came on, and Dale stood in the doorway. Unlike any other night, when he wore a ratty blue robe, its pockets stuffed with a fifth of whatever was on sale, Dale was waiting in jeans and a plaid shirt.

He smiled as if she had just returned from coffee with the ladies at church. "I knew you would come back tonight to fetch him."

"Where's my son?"

"You mean our son, unless that's a lie, too?" He walked away, and she followed him to the living room. He sat down in the recliner and picked up the tv remote.

Before she could control herself, she tore the remote from his hand. "Where the hell is Sonny?"

Dale looked at her and laughed. "There's the Spanish blood I love! I get a kick at how excited you can get, and miss how it used to be for me."

She thew the remote and hit him in the shoulder. "Where is he?"

"Why would you care? He said you ran after the monitor came off, but I knew he was fibbing." He cocked his head. "My question is, who gave you a ride?"

She kicked his shin. "Where is Sonny?"

He laughed like he did not feel it. "Go ahead and ignore the question. I'll find out and then talk with the Chief about accessory charges for whoever it was." He stood up. "So, you were looking for Sockeye in Salem? What a funny family we have. Sort of like, *Where's Waldo?*"

She looked past him at the dark hall. There was no way Sonny was sleeping in their bed or at his friend's house. There was only one other location and her stomach sunk. This was on her.

"You're going to tell me where our son is and then you're going to pack a bag and get out."

He screwed up his face. "You must be having a brain seizure because you're not making any sense. This is my house!"

"No! This is supposed to be a home for our family."

"You mean our son. Your boyfriend knocked you up and now Sockeye is running wild like I always said she would."

"You're a monster! You brought me here because you said you loved me… wanted to make a home … needed a real family."

"Sure, but you made it impossible."

"Why? Because you expected a mail-order bride that would cook and clean and…" she pointed at his crotch, "be on call and beat me if I didn't please you?"

He ignored her and walked to the hutch in the corner and opened a drawer. "I can't trust you."

"Your buddy might be blind, but the State Police will look into the abuse. They will listen and see the truth."

He rushed at her with a pair of handcuffs. She swung at his head, but he ducked and grabbed her around the waist and threw her on the floor, cuffed one hand, and then attached the other end to the arm of an oversized rocking chair.

He backed away and wiped sweat off his brow. "We both need some quality sleep, since tomorrow is a big day. You're going to be arrested for trying to kill me."

"What are you talking about?"

He walked back to the open drawer of the hutch and took out a long knife. "I will call 911 in the morning and tell them how you snuck in and tried stabbing me while I was sleeping."

"They won't believe you!"

"Of course, they will, especially after I cut myself. Too bad Sonny wasn't here to see the attempted murder, but he's doing time in the hole for being so disobedient and making me lose a day at work."

She could still smell antifreeze and exhaust. "Sonny isn't strong like Olivia. You will break him."

He took an iPhone out of his back pocket. "No issue. The video has gone viral. Sockeye can cure him."

She sat silent on the hard floor. Maybe she was wrong, thinking she could out-stare the darkness.

CHAPTER FORTY-FOUR

Olivia noticed how things looked different after midnight as nature asserts its primacy on dark, deserted roads. She eyed the passing trees which swayed in the light breeze, no doubt in a gab session about all the stupid things the two-legged animals did that day.

The country road curved to the right around an outcrop of granite. Legend had it that a hundred years ago, the construction crew ran out of dynamite on a Friday afternoon. Since it was payday and the boys were mighty thirsty, they beat a path around the problem to the McAllister Saloon.

Olivia wished she had a stick or two of dynamite for tonight's homecoming, but given what she uncovered yesterday morning, she was the gunpowder now. The long ride home had been quiet, except for a few pleasantries to break the growing awkwardness.

"My house is just up the road," she said, holding back the sigh of relief. The address was correct, but it had never been her house. Just Papa Dale's and Sonny's.

"I don't feel comfortable dropping you off without coming in and explaining why you let a stranger bring you home," Nancy replied.

Feel comfortable? She considered it an odd concept unless she was in Luke's arms, dancing in small circles or making out in the den. Now that was a lie, too. She looked at the kind woman. "You're not a stranger after all you've done for me. I'm sorry, but everyone will be asleep and I'm in trouble enough without causing a big scene." She took a deep breath. "It's too bad you have a long drive home."

The driver nodded. "I'll apologize again for the late start...but I'll come clean and share that I had to get someone to watch Mom. After bringing up three kids, I assumed I was through with all-nighters. But my mother has Alzheimer's and struggles at night. Thankfully, my sister came through in a pinch." She shot her a quick glance. "Getting old is not for the faint of heart. Don't worry about me none. If I get drowsy, I'll listen to talk radio, which is better than caffeine these days."

She laughed as Papa Dale liked to sit in the Catalina after dinner with a six-pack and listen to the radio, too. Mama teased him about it, because he would come in the house cursing about the deep state.

"I feel bad you drove me all the way home. The bus from Portsmouth would have been fine," she said, finally at ease and sorry it took so long.

"But you would have missed my fried chicken!"

"Yes, it was delicious."

Nancy shook her head. "But, I couldn't in good conscience put you on a bus after seeing that Luke guy hanging around the church all afternoon. You say he's a friend of yours, but there's something about him that gives me the creeps."

"I agree he's...." she hesitated and then almost laughed, "out of this world."

"Is he your boyfriend? He looks old for you."

Had they been together long enough to meet the definition? "More like a crush gone bad."

"Did he take you on this road trip?" Nancy asked, still probing.

She thought back to meeting Rezi. "No, and it's a long story... I stayed with someone that claimed to be a friend of my mother, but that turned out to be a lie."

The driver glanced at her again and, if not driving, it would have extended into a stare. "Okay, I'll stop the interrogation, but one more question. You look familiar and I can't place why. Have we met before," she smiled, "or have you been on tv?"

She tried to laugh, but it sounded forced. The good Samaritan would find the answer in the browser history on her phone. In the meantime, she changed topics.

"Do you believe in UFOs and aliens?" she asked.

Nancy sighed. "That's a weird pivot."

"Well, do you?"

"Who knows? If they're real, I hope they can save us from ourselves. Sometimes it seems like we're bent on bringing it all crashing down." She blessed herself. *"Father, forgive them, for they do not know what they are doing."*

But Seth, Luke and Rezi sure do, she thought. "Then why doesn't everyone just give up?"

The driver thought about it for a moment. "I believe in the butterfly effect, meaning the world is interconnected and you can make a big difference even by doing the smallest thing. No matter the frustration, I try to be God's hands and feet in this broken world. It makes me feel like I'm walking with Him when I help others. It's as simple or complicated as that, and often difficult. Some days it's all I can do to put one foot in front of another. But then I see the smiles on the faces of the people we help at the food pantry or during home visits where we strive to be a bridge over troubled waters. And if you talk with the people we help, you find they share what little they have with their neighbors. It gives you a new perspective on what heaven on earth would look like. One big home where everyone belongs."

If Firth were real, they would leave us alone after probing this lady, she thought. "We're here!" she said, trying to sound excited. "My house is the next one on the right."

Nancy slowed down and pulled into a short driveway.

Olivia eyed the Nelson ranch, which had been dark since Mrs. entered a nursing home last year.

"Is anyone home? I don't see any lights on," Nancy said in that motherly voice again.

"That's because my mom believes Jesse James owns the utility company." She leaned over and gave the kind woman a tight hug. "Words cannot express how grateful I am for everything."

Nancy touched her arm. "After raising three daughters, I have radar for sniffing out trouble. Regardless of the details, I wouldn't leave my sixteen-year-old daughter stranded a couple hundred miles from home. I will keep you in my prayers."

"I'll take all you have," she replied.

Before tears flowed, she left the car and waited for the taillights to vanish before returning to the road. The chill in the air made her question if summer would ever come.

A half mile later, she walked up the long driveway and stood looking at the house she grew up in. It looked as dark as the Nelson's, but the insides were hotter than hell. In front sat the Catalina with its cramped trunk. It was where she might end up if things unraveled.

Willing herself forward, the blood seemed to accumulate in her legs, resulting in each step feeling heavy and causing a sensation of lightheadedness. She slipped in the front door and steeled herself as the darkness swallowed her. Mama often recounted the tale of Jonah trapped in the whale's belly, and bet he experienced a similar sensation — a feeling devoid of sight and sound, except for the rhythmic thumping of the heart. The intensity froze her in place, which was beyond dangerous. Her thoughts went into overdrive, urging her to sneak into Sonny's room. She would be careful waking him, so he did not scream, assuming she was a ghost. Then they would plan for the morning.

Sweat pooled on her forehead as she tip-toed across the living room. Half-way to the hall, she heard movement in the room's corner and braced, waiting for the whale to vomit her out onto the front lawn. The trunk would be a hamster cage minus the cozy shavings.

"Who's there?" The question came not from a drunken, lustful man, but from the one voice she craved.

"Mama?" she asked in a whisper.

A muffled cry rose in response, and she rushed to the corner of the room and fell to her knees. Her mother pulled her in and their tears came in great waves. When the cries became too loud, they buried their heads in each other's hair.

After the tears subsided, Mama touched the gold earring in her ear and she thought back to receiving it moments before Rezi whisked her away.

"My dear, sweet girl. All of this is on me. I'll never forgive myself," her mother whispered.

"Don't say that! It's not true!"

"It is because I've been afraid since I crossed the border. But when you jumped off the bridge, that person died. I knew God took pity on me when I saw you on the video healing people."

She nodded her head as the memories of everything that had happened since leaving Maine flooded her mind. It was too much to take in. "I thought I lost you, too. They told me you died in a car accident!" Her leg cramped, and she adjusted her position. "Why are you out here sleeping on the floor?"

"Because Dale cuffed me to the rocking chair."

"What?" She crawled around her mother and found the cold metal curled around the chair baluster. Without considering the consequences, she started tugging on the wooden dowel. She could not make the disabled walk or the blind see, but snapping an oversized popsicle stick should not be a problem.

Her mother pulled her hand away. "I've already tried that. You're going to wake him up! Then he will chain you up too, or something worse."

She sat back. "I'll wake up Sonny. He can break it in a second."

Mama sighed. "He's locked in the trunk."

Her stomach dropped. She half listened to Mr. Reese ramble on and on about WWII in history class, and remembered him talking about the danger of going behind enemy lines.

"Maybe I should hide until Papa goes to work?"

"No, patience has gotten me into this mess. The car keys are in the kitchen. Get Sonny out of the trunk and have him get hold of Billy. Maybe the State Police can help."

The image of Lori at the gas station crossed her mind. She was of little help and now they depended on her brother? "Why Billy?" she asked.

"No time to explain. He's been a lifesaver."

New tears came. "I'm not leaving you here. He will kill you before I can get help."

Her mother let out a low growl. "You heard me! Now get going!"

Olivia pulled herself to her feet and tip-toed to the kitchen. Papa Dale left the keys on the counter next to the coffeemaker. Whenever he forgot, hell would follow.

Fortunately, the steel ring which held the idols in Papa's life — the keys to the Catalina and the store sat on the counter close to Mr. Coffee. The injured bird flashed in her mind as she grabbed the keys and headed for the living room. Although she considered it dead, Seth showed her that not everything was as dire as it looks. Turning around, she headed straight for the utensil drawer. There, way in the back, she felt the weapon reserved for Thanksgiving and Christmas.

"Trust my heart," she whispered.

"Do you have the keys?" Mama asked when she returned.

"Yeah."

"Then get out of here!"

She crouched down next to her. "Not without you," and held the electric knife in front of her face.

Mama looked unimpressed. "Are you kidding me? It will make too much noise. Now leave!"

She ignored the order and plugged in the knife. The cord barely reached the chair. "The blade is sharp. I'll only need a few seconds."

Her mother went silent for a moment. "I'll count to ten and then you have to run."

"And when it works?"

"I'll hold Dale off until you get Sonny out of the trunk."

But where would they hide? A golden idea struck. "If we get separated, let's meet at the treehouse."

Mama nodded, and they hugged for a long moment.

"Dear God, help us!" her mother whispered and then leaned back and raised her hand to give her daughter a clear view of the baluster.

The knife made a horrible, jarring noise when she turned it on. It seemed like the knife was barely making a mark on the wood, but with a little more force, the teeth of the blade finally caught.

Mama shook her after counting to ten, but she kept at it. The wood slowly surrendered, and using her free hand, she shook the wooden dowel and it finally snapped.

The sound of yelling filled the house. She left the knife on to distract and buy time. Mama helped her to her feet and pushed her toward the front door.

The car was only a hundred feet away, but it gave the sensation of being trapped in one of those dreadful nightmares where a monstrous creature is approaching and your feet are as heavy as stone. When she reached the Catalina's trunk, she dropped the keys and panic set in. Her eyes scanned the cracked pavement for too many seconds before finding them. When she glanced toward the house, the front lights were on and Mama was on the top stair, holding the door shut.

Her trembling fingers put the key in the lock. The trunk lid popped open and revealed Sonny lying curled in a fetal position. His eyes lit up with a sense of warmth and acceptance, as if he believed he had found his place in heaven.

"Liv?" he asked.

"Hurry-up-we-have-to-run!" she replied in one word.

Sonny held up his hands, which were duct taped together. She glanced at his feet, hoping they were not tied, too. Luckily, the feet were shoeless but free.

She helped Sonny out of the tomb and heard Mama screaming. The words were unintelligible, but sounded like prey wailing for mercy.

Without time to free Sonny's duct-taped hands, she grabbed his arm and went to the car's front. She discovered her mother had retreated from the front stairs to a small tree planted in a new garden. It was her last stand, and she threw rock after rock at Papa Dale. He dodged all of them and was only a few feet away from reaching her when one missile connected with his forehead and knocked him to the ground.

"Mama!" she yelled at the top of her lungs. Her mother glanced over at her and Sonny. She pointed toward the woods and the three of them began running.

Olivia saw the tips of the tall pines swaying in the breeze as they approached. She could hear them whispering, "Hurry!"

CHAPTER FORTY-FIVE

As they ran toward the woods with the dangling handcuff whipping her leg, Gabrielle noticed Sonny's taped hands, a clear sign Dale's abusive tactics were escalating. She slowed her pace so her children could get a good lead. Dale sucked at running, but if anger made him a world-class sprinter, let her be the finish line.

Her right foot tripped on something and she went airborne before landing in the dewy grass. Seconds later, she was back on her feet and ignoring the pain, continued the race.

As they neared the woods, she worried how they would locate the narrow path in the darkness. If they missed it, they would have a nasty time pushing through a deep hedge of picker bushes. In the dim light of a crescent moon, she saw Olivia and Sonny vanish and aimed for the same entry point. Moments later, she saw the thin opening in the picker bushes and barreled into the darkness.

Some places are never forgotten, she thought as she slowed to a walk. Even now, she remembered every twist and turn when she walked a mile to school. It was the same with her children. They grew up in these woods, picking wild blueberries, playing hide and seek, building forts. Sonny's crown jewel was the treehouse he constructed a few years ago with pallets from the store. He started it after his buddies went on a camping adventure with their fathers. Dale wanted no part of the outing and told his son he had a bad back and the men organizing it "should grow the hell up." Sonny channeled the frustration into the treehouse project and kept it a secret. Then one Sunday afternoon, he led them out to see it. Dale walked around the structure, smiling, but also pointing out areas where things could have been done better. Sonny was okay with the feedback until Dale threatened to charge him for the pallets.

She slowed her gait to a crawl not to trip in the dark. As the trail curved around a large oak, she almost ran into Olivia and Sonny, who were waiting for her. She threw her arms around her son and felt surprised when he hugged her back, his hands now free. Olivia embraced them both.

The reunion was short-lived.

"Now what?" Olivia asked.

She wiped sweat from her brow and continued working on catching her breath. "Sonny, do you… have your phone?"

He winced. "No. It's back in the trunk."

Olivia slapped her arm as the mosquitoes saw an early breakfast. "Let's figure it out at the treehouse."

They set out for the quarter mile hike and reached a short hill. At the top sat the treehouse, which was a misnomer as it was more of a lean-to which sat on the ground between two maple trees. It had three walls and pine branches for the roof.

Sonny stopped and spun around. "Don't take another step!"

"What's the matter?" Olivia asked.

"Some jerks wanted to burn it down last year, so I booby-trapped the area. Follow me."

He led them off the path and through thick brush until they reached the edge of the platform. Sonny jumped up first, followed by Olivia.

Her daughter extended her hand and helped her up.

"How are we going to get that off you?" Olivia asked, pointing at the handcuff.

"That's a problem for later. Right now, we'll wait until morning and figure out our next steps."

"But Papa knows about this place. What if he comes?" Sonny asked.

She laughed. "Your father complains about the distance from the bedroom to the kitchen. I don't see him walking a mile in the dark."

"No, he'll call the Chief instead," Olivia countered. "I always wondered what he has on him because he jumps whenever Papa Dale asks."

Sonny went to the corner and opened a plastic storage container. Inside were blankets, and he gave each of them one. They wrapped themselves up and sat down facing the path.

"About that video," she said, eyeing her daughter, "tell me about the healings."

"It's a long story, but turned out to be a sick fantasy."

Sonny chuckled. "Well, you've had enough practice. Remember when you wanted to stay home from school and you ran the thermometer under hot water?"

Olivia laughed.

"And you think your Mama didn't know?" she chimed in. "Give me a break! The thermometer read a hundred and ten degrees. You would have been dead with a fever like that!"

"Then why did you let me stay home?"

"Because I knew about the bully on the bus. The next day, you marched out and confronted her. I should have taken your lead sooner."

Sonny cleared his throat. "No, I should have. We've been living a nightmare for too long." He touched Olivia's arm. "I'm sorry for everything you've gone through. I should have been a better brother."

"I've always loved you, even though you hog all the hot water," Olivia replied.

They hugged for a long moment.

Exhaustion and fear extinguished the conversation, and they listened to the crickets and swatted mosquitoes every few minutes. The extremes of anxiety and monotony pulled on her eyes and she leaned against the sidewall. She felt herself drifting away.

Suddenly, someone shook her. Opening her eyes, she found Sonny's face looking like it did when he used to wake her up in the middle of the night to check under his bed for monsters. Olivia was behind him, pacing.

"Mama! Someone is coming!" Sonny whispered.

She threw the blanket off and jumped up, feeling stiff. The sky looked pink, the air silent, the path empty.

"We're sitting ducks if we stay here," she said to her son. "We should take off through the woods! Find somewhere else to hide."

Sonny shook his head. "Behind this is wetland, and it's pretty muddy."

"But he wouldn't chase us through that!"

"How do we know he isn't making noise trying to make us leave so he can jump us?" Olivia added a bit too loud.

"Good point Sockeye!" a familiar voice boomed as Dale appeared on the path. He was wearing his day off getup; jeans and a gray sweatshirt. In his right hand was a baseball bat.

Motherly instinct took over, and she stepped forward and kept her handcuffed hand behind her back.

"You can turn around and go back to hell," she said.

Dale laughed. "You mean heaven. Your American dream ends here and I find it fitting. You're back in the wilderness with wild animals."

Olivia responded, "You're the one that's lost and should be deported."

Dale nodded. "I expect that coming from you, Sockeye. I mean.... you must be itching to get south of the border and spawn. Don't worry, the boys will line up for you." He took a few steps closer. "Come on, Sonny, let's get home. All is forgiven. We can have a big breakfast and wait for the Chief."

"No Papa. I'm staying here with Mama and Liv."

Dale pointed the bat at him. "Listen to me good, boy. Your Mama is in a heap of trouble. After last night, the Chief will add attempted murder."

"This is the end of your lies!" she yelled back.

Dale pointed at the ugly gash on his head. "You tried killing me with a rock. I have the murder weapon on the kitchen table for the Chief. Rest assured, if he refuses to punish you, I will."

"A friend told me it was time to man up," Sonny said, stepping to the edge of the platform. "I won't let you touch her!"

Dale let out a bloodcurdling yell and rushed forward, and she pushed her son away so she could face the fury. Dale raised his bat like her head was a baseball destined for the next town. She put her arms up, bracing for the bone crushing impact, when he suddenly vanished.

The air fell silent for a second, followed by a loud scream.

She looked over the edge of the platform. Dale stood upright in a hole a good six feet deep. His head and shoulders were movable, but everything south wedged into the hole. Broken pine branches outlined the pit.

Sonny came alongside. "This is the trap I warned you about," he said to her in a low voice.

"Hurry and get me the hell out of here!" Dale screamed. He thrashed about, but remained locked in place.

Sonny kneeled down. "First, promise you won't beat them."

Dale moaned. "I'm hurt and you're negotiating with me? What the hell is wrong with you?"

"I mean it Papa. Promise me you won't hurt Mama or Liv," Sonny repeated.

"I promise you have nothing to worry about. You're my blood. But your scheming mother deserves to be locked up, and I don't give a damn about the other one."

Sonny hung his head momentarily and then stood up. Tears streamed down his cheeks as he retreated to the rear of the platform.

"Okay, that's it! I'm calling 911 and they will arrest all of you!" Dale yelled.

Olivia took her turn and kneeled down. "That would be a neat trick to watch seeing how you're wedged in like that! I could make the call for you but—" She smacked her head. "I don't have a phone."

"Why you little insolent…." He looked at her and laughed. "Then do your magic trick Sockeye and heal me!"

Olivia shook her head. "That's impossible, because I can't cure a diseased soul," she replied and stood up and joined her brother.

Gabrielle went over to them. "Go back to the house and pack your things." She looked at her son and whispered, "Call Billy and tell him we need a ride."

"We're not leaving without you!" Olivia said.

"I won't be far behind. Now go!"

Sonny nodded and pointed at his sister. "Follow me so you don't fall into the other holes."

As they made their way into the brush, Dale called after his son. "Sonny, don't leave me like this!"

Once they were out of sight and the air fell silent, she sat down and studied the man she once loved, regardless of his worthiness.

"I know what you're thinking! Leave me here and make it appear like an accident. But I know you. The guilt would be unbearable," Dale said like he was trying to convince himself.

"You threatened my children. I'll have no trouble sleeping."

"And one of them is mine and the other I raised. I'm not the monster you make me out to be. I'm a hard-working Christian man that makes mistakes."

"That may be true. When I pick out your tombstone, it will say: he loved the Lord, but no one else."

"Hate me all you want, but you owe me!"

"Owe you?" She had a flashback of lying in bed with him after arriving in Maine. Rain pelted the windows and the only defense against the cold which infiltrated every nook and cranny was spooning with the man that promised to take care of her and Olivia. She noticed the hundred things he took for granted: hot water, stocked shelves, clean clothes, good health. But in those first days, she also saw micro flashes of something darker in the way he treated people he came in contact with: clerks, servers, janitors. As time passed, she questioned whether she was sleeping with just another flawed human or a snake that no matter how often sheds its skin, is still a snake.

She watched his face. "When we first met, you said you wanted me; after I moved up here, you said you needed me. But never in all the years we've been together did you ever whisper you loved me."

He gave her an expression of frustration and asked, "Do you have dementia? We've been through all this! Sheila took a knife to my heart the night before our wedding, when she ran away with my best man. I was devastated and heartbroken.

"But I'm not Shiela! After giving you everything I have, you still can't say it."

"If I say I love you now, they will be empty words." He let out a long moan. "I think I have a broken foot."

The admission gave her pause as she recalled many times when he put on his best clothes for work and doused himself in cologne. "When was the last time you saw her?"

"That's a stupid question. She lives a hundred miles away in Bangor."

"Funny you know where. You still didn't answer the question."

He looked away and winced. "My tenth high school reunion."

The only one he attended and wouldn't let me come. She stood up. "Tell me the truth."

"Okay, I'll come clean because it's no big deal. Ned stays in touch with Sheila and the three of us had lunch last year. She's going through an ugly divorce. But you're the only one that matters to me. Get me out of here and I'll show you."

"How? By planting me in this hole?"

He closed his eyes like he did not trust his poker face. "You just have to trust me."

"If I follow my heart, I should fill in this hole because I know what happens if you get out." She stared at the top of his head and the thick hair that he combed so meticulously.

"Please help me! Let's go home and we can talk things over," he pleaded.

She stood up and picked up the baseball bat. "I saw a quote only strong women are remembered in history. I want to join that club."

"What does that mean? Bash my brains in with the bat?"

"No, use it as kindle wood to start a fire." She walked over and took a half dozen pine branches off the roof, their needles deep orange.

"You're going to cremate me?" Dale asked, in a high-pitched voice she did not recognize.

She placed the first branch over his head. "You always had an active imagination, although Sonny said some kids wanted to burn this place down. No, I would never put you out of your misery like that.... it's much too quick. I just want to make sure you don't catch a sunburn or have wild critters nibbling on your head."

"I'm begging you, Gabrielle! Please don't do this! I'll give you anything you want!"

"Including a path to citizenship and adopting Olivia?"

He did not respond.

"No worries, as I don't want that either." She placed a couple more branches over the hole. "We should reflect what brought us here. I was going to start with Atlantic City, but I believe it goes much further back than that. We should explore your childhood and all the cruel habits you picked up, but you won't because I'm just one of those dumb illegals that only knows how to pick fruit and vegetables so this country can eat. I guess you will have to figure it all out by yourself. But if you want my honest opinion, you should have gotten a dog if you were so lonely back in Atlantic City." She thought for a moment. "Strike that. No dog deserves you."

"But you don't understand. I'm claustrophobic! You can't leave me in this hole."

"That's priceless." She leaned over and noticed how his head covered in orange needles communicated the same thing — they were both dead. "Be brave and face your fears like Olivia, Sonny, and I did in the trunk. I'm also hoping you had a big cup of coffee before coming to hunt us down. You'll also learn how hard it is to deny a full bladder."

CHAPTER FORTY-SIX

Opposite the race into the dark woods and straining to find the path, Gabrielle walked back to the house, bathed in soft morning light. To her surprise, Olivia and Sonny were waiting next to the Catalina with the trunk open like a lid of a coffin.

Even before she got there, she could read the crucial question on their faces.

"Mama, what did you do?" Olivia asked, looking at the bat she was holding.

"Do you think I'm the type who believes in an eye for an eye? If so, Papa Dale would have been six feet under many moons ago."

"What are you going to do with him?" Sonny asked as a follow-up.

She held up the bat. After a few beers, Dale would sometimes take a pail of river rocks and stand in the field and take batting practice. He hollered every time a stone made it to the woods. The bat had countless dings, but free of blood.

"Papa Dale is mulling over his mistakes, and that will take quite a while, I'm afraid." She threw the bat in the car's trunk and looked at the small prison. "Funny the things you discover after so many years. Seems he doesn't like confined spaces." She glanced at her son. "Did you call Billy?"

"Yeah, he's on his way." He pointed at her wrist. "He said he can get that off you in no time."

"Whatever. If not, it's my new charm bracelet." She pointed at the house. "Now let's hurry and pack."

The front lawn was littered with the rocks she threw. As she walked into the house, her gaze fell upon the broken chair, the electric knife, and an empty fifth of whiskey in the recliner. *This time, the liquid courage did him in.* She led her children down the hall to their bedrooms and continued on to hers. Standing in the doorway, she eyed the queen-sized bed: the place where they made love, war and spent most of their relationship in the spaces in between. Her grandfather told her stories about relatives in WWI. He enjoyed watching her eyes bulge when he described the horror of trench warfare; rats, disease, and mustard gas. It felt like a kindred world.

She retrieved the trash bag under the bed, the one that felt like a jilted lover. She shuffled over to Dale's bureau, a sanctuary where she stocked his ironed golf shirts, underwear and matched socks. He gave her access to the lower four drawers but prohibited her from the top one, which contained personal items. The way the order came down with the vein in his neck protruding, she thought it held remnants from the tree of life. No serpent ever tempted her to open it, but a nine-year-old Girl Scout that knocked on the door selling cookies did. She went searching for a couple dollars to surprise Dale with a box and found a five-dollar bill in the top drawer. After she told him, her bruised arm had more stripes than his favorite Samoas cookie.

She opened the top drawer much too fast and felt adrenaline coursing through her veins. The black wallet sat in plain sight. She experienced momentary disappointment when she discovered that the money sleeve only held three twenties and five singles, but the emotion vanished as she touched the ATM card. Dale had the impression that she was illiterate, but she memorized his PIN number years ago and had knowledge of the checking account's average balance of three thousand dollars. The wallet also held a gold Mastercard. From watching enough crime shows, she knew that using either could be tracked, so she planned to empty the bank account and use the Mastercard for needed supplies before heading south.

She continued rifling through the contents of the drawer. Most of it was junk; paper clips, rubber bands, but she found a watch and a couple of gold chains she could hawk. Underneath the mess, there was a receipt from last month for Home Away Motel. She remembered Dale telling her he had to work all night on a new display.

"He's all yours, Sheila!" she whispered.

Olivia and Sonny wandered into the room.

"Are you all packed?" she asked, shutting the drawer.

"Yeah. Where are we headed?" Olivia gushed.

"South of the border." She shot them both a smile. "It's time you met your grandfather. I'll be a couple more minutes. Meet me out front."

She took a few more shirts out of the closet and stuffed them in the trash bag along with some toiletries. Then she headed to the kitchen, retrieved the hidden thousand dollars, along with a pack of matches. After one last glance around the kitchen, she exited through the back door to the small utility shed. After stepping over the lawnmower, she retrieved the five-gallon gas can. Luckily, it was half full. The sun was over the pines when she came around the house and walked over to the Catalina.

Dale said the gas can had a self-sealing spout but in the first few years mowing the lawn she ruined many a t-shirt spilling the gas. The only way to outmaneuver the spout was through patience. She extended the plastic hose and poured a quarter of the container in the trunk, soaking the bat. Next, she opened the driver's door and poured gas in the front and back seats and popped the hood and made sure the V8 engine had a good drink too. After allocating every drop, she threw the spent container in the trunk.

When she turned around, Sonny and Olivia were standing a few feet away, watching her.

"You can't do this, Mama!" Sonny said, shaking his head. "Someone will call it in, and we'll get caught!"

"That's fine with me. Just trying to build my rap sheet." As she took the matches out of her pocket, she heard a noise behind her and saw a large white van coming up the driveway fast.

"Does Billy have a van?" she asked.

"Not that I know of," Sonny replied watching.

The vehicle veered around the last pothole and stopped fifty feet away. A second later, a thin woman emerged from the passenger side, while the rear doors opened and a half-dozen men wearing black hoodies emerged.

She looked again at the woman and though she did not recognize the black hair, the porcelain face said enough and she rushed forward, wishing she had the bat. Two men in black hoodies stopped her from reaching the traitor. Sonny jumped to help, but four others intervened.

"You're just in time. Why don't you get in my car so I can roast you with the other garbage I'm burning this morning," she yelled.

Rezi looked unfazed and walked over to her daughter.

Olivia shook her head. "This is like a bad dream. How do you and Luke keep finding me?"

Rezi smiled like she would never figure it out.

Olivia glanced at her mother. "I don't have a phone that anyone can track or a pocketbook where someone could hide an air tag." Her face suddenly darkened. "Wait, a minute! Seth gave me this!" She pulled the turquoise necklace off and threw it on the ground.

Rezi responded with that funny laugh of hers. "You think we have a homing device on a piece of costume jewelry? C'mon Olivia! After everything we've been through, how can you continue denying them? Trust us."

"Trust liars?" Olivia replied.

Gabrielle broke away from the men holding her. "I asked for your help and you kidnapped my daughter and tried to brainwash her."

Rezi pointed at her chest like she was addressing her heart. "Remember, you were the one that gave her to me because you were desperate and afraid. Let me assure you this is no Stockholm syndrome, where we took Olivia for some evil plan and she developed a tie with us." She laughed. "The fact is, Firth has always been watching Olivia."

"Who the hell is Firth?" she asked.

"Aliens," Olivia chimed in.

"I don't understand."

Rezi sighed. "Remember that summer day about fourteen years ago when the man you live with went on a fishing trip with his buddies? After lunch, you brought two-year-old Olivia into the backyard to play in the sandbox. It was a little after noon, and you fell asleep for a moment. When you looked up, your little girl was sitting fifty yards away under the shade of a white birch. After you ran and scooped her up, you noticed it was three o'clock. It haunted you for years. If you remember that, I can tell you about the night your daughter was conceived. It was during the spring planting. You and Luis made such a handsome couple."

Gabrielle experienced the sensation of the air leaving her lungs, making it difficult to breathe. "You're making this up!" she said, too afraid to confirm the incident. She remembered the sandbox scare and believed she had fallen into an exhausted sleep but never understood how much time elapsed. She worried for years about what could have happened to her daughter.

Rezi nodded and looked at Olivia. "Those chilly nights in the trunk when you slept so well…. I bet if you talk with your brother, you will find he didn't sleep a wink. Do you think that was by accident, too?"

"What do you want?" Sonny asked.

"Wrong question! The correct one is, what can your sister do to help the cause?" She continued staring at Olivia. "You heard Seth fill in the blanks."

Olivia laughed. "Yeah, with lies. I discovered the truth about Luke faking blindness and—"

"I'll admit we used poor practices to speed up acceptance, but it doesn't change the core message," Rezi interrupted. "We launched the plan, and rejection is not an option. Firth promised to begin with a carrot by enabling people like you to act as a conduit for showcasing what we can achieve if we cooperate. But if that doesn't work, they will use the stick instead... and it will get ugly fast. Firth will not let our poor decisions impact their world."

The truck came screaming up the driveway, and it took Rezi and her entourage by surprise.

The truck came to a stop in front of the van. Billy jumped out and Lori followed.

"Is there a problem here, Sonny?" Billy asked, looking at all the hooded men.

"Not now," Sonny replied admiring the hulk, and smiling at Lori.

"Well, get your bags. Time is wasting."

Rezi held up her hand. "We're not done here. Olivia, you need to come with us."

"No way!" Olivia replied, and took her mother's hand.

Gabrielle led her daughter over to the trunk of the Catalina and then lit a match and threw it in the trunk. The car burst into flames.

Billy let out a whistle. "I didn't see that coming."

She walked over to Rezi and got in her face. "Bother my little girl again, and I'll take a match to you next."

CHAPTER FORTY-SEVEN

The small ranch sat on the edge of town, under the shade of a large Montezuma bald cypress. From a distance, the bright yellow home with the clay roof tiles looked the same as it did every night in her dreams. But everything surrounding it moved on — or "evolved" as people in the States bragged. The dirt road that once memorialized footprints and tire marks from every variety of bicycles, scooters, and trucks and deposited dust which her mother battled every day was now paved. A streetlight adorned the corner, the spot where Luis used to hide in the shadows and kiss her as they made plans for the future.

"How much further is it, Mama?" Sonny moaned. She glanced back at her son and daughter, who were struggling to keep up. They looked hot, hungry, and exhausted. The trip had been long, and she expected the burden would lighten as the distance from Maine increased. Instead, fresh worries emerged about getting into Mexico without documentation, but the bus sailed through without incident to the station. She barely walked a hundred steps before Carlos eyed her and she pretended not to recognize the porter, a rude skill she picked up from Dale. The skinny kid from high school had filled out nicely. Once upon a time, he had a crush on her and would run errands for her mother, hoping she would put in a good word. Now, as she stood on the street that was the dividing line between the old and new world, she wished she had said hello. Perhaps Carlos could have been a bridge from the past to the present. Instead, she stood looking at her children, wanting to tell them she only had enough courage to get them to this point and not a step further.

She looked once more at the homestead, sensing the emotions of being an orphan.

"Gabrielle…you're my oldest…and supposed to set an example for Roberto! I'm glad the cancer took your mother — God rest her soul… because this would have broken her worse than it does me." She could not tell if Papa's voice was breaking or the phone connection was spotty.

Tears blurred her vision, and the ache was so bad in her chest she could not reply.

"I work and work and work some more … in too many farms with too little respect… to support my family," he continued with his voice rising. *"My hands ache so badly I can't make a fist anymore… and my back feels like I have broken wings… all to harvest fruits and vegetables. It's honest work that no one appreciates. Like we talked, I did not want you following this wandering life."*

"There's no shame in hard work. If it was good enough for you, why not me?"

"For your brother, perhaps, but you had a different calling! After all the English lessons I paid for, you could have been a teacher. You speak better than the Americans that I work for. But Luis! He was the snake in Eden, whispering words in your head and Roberto's. Now my son is dead! I hope he rots in hell."

She thought of the baby growing inside her, but how could she tell him he would be a grandfather under these circumstances? *"We just wanted to make some good money in New York. You always said what you make in six months in the States would take three years to earn at home."*

"Which would have been fine if you stayed on the farm! But you listened to that devil that is tired of hard work and took off for the city."

"But… I love Luis!" she said, not able to put him in the past tense.

"What do you know about love? The way he leered at you made my blood boil! Reminded me of a hungry, rabid dog in heat. He only wanted to ravish—"

"He didn't take advantage of me, Papa!" she interrupted as the party at the lake flashed in her mind. *The others had left, and they were all alone under the stars. Time stood still as they got lost in one another.*

"Now your brother is gone and you're thousand miles away from home. Happy?"

She filled her lungs with a deep breath. Poor Roberto, hungry for a better life but thought he deserved it yesterday. They no sooner got to New York when his new friends sold him on the promise of easy money by boosting a few cars. Luis tried to stop him the night he picked the wrong neighborhood, and someone gunned them down. The truth would kill Papa.

"I just want to come home," she cried, rubbing her belly that held all she had left.

"Well, you can't! Not now or ever! You took my son away, and the penalty is you will share my grief. You don't have a home or a father anymore!"

Even after all these years, the memory took her breath away, and she bent over and put her hands on her knees. But this time, she heard her mother whisper: *"unless a grain of wheat falls into the earth and dies, it remains alone; but if it dies, it bears much fruit."* She took a deep breath and stood up and looked at her children. *Tears watered my secret seeds, and we grew resilient.*

Olivia read her face, and grabbing her hand, pulled her forward. They were still a respectful distance away when the front door opened and a bald, stocky man wearing a white t-shirt and jeans came hurrying out.

Gabrielle braked and waited for the coming storm.

Her father looked shorter than she remembered, but just as tanned, and moving so fast his feet were trying to keep up

"Is that him?" Sonny asked, coming alongside.

She nodded. "Just be quiet and let me do the talking." She thought if things went bad, maybe Carlos would find them a place to stay for a while. She had enough money.

As he got closer, the speed walk turned into a sprint and she feared the charging bull. Gabrielle tried to get a look at his dark eyes despite remembering they were like the ever-changing weather in Maine.

She took a few steps forward and opened her mouth to hurry through the words she rehearsed. But as she feared, emotion overwhelmed her. All she could do was cry from a wound so deep that it could never be repaired.

Her father came at her so fast, she thought he might tackle her and throw her on the bus north. But at the last moment, she noticed his quivering lips. Before she could process it, he picked her up like he used to when he came home after months of being away in the fields. When her feet touched the ground, he held her tight and his chest heaved as he cried.

A long moment passed before he let her go and when he did, he fell to her feet. "My dear daughter…. my lovely …. beautiful little girl…. I have prayed for this day for what seems like an eternity. The Lord can summon me home now, as I know you are safe."

She experienced a release in her gut, a tightness that lasted too many years. "I love you so much Papa and missed you!" she cried and pulled him up and they embraced again.

After a long moment, Papa stepped back and, wiping his eyes, turned to Olivia and Sonny. They both looked uncomfortable watching the emotional reunion.

"And what angels are these?" the old man asked.

"Papa, this is Olivia and Dale Junior, though we call him Sonny," Gabrielle replied, beaming.

Before they could say hello, he pulled them both in and kissed their cheeks. "Call me Abuelo!" He kissed them again and then backed away. "Look at me! An old fool visiting with my daughter and grandchildren in the middle of the street! Come inside quick!"

He guided them inside the house, leading them to a cozy living room furnished with a couch and recliner. "Please sit and relax while I get you something to drink."

Sonny and Olivia did not need to be asked twice and collapsed on the couch.

Gabrielle felt an overpowering surge of memories as she followed her father into the kitchen. Her father opened the refrigerator. "What do the children like? I have Coke and lemonade." He shot her a worried glance. "Would they rather have tea or coffee?"

"Coke is fine," she replied. She watched him take out a few cans and noticed his face had a red glow and he was breathing hard. She took the beverages out of his hand and put them on the counter.

"Papa, I'll never be able to say sorry enough for what happened. You were right. I should have talked with you before we left for New York." She took a deep breath. "Look, I don't deserve to be your daughter, and wouldn't have come if we had anywhere else to go."

Her father pulled her in for another embrace and held her tight. "Regret is a worm worse than the grave. Whatever guilt you experience pales compared to mine. When Roberto died, I said things, horrible things that I will always regret."

The secret of how he died stealing cars pulled at her heart. "Then why didn't you search for me?" she asked, pulling away.

"I did and traveled to Atlantic City searching for you after I heard you were there. I found the hotel, but they didn't know where you headed after having the baby." He rubbed the heavy bags under his eyes. "I didn't know you were with child! Why didn't you call me?"

"I've been asking myself the same question all the way here. Time doesn't heal all wounds, but I should have recognized the pain you were going through and my reaction only made things more difficult. When we lost Roberto and Luis, a piece of me died. I wanted to just fade away, and I did for a long time." She looked toward the family room. "But I still have a piece of Luis with Olivia. I also see some of Roberto... like his courage."

He nodded. "A true blessing. And your boy?"

"Sonny is a gift from God, but his father fits your saying about regret being worse than the grave. It's a complicated story and part of the reason you never heard from me."

"I want to hear the whole thing." He hurried over to the other side of the kitchen and picked up the phone.

"Who are you calling?"

"The entire family! We're going to have a fiesta tomorrow night."

"C'mon Papa. Everyone will point their fingers about celebrating the prodigal daughter that squandered everything!"

Papa stopped dialing and smiled. "Don't you remember how the parable ends? *But we had to celebrate and be glad, because this brother of yours was dead and is alive again, he was lost and is found.*" He let out a laugh. "But instead of a fatted calf, we're going to roast a pig!"

CHAPTER FORTY-EIGHT

Olivia made a beeline for the couch and collapsed on the soft leather.

Mama followed and sat down next to her. "I haven't partied like that in twenty years! My feet are killing me from dancing. I must be getting old, because the music was way too loud. My ears are ringing."

"Abuelo is a hoot. I thought I was a princess with the way he introduced me to everyone," she responded.

"Beats being called Sockeye!"

She shrugged. "I told him how Papa Dale called me that, and he made me see things differently."

"How? I've been trying for years and you wouldn't listen."

"He likes to fish and told me all about the lifecycle of sockeye salmon. The young spend time in rivers and lakes before migrating to the ocean. Then a few years later they head back to freshwater to spawn—"

"Yeah, like Dale teased." Mama said, interrupting.

She nodded. "But I didn't know they stop eating once they enter freshwater and rely on their energy stores to travel hundreds of miles fighting to make it back where they were born. Only one out of a thousand make it home to spawn, but none of them get lost. It's like they follow a beacon home. Afterwards, they have no energy to return to the ocean and die. Bears, wolves, and eagles eat them or they decompose and add nutrients to the land and water."

"That's my father ... the walking encyclopedia," Mama laughed.

"I feel like we've been on a long journey, too," she added. Seth elbowed his way into her mind, explaining how Firth was persevering because they shared this small oasis with us. She wanted to discard the crazy idea, but heard Abuelo explaining how during the marathon home, sockeye turn from silver to red, and the males get hooked jaws and teeth. The courage and determination her mother showed summed up how they had changed too. Perseverance does that.

Mama pointed toward the kitchen. "I can still see my mother hovering over the stove. Tomorrow, we will visit her grave." She took a deep sigh. "But this isn't home for you or your brother."

"Abuelo already sensed that. He thinks it's better if I change my Sockeye nickname to a ruby-throated hummingbird. They spend summer in the States and winter here."

"Have two homes?" Mama asked and fell silent for a long moment. "I'm not sure how that would work, but we can explore it. At the party, I talked with my cousin Pedro, who's a lawyer. He's going to investigate the charges and determine if he can have them dismissed. He has a few ideas too about getting me a job where my English would be helpful."

"How can he do that? You left Papa Dale to ...." her voice trailed off. She could not allow the word to take shape in her mouth, even if it had been a burden in her thoughts since they departed Maine.

Her mother looked shocked. "I thought you knew me better than that! I told Billy to rescue him after he dropped us off in Portsmouth. Hopefully, the day in the hole changed him."

She shrugged. "I doubt it. He is out for revenge."

"Yeah, for the Catalina. But he will have to get over a lot of things if he wants to see his son again. If he waits too long, the question will go away, when Sonny turns eighteen. In the meantime, Pedro will ask about custody."

"Are you kidding? I want no part of that!"

Mama laughed. "Yeah, no worries there. You're not his blood, remember?"

"I think Sonny is done with him, too."

"But his friends are in Maine…. along with Lori."

She rolled her eyes. "They haven't stopped texting since we left."

Mama laughed, and she sat back on the couch. As they listened to the wall clock ticking, Olivia felt herself slipping away and stood in a fast-moving stream with the sun overhead. Suddenly, the current strengthened and carried her into foaming white water that did not roar as much as buzzed, electrifying every pore of her skin. In the chaotic stream, she could make out an enormous head with dark eyes scrutinizing her.

She bolted upright, gasping for air. Her mother was asleep beside her. The dream evaporated, but the buzzing sensation continued. She strained her ears, telling herself it was impossible.

Sonny came running into the room.

"Come quick!" he said, panting. "You have to see this!"

"What's the matter?" Mama asked, waking up.

Sonny had a peculiar expression on his face, as if he couldn't find the right words to describe it. He just pointed outside.

She rushed to the front door and opening it, gasped. A line of people stretched from the front walk down the street as far as she could see. Many were in wheelchairs, others in leg braces, some propped up with crutches and walkers. Many were silently holding candles and flashlights from iPhones.

"What are they here for?" Mama asked.

Olivia glanced at her mother and brother. "Do you feel anything or hear the loud buzzing sound?"

Mama gave her a strange look. "No."

She looked at Sonny. "How about you?"

He shook his head.

"Olivia!" a familiar voice boomed. She took a few steps outside and found Seth standing at the front of the line. He had on his event garb.

"What do you want?" she yelled.

Seth shrugged and pointed at the crowd. "I'm the wrong person to ask, but I'm guessing they want to be healed." He looked up at a bright light in the sky. "Your neighbors heard you were here and word spread. Tonight, the possibilities are unlimited."

"Quick! We can escape out the back!" Mama said, pulling on her arm.

Olivia looked at her hands and felt electricity flowing through them. Rezi's words about sticks and carrots played a tug-of-war in her brain. *Will I get zapped if I ignore it?* She scanned the crowd and the expectant faces and felt something inside shift. *Could I cure one or a thousand?*

"What's that weird light hovering over the trees?" Sonny asked, pointing.

She broke away and headed toward the crowd and focused on a man cradling a small boy wearing a bandage around his tiny head. The image of the pale blue dot captured in a grainy sunbeam came to mind. Firth and Seth were terribly farsighted and missed seeing the endless array of selfless acts on this speck of dust; from salmon runs sacrificing everything for the next generation, to good Samaritans helping those without food, clothes, and shelter, or her mother risking all to save them from a sick tyrant. She remembered how two fish were central to a miracle feeding thousands. No one was left out. Everyone was welcome.

"Where are you going?" Mama asked, taking her hand.

"To share what I have… because this home is big enough for everyone."

ACKNOWLEDGEMENTS

Nikki is part of my MilliporeSigma family and sends me an amusing text every year. *Happy St. Patrick's Day, enjoy your bubbling vat of meat and potatoes.* After finishing *Secret Seeds,* a bubbling vat is a fitting summary. In retrospect, my daily newsfeed provided a plentiful supply of the key ingredients: aliens, immigration, cult worship, abuse, and dysfunction. The pairing would have been toxic without seasoning it with love, courage, perseverance, redemption, and self-discovery. But more than a good meal shared with family and friends, I hope this story both satisfies and causes a bit of indigestion of what it means to belong.

Given the length of winters in New England, the first draft came together quickly. As always, it's the editing that makes me feel trapped in *Groundhog Day.* As with everything I attempt no matter the season, special thanks to my wife and best friend, Robin. Her support and patience during these marathons mean the world. I remain indebted to my daughters, Heather and Taylor. It was their encouragement twenty-five years ago that revived a dream delayed too long. Their critical feedback and support, along with son-in-law Michael, are a constant lifeline. I also want to thank my grandsons Nolan and Wesley, the Grand Wizards of Imagination, who continually teach me there is no shelf-life on creativity. I am also blessed beyond measure with family and friends, and their love sustains me. The true reward of this endeavor are the people I meet and the feedback received. Most importantly, I continue to be especially thankful for being part of the Black Rose Writing family.

I hope you enjoy this story of belonging and post a review. I look forward to hearing from you on my author website: vincentdonovanbooks.com.

ABOUT THE AUTHOR

Vincent Donovan, a two-time quarter-finalist in the highly-competitive Amazon Breakthrough Novel Contest, graduated with a B.A in English from Merrimack College and an M.B.A from Rivier University. For over twenty-seven years, Vin worked in leadership positions in the biopharmaceutical industry, allowing him to bring a unique blend of creativity and business acumen to his writing.

A runner most of his life, Vin uses that time to work out plot lines and characters. He has a large family with crazy and creative grandsons but is especially passionate about being the change you want to see in the world by volunteering with the Society of St Vincent de Paul to help many who have nowhere else to turn. No work of charity is foreign to this ministry.

NOTE FROM VINCENT DONOVAN

Word-of-mouth is crucial for any author to succeed. If you enjoyed *Secret Seeds*, please leave a review online—anywhere you are able. Even if it's just a sentence or two. It would make all the difference and would be very much appreciated.

Thanks!
Vincent Donovan

We hope you enjoyed reading this title from:

www.blackrosewriting.com

Subscribe to our mailing list – *The Rosevine* – and receive **FREE** books, daily
deals, and stay current with news about upcoming
releases and our hottest authors.
Scan the QR code below to sign up.

Already a subscriber? Please accept a sincere thank you for being a fan of
Black Rose Writing authors.

View other Black Rose Writing titles at
www.blackrosewriting.com/books and use promo code
PRINT to receive a **20% discount** when purchasing.

www.ingramcontent.com/pod-product-compliance
Lightning Source LLC
Chambersburg PA
CBHW030806210726
48290CB00002B/446